Painted Upon a Cloud

E. Costantino

ISBN-13: 9780578901619

The cover pic is the fabulous work of Karen Cantú.

Many thanks to Tabitha and her red pen.

Contact: daystarprint7@gmail.com

Table of Contents

Chapter 1

I'm not going to lie. I struggled with my faith in God. Not that I ever reached the point where I rejected him altogether, but the idea of his still existing and presiding over this world only aggravated me—especially in a world of two billion people. God seemed nowhere to be found. Then to make matters worse, I came to believe I was cursed. Downright cursed. This was confirmed in my mind on an unforgettable September day.

I sprang up in my bed and leaned over towards the window. The sun was already shining on the deserted horse-drawn reaper in the field across the dirt road. *I should've never gone back to sleep! What was I thinking?* I flung the blanket aside and jumped out of bed. I threw on my knee-length trousers and knitted pullover then slipped into my socks and shoes. I ran a comb through my hair and hurried downstairs into the kitchen.

"Good morning, Mother." I kissed her on the cheek. "Dad already leave?"

"You mean you didn't hear the wagon jangling through the yard?" Mom said, scowling. "Don't tell me you overslept."

"I won't then. I was only asking a simple question." I couldn't admit to sneaking a cup of coffee before bed, which kept me up till the wee hours of the morning.

"Well, the simple answer is *yes*," Mom said. "You just missed him."

"Pshh! He didn't even say goodbye."

Mom eyed me in her usual way, tilting her head down, peering over her glasses. "And to think *you* didn't even say goodbye to *him*."

"He's supposed to say goodbye first."

"Horsefeathers! Your lazy bones should've been down here already. Now get a move on it."

"I'm not running late. I'm doing just fine."

"Sure you are," she muttered. She stood at the sink in her sturdy ankle-length dress, her pearl drop earrings bobbing as she scrubbed out the pan. "Ready for another year of school?"

"Ready as I'll ever be." I heaped some scrambled eggs onto my plate. "Though I'm not looking forward to seeing Dominic."

"Oh, stop it."

"No, I'm serious. He's such a troublemaker. And he's gotten worse over the summer. And if you had to spend an entire day with him stuck in the same classroom, you'd understand."

"Just mind your own funeral."

"That's what I mean; you don't understand. I could be sitting there doing my work, keeping to myself, but that doesn't stop him from causing trouble. Besides, it *is* my funeral. That no-good mischief-maker will probably be the death of me."

"Boo-hoo."

"See? You don't care."

"Would you like a shoulder to cry on?"

I rolled my eyes and turned the other way. "Go ahead. Think he's an angel for all I care."

"I never said I thought he was an angel, and I know better than that. But you can't control other people. You can only control yourself. That's all I'm saying."

"It's just that he thinks he's so much better than everyone just because he's the sheriff's son. You wanna talk about minding your own business, he's the one who thinks it's his job to take charge of every situation. Like he's some great general or something and we're his army of schoolmates. And then the way he looks at you, like he's so high-and-mighty—makes me wanna punch him in the face."

"David Hayes! Listen to yourself!"

"I didn't say I was going to, Mom. I said it makes me *want* to. There's a difference."

"Well, that's the problem, that you even want to—and don't talk with your mouth full like that! My stars! You're fifteen years old now, and I need to still tell you that?"

I wolfed down the last piece of toast then washed it down with some orange juice. "All I'm saying, Mother, is that you'd wanna punch him too if you had to spend one day with him."

"Well, good for you. You could've had a great day of school for all you know, but it looks like you already got other plans, don't you?"

"No, not that at all. I'm just worked up. The first day's always the worst for me. Once I get through the day, things end up feeling normal again and then I don't mind as much."

"Well, I remember those days. You'll do fine. Just be sure to mind your business, pay attention, and be respectful to your teacher. And don't go around waking snakes, you hear?"

"I'm not gonna start trouble. What kinda son do you think you have?"

"Well, I wasn't born yesterday, David. You're usually up to *something*. In fact, I wouldn't be surprised if you were up to something *now*. You've got that look on your face."

My mother had keen insight. I quickly changed the subject. "Oops!" I said, examining one of the pans on the drying rack. "Looks

9

like you missed a spot. You know that's a sin to Crocket to leave a pan dirty like that."

She gave me a light smack on the face. "Now watch it there, young man, or you'll get a pan to the back of your head, dirty or not."

"Phew! This place is dangerous."

"What's dangerous is the way you go about scarfing down your food. You're bound to choke to death one of these days. My stars! The dog eats slower than you."

"I gotta get going. You want me to be late for school?"

"But I thought you said you weren't running late, hmm?"

I shoveled the last bit of breakfast into my mouth and set my dish and fork in the sink. "I'm not. See? I'm right on time."

I retreated into the living room. My older brother was seated by the window, gazing out.

"Good morning, Andrew," I said.

He didn't reply. He didn't look at me. He just nodded while stroking his thin scraggly mustache and scruffy chin.

Just then, Evelyn came fluttering down the stairs in her velvet dress and wavy brown hair. She paused in front of the dining room mirror to even up her sash and arrange the shawl around her neck. Then she proceeded into the kitchen where I overheard her tell Mom that breakfast was going through her "like a dose of the salts." So I knew exactly where she'd end up—which happened to be the perfect place to hide!

"This is gonna be perfect, Andrew," I whispered. "She's gotta go iron her shoelaces. You know what that means?" I left the living room and made as if I were going upstairs. "Evelyn," I called, halfway up the steps.

My sister emerged through the doorway with her hand over her belly. "Yes, Davey."

"I'm gonna be in my room, so gimme a holler when you're ready to leave for school."

"Will do."

As soon as she returned to the kitchen, I slipped back into the living room.

Andrew leaned back in his chair and gave me the sort of look that said I was asking for trouble. I ignored the unspoken admonition and headed for the front door.

Rouge, our fox-red Labrador, must have sensed I was up to something. She followed me to the door, wagging her tail.

"No, Rouge. Stay here, girl—Andrew, call her for me."

"Come here, Rouge," Andrew muttered.

As usual, she listened to him. Rouge belonged to the family, but she might as well have been Andrew's dog. She adored him. When it was time for bed, she followed him up the stairs and lay down beside him on the floor and stayed there throughout the night.

I sneaked outside and ran around back and hid in the outhouse. I peeked through the moon-shaped hole in the door and waited patiently for my sister.

A couple minutes passed. I began to doubt my plan. It seemed Evelyn was never coming out.

At last, I heard the back door open and Evelyn singing *Shoo, fly, don't bother me.* I was so excited about my scheme; my heart was racing. My sister's footsteps drew closer. At just the right moment, I burst from the outhouse, shouting—

"Boo!"

Evelyn flew back, shrieking, as if she were being ambushed by a grizzly bear.

"David Millard Hayes!" she screamed. "You're dead!"

"Man alive!" I said. "I didn't know it would scare you *that* badly. Ha ha!"

"It's not funny!" Evelyn said, huffing. She marched straight to the outhouse, shoving me out of the way. "Get out of here, David. You're dead!"

I knew I had crossed the line with her. I had never seen my sister get that angry before.

I started for the house and looked back one last time. She glared at me from inside the doorway of the outhouse.

"I said I'm sorry, Evelyn. I didn't realize—"

"I don't care! You're dead! This is the last straw. You wanna keep scaring me the way you always do? Well, I can play that game, too. And believe you me, I can play that game just as well—if not better! I promise you, David. You're—so—dead!"

She slammed the door shut.

As soon as I got inside, Mom came storming down the stairs. "What in the world is going on? Sounds like crying murder!"

"I was just joking around with her. I jumped out of the outhouse and spooked her, but I didn't know she was gonna get so steamed up about it."

"You scared her half to death for goodness sake! What do you want her to do? And didn't I just tell you moments ago not to go stirring up trouble? I'm telling you, David, you're walking on thin ice with me. I'm gonna have a talk with your father about this. Your scaring antics better stop if you know what's good for you!"

"I'm sorry. It's been two weeks since I scared her."

"I don't care if it's been two whole years! You are *never* to scare your sister again. Do you hear me, mister? Neeevvver!"

"Yes, ma'am."

"Now get going to school!"

"I'm waiting for Evelyn. She wanted us to ride together."

"Well, I have a mind to have you go on without her. But if she said she'd ride to school with you, then that's her business." Mom stomped back upstairs. "We'll see if she even wants to after all the blood and guts you caused this morning!"

Evelyn came back into the house. She had settled down, but I could tell she was still upset. She wouldn't even acknowledge me.

She gave Andrew a hug and then kissed Mom goodbye at the door. I muttered my goodbyes and patted Rouge on the head. Andrew looked up at me and just shook his head.

My sister and I left the house. Mom stepped out onto the porch and pointed her finger. "I'm telling you, David, mind your own funeral today. And don't—go—waking—snakes!"

"I'm done, Mom. I'm done."

"You better be. Now let's have a good first day of school."

Chapter 2

Evelyn and I went out back to the storm cellar where our bicycles were propped up. We hopped on and pedaled through the yard then down the dirt road together. We attended school in Avondale, a mile or so from Belfast where our family resided. We lived on Healy Road, which would lead you straight into town.

"I bet you're looking forward to seeing Beth and Alice and Mattie again," I said. "It seems the four of you just like being together, even if that means being cooped up in a classroom."

She kept pedaling and surveying the countryside, her hair cascading from her pretty little head with the free strands fluttering in the breeze.

I tried again. "I can't tell you how happy I am Miss Jefferson teaches the lower grades now and that we don't all have to be squished in that old schoolhouse with all those annoying ragamuffins. Besides, I really like Mr. Wagner. I think he's done a real good job with the high school if you ask me."

The truth is she *hadn't* asked me, and it appeared she wasn't going to answer me either.

"It's nice we have fewer students dropping out or staying home to work the farm…Though I don't think the Sawyer boys will ever come back to school. Do you?"

She shrugged her shoulders.

"Not that I can blame them or anything; I'm just saying. They already had a good-size farm with all that corn and snap-bean, and now they've gone and added all those cattle. Pshh! And then the hum drum of milking cows and gathering eggs every blasted day, no thank you. Is it just me, or does it seem they can barely get ahead?"

"Uh-huh."

"If only Irvin came to school, then he could beat the snot out of Dominic. I'd pay to see that fight... Well, at least we've still got Kingsley. I think Jack Kingsley could take him on, don't you?"

My sister persisted in giving me the brushoff, so I stopped trying for the time being.

Evelyn and I had our fights, but I truly loved my older sister. The center of her soul was genuine sweetness, and she had a countenance that matched her heart, too. Evelyn looked like a little bundle of joy, her eyes so full of sparkle and life, which was a testimony to her personality considering all our family had been through. But for now, she was not happy to say the least.

We pedaled on in silence, aside from the melodies of cardinals and finches that floated through the countryside. When we arrived in town, we were greeted by the clatter of horse-drawn carriages and the sputtering of motorcars. I followed Evelyn's lead as she made a last second turn down Allen Street. Then she veered onto the path next to Eva's Bistro Kitchen, into the woods.

"Why you going this way?" I said.

"I like riding through the woods, alright?" she snapped.

"That's fine...I was just wondering." At least she responded to me. "Don't get me wrong, I like riding through here. It's like being in a tunnel of trees. Though it looks like they need to trim back some of the ivy and snakeroot, don't ya think?" I gave her a chance to reply. "Don't ya think, Evelyn?"

She was flat-out ignoring me again.

About a minute later, we came out the other side of the woods onto Newbury Terrace, right alongside the property line of the Tamases. Mrs. Tamas happened to be sweeping her porch and spotted us careering by. She smiled and waved to us.

Evelyn smiled back—the first time she had done so since we left the house.

We wheeled around the corner then pedaled down the sidewalk, right up to the porch steps.

"Good morning, Mrs. Tamas," Evelyn said.

Mrs. Tamas set her broom down and brushed off her skirt. "Good morning! So good to see you. How are you both dis vonderful morning?"

I forced a smile. "We're doing well, thank you."

"I couldn't be better," Evelyn said. "It's such a beauteous day." She held up her schoolbag. "Today's our first day of school. And what better way to start the schoolyear than with sunshine and fresh skies!"

"Dat's right," Mrs. Tamas said, clasping her hands together. "Oh, good for you. You'll do vell. You are such good children. Now you study—You learn all you can—You do your homevork—And you vill do vell on your tests, I can promise you dat."

"I always do," Evelyn said.

"Good. Good for you. Keep up da good work."

"Yes, ma'am. Is Mr. Tamas here?"

"No. He vent to da factory early. Day needed him badly. I guess a problem vid another machine. You know, alvays problems vid deze machines."

"Well, they couldn't do it without him," I said. "He does a fantastic job keeping that place running."

"He does. He does. Now me? Nah, I'm just a seamstress. I don't know nudding 'bout fixing machines. Give me a needle and some thread, and I'll make it fit, alright? Now give my husband a rachet and a wrench, and he'll make it run. Ha!"

"Well, you're a fabulous seamstress, Mrs. Tamas," Evelyn said.

"Vell, dank you. You are a sveet girl, Evelyn."

"Is Stephen here?"

"Yes, he is. Hold on. My son vood very much like to see you two." She opened the door and called into the house. The only word I understood was his native-born name: "Istvan!"

Stephen came out onto the porch, freshly shaven and in his white shirt and necktie. He was a young man in his early twenties. His suntanned hair was parted down the middle, and his light blue eyes added to the amiable expression on his face. "Oh, it's de Hayses! Vell, good morning to you!"

"Good morning, Stephen," I said. "We thought we'd just stop by to say hello. We're on our way to school."

He stuck his hands in his pockets like he usually did when he gave you his undivided attention. "I see, I see. Vell, dank you for stopping by. So good to see you. How are you both?"

"Pretty good," I said.

Evelyn nodded her head, her face beaming.

Stephen pointed to my sister's schoolbag. "I see you are a prepared young lady. Is dat all your paper and pencils and dings?"

"It sure is," Evelyn said, touching up her hair. She went to grab the bag from the handlebar and fumbled it. All her belongings spilled out on the ground. "Goodness gracious, I'm so clumsy!"

"Oh, no," Stephen said, folding his arms across his chest. "Dat is terrible. Now all your dings are all over da place."

Evelyn looked down at the mess with her hand to her face, as if she didn't know what to do. She looked up and gazed at Stephen again, full of smiles.

Stephen put his arm around his mom. "Good ding day don't make pencils out of glass, huh?"

"It is," Mrs. Tamas said. "But it vood also be good to give the lady a hand, Istvan."

I felt embarrassed for my sister. "Don't worry, I got it." I hopped off my bicycle and went over and gathered up all her belongings. I swept them back into the bag and handed it to her. "Here you go."

The smiles had vanished from my sister's face. She snatched the bag from me and hung it back up. "Well, we don't wanna be late. We should get going now."

"Alright now," Stephen said. "Danks for visiting. You have a vonderful day at school."

Mrs. Tamas took up her broom again and waved goodbye. "Tell your parents I said hello."

"Will do," I said. "Take care now."

Evelyn looked back one more time. "Bye, Stephen."

We continued pedaling down Newbury Terrace, which eventually curved its way to Mill Street.

"How long's it been since the Tamases moved here?" I asked. My sister shrugged her shoulders, but I pretended not to see. "Let's see, they came to America in what…1910? I think that's what Mom and Dad said. So it's been about fourteen years now…Hmm. To think that Mikklos and Csilla got to come here and work at the Grisham Textile Factory together. I mean that's pretty amazing, the way that worked out for the both of 'em. I wish everything worked out that way. Don't you?"

"Uh-huh."

At last, we steered onto Mill Street, the prospect of the school before us. It was a respectable three-story brick building with arched windows and a bell tower.

I decided I was going to hazard one more apology before we arrived. "Listen, Evelyn, you don't have to say anything at all to me, alright? I don't blame you for being upset with me and for not wanting to talk to me; I completely understand. What I did this morning was rude. It was inconsiderate. But I want you to know, before school starts, that I *am* sorry just so you know. I'm sorry for scaring you."

She finally turned to me. "You're gonna give me a heart attack one of these times, Davey."

I breathed a sigh of relief. I was Davey again! And with that, I felt confident the storm was past.

But I didn't know any better.

Chapter 3

School had barely gotten underway when I had an unfriendly encounter with Dominic. We were both headed to the front of the classroom where a single sharpener was fastened to the wall. It was not a contest for me, but it so happened I got there first and proceeded to sharpen my pencil. He nudged the back of my knee with his foot. "Knock it off!" I said, catching my balance. He leaned in and whispered, "You best mind your manners."

Later during recess, I was sitting against the tree reading a book when Dominic approached me. He crouched down and stared at me with his widely set eyes. "Be thankful your sister's gorgeous," he said. He smacked me on the head then walked away.

The thing that frustrated me to no end was that Dominic was a terrific boxer. He bragged about being the next Gene Tunney. No one ever won a fight against Dominic Lockhart. And ever since he whipped Carl Slack the year before, no one dared to challenge "the sheriff's son." Jack Kingsley was the one guy left I thought could possibly take on Dominic. Jack was a sturdy fellow with a big bicep and seemed to have every bit of confidence in himself. He wasn't proud though. He was just a friendly fellow with nothing to prove at all, except that he could crack a baseball out of the field, all the way into Hillcrest Cemetery. Something Dominic couldn't do. Jack was the only guy Dominic seemed to respect.

Class let out early and we decided to break in the new schoolyear by playing some ball. We agreed upon five innings. I remember Daryl Mitchell, Jack Kingsley, Walter Davis, Carl Slack, and me on one team. Henry Brook, Robert Bellman, Dominic, and his two younger brothers, Harvey and Sam, were on the other team. Harvey Lockhart was the best pitcher in Avondale and could throw an accurate fastball. No doubt, the best weapon Dominic's team had against Kingsley.

We reached the bottom of the last inning and found ourselves down by two. However, things looked brighter with Jack, in his denim bib overalls, stepping up to the plate once more. Harvey had held Jack to a base hit in the first and third innings, but Jack cracked a homerun in the fourth and brought two additional guys home with him. Now, with only a single out and Carl on second base, we had a good chance to at least tie the game.

That's when the drama unfolded. The Lockhart boys and Robert Bellman broke from their huddle with smirks on their faces.

Jack gave a couple practice swings. "Show me whatcha got, Harvey. We're about to tie this baby up."

Harvey spit on the mound. "I don't think so."

"Are you sure about that?"

"Trust me. You won't be bringing anybody home this time around."

Harvey wound up and pitched a ball to the outside.

"Ball one."

"Seriously?" Jack said.

Harvey just smirked.

He pitched another one.

"Ball two."

At that moment, we figured their game plan was to let Jack walk rather than risk being scored against.

21

"You've got to be kidding me," Jack cried. "You're that scared, Harvey?"

"I ain't scared of nothing," Harvey said.

"Then let's see what you got."

"Come again?"

"You don't trust your own pitching. You're too afraid I'm gonna hit one out of the park."

"I'm not afraid."

Kingsley turned to us. "Look at this rube, boys. He's nothing but a scaredy cat!"

Harvey looked daggers at Jack.

"Don't get me wrong," Jack said. "I don't blame you. I'd hang up my fiddle, too, if I were you. 'Cause you know I'll crack that ball!"

At long last, Harvey wound up and let it go. It whizzed straight for Jack and pelted him right in the leg.

"Man alive!" I said. "You alright, Jack?"

Jack grimaced and limped around. "Wow! You've got problems, Harvey."

Harvey spit on the ground again. "Looks like you're the one with the problem."

Jack glared at Harvey, still trying to walk it off. "You could've struck me out. You missed a golden opportunity."

"I didn't miss nothing," Harvey said. "I hit it dead on."

Jack stopped. "What are you trying so say?"

"I'm not *trying*. I said I didn't miss nothing."

Jack started toward the mound. "So you hit me on purpose? Is that what you did?

"Ha! I didn't miss nothing!" Harvey hollered, pointing his finger at Jack.

Jack got right in Harvey's face. "You could've struck me out!" Harvey shoved Jack away. "I struck you, didn't I?"

And that's when it all made perfect sense: I wasn't the only one who had wanted to see Kingsley versus Lockhart. As soon as Jack shoved Harvey, Dominic rushed over.

"What are you pushing my brother for?" Dominic said, bumping Jack off the mound.

Jack came right back. "He pushed me first."

"'Cause you got in his face, that's why."

"'Cause he pitched a hit on purpose. That's why."

"Prove it. Prove he hit you on purpose. Prove it!"

"I don't need to prove nothing. He said so himself, and you heard him."

"You got a bee in your bonnet, Kingsley!" Sam chimed in.

"Yep!" Harvey said. "I was just joking. You obviously can't take a joke."

Jack started toward Harvey again. "It wasn't a joke! And if you were aiming at one, it wasn't funny!"

Harvey burst out laughing. "You just called yourself a joke because I was aiming at you—that's what you just said. *You* said it! Not me!"

Jack lurched forward at Harvey, and Dominic immediately intervened.

"Get out of my way now, Dominic," Jack said. "I'm not playing anymore. This ain't your fight."

"Leave my brother alone."

"Don't you shove me. I said get out of the—" Jack rammed Dominic in the chest.

Dominic caught him in the face.

Jack charged Dominic, throwing his weight into him. But Dominic shifted backwards, causing Jack to trip himself up.

Dominic sprang forward and caught him again with a right.

Jack returned a combination, landing a blow of his own. But whatever hope I felt at that moment vanished as Dominic laughed it off and began urging him on. Dominic was bobbing and weaving comfortably and began picking Jack apart with a solid jab here, a solid jab there.

Jack looked dispirited now. He had no answer for Dominic's light feet and quick hands. Before long, Dominic assailed him with a series of combinations followed by a hook that clipped him right on the jaw. Try as he might, Jack hobbled around like a drunken man before stumbling to the ground.

Carl, Walter, and Robert moved in to see if he was alright.

Meanwhile, Dominic put his belted jacket back on, as well as his fedora hat, then went and stood over. With his hands on his hips, he peered down upon his beaten opponent.

The question that once lingered in my mind was put to rest by the pit in my stomach. The matter was settled: Dominic was the undisputed champ of Avondale.

Jack sat himself up on the ground, his face already swollen.

After a minute, he got up and shook Dominic's hand. "You won fair and square...but what happened to me wasn't right."

Dominic turned to his brothers and nodded. "It's not the way we wanted the afternoon to go, right boys? But it's all water under the bridge."

"That's right," Sam said. "Hopefully we all could have a second go with the same teams."

"With a more friendly outcome next time," Harvey added.

Jack bid us all a good evening, then turned around and headed home. Daryl and I said we would go with him, but he insisted on walking alone.

As if Jack's loss wasn't bad enough, the Lockhart boys decided to accompany me, Daryl, and Carl as we started for home. The final frames of the fight played over and over in my mind as I walked my bicycle. Dominic could hardly hide his triumph. He sauntered up the street in his two-toned oxford shoes and was cheerier and more talkative than usual, which made me even more sick to my stomach.

Just then, a horse and carriage could be heard bowling down the road. The driver came around the bend right where Ervin's Tavern once served beer and "pick-me-ups" before Prohibition took effect.

"Hey, look!" Harvey shouted. "It's Dad!"

Sam and Harvey waved their hands around excitedly.

The horse and carriage slowed down and pulled up alongside us. Sheriff Lockhart was in uniform: gray slacks, a button up shirt and tie, and his badge. Roy Schnilbacker was seated next to him, in handcuffs.

Sheriff Lockhart looked us over with his usual searching gaze. "Gentlemen, how ya'll doing?"

Daryl and Carl said hello. I nodded my head.

"Hey, Dad," Sam said. "What did ole Roy do this time?"

Sheriff Lockhart turned his head. "He did enough. Right, Roy? Enough to land you in the big house again."

Roy smirked. "Your pa thinks he's so big and powerful...but he'll get his."

Sheriff Lockhart grasped the young man's shoulder. "Is that a threat?"

"You can let go of me, Augie. Everyone knows you're so brave and strong and tough."

"Answer me. Is that a threat?"

Roy tried pulling away from him. "Call it a promise. I never said I'd have anything to do with it. It's just that you think you're the king of this county, and you ain't."

Sheriff Lockhart chuckled. "That's what I thought. 'Cause I'd put a hole in your head so fast, boy."

"An eye for an eye, and a hole for a hole," Roy mumbled.

"How's my dad gonna get a hole in his head if you're already dead?" Harvey said.

25

"No kidding," Sam said. "What a dim-witted thing to say."

Roy heaved a sigh. "If I'm not mistaken, we've got somewhere to go. Right, Augie?"

"You're right about that much," Sheriff Lockhart said. "'Cause if I'm not mistaken, you're headed to the jailhouse, and I'm headed home to my charming wife—You boys want a ride?"

"Thanks, Dad," Dominic said. "But it's such a beautiful day, I think I'm gonna walk the rest of the way with my friends."

I wanted to gag.

"That's right," Sam said. "Dominic had a good first day of school."

"Did he now?"

"Yep. He got to be teacher today."

"Whatta ya mean?"

"Well, let's just say he taught Jack Kingsley a lesson."

The Lockhart boys burst out laughing.

"What's so funny? What happened?"

"Jack Kingsley picked a fight with Harvey. That's what happened."

"And Dominic set him straight," Harvey added.

Sheriff Lockhart smiled down upon Dominic. "Did ya give him the one-two treatment?"

"More than that," Dominic said. "I dropped him."

"Attaboy! That's what I wanna hear." Sheriff Lockhart turned to Roy and patted him on the back. "Ready, Mr. Schnilbacker?"

Roy kept straight ahead and said nothing.

"I'll take that as a yes. Alright, boys, this man looks like he's in a hurry to keep his schedule. We wouldn't wanna make him late for his appointment." Sheriff Lockhart tipped his hat. "Ya'll take care— Let's go!"

The horse and carriage took off down the road. There I stood, still stuck with the Lockhart boys.

We proceeded up the street and came upon the old Mill Street Factory where they used to manufacture boxes during the 1890s. The building had been abandoned for the last seven years, and the property was taken over by weeds and brushwood.

"Hey, Harvey," Dominic said. "Try your hand at that window over there."

"That one?" Harvey said. "Easy. Let me find a good rock."

He found one alright and pitched it, shattering the glass.

"Dead on!" Dominic cried.

Harvey sneered. "You betcher. I always hit what I aim for."

Dominic and Sam glanced at each other and snickered.

Then Dominic picked up a rock and threw it. "Oh, so close! C'mon ladies, give it your best shot."

I knew the building was abandoned, but there was something about breaking the surviving windows that didn't sit well with me. I didn't think my parents would approve of it either, so I just watched.

Evidently Daryl and Carl didn't mind. They pretended to be launching mortars in battle, the sound of shattered glass bearing witness to their military success. "Woohoo!"

Sam hurled another stone. "C'mon, David. Stop piddling around."

"I'm not," I said.

"You're such a spoilsport," Harvey said.

"I'm having fun watching," I said.

"Nah," Dominic said. "The little twerp's too scared. Look at him; it's written all over his face."

"I'm not scared," I said.

"Then why in the name of Sam Hill aren't you joining in?"

"I just don't think it's a good idea, that's all."

"Pshh! They don't even use the old building, so what's the big deal?"

"I didn't say it was a big deal."

"Then don't be a pantywaist. "

"Don't call me a pantywaist."

He got right in my face and folded his arms. It was like he could peer into your soul and then tacitly inform you of the weakness he had spotted inside.

I bristled and said it again: "I'm not a pantywaist."

He smacked me on the side of the head. "Then don't act like one."

I came close to pushing him away to preserve some smidgen of self-respect, but visions of the recent fight continued to flash across my mind. Instead, I stepped back.

Feeling the need to prove myself now—I'm ashamed to admit it—I set my bicycle down, at which point I insisted on it one last time, while picking up a rock, that I was *not* a pantywaist. I selected a window and threw it—more out of anger that I had caved to someone who was no friend of mine.

I picked up another rock and flung it as hard as I could.

"Good heavens!" Dominic said. "You nailed that bird! Ha ha!"

The guys were hysterical. Each one thrashed his arms around and stomped, roaring and laughing like mad all at the same time. They couldn't believe it.

Neither could I. I was thunderstruck.

But then I felt proud. I may have missed the window, but at least I hit *something*. A smile stole across my face.

Dominic ran over to where the bird had fallen from the ledge. He scoured through the weeds. "I found it!" he yelled. "Good heavens, David! You murdered a sparrow!"

The smile on my face died out. "I didn't murder anything! It was an accident!"

"Accident or no accident, you killed it—Get a look at this, fellas!"

Everybody waded through the brush to catch a glimpse of the bird.

"That's a sparrow alright," Sam said. "That don't promise no good for you."

"Why not?" I asked.

"It's bad luck to kill a sparrow," Carl explained.

"Or even to have one fly into your house," Daryl chimed in. "My cousin said her aunt had it happen to her, and she died soon after."

"Since when are you superstitious, Daryl," I said.

Daryl shrugged his shoulders. "I was just telling you what my cousin said."

"If you ask me," Carl said, "that sure as heck is a sign."

I rolled my eyes.

Just then, Dominic sprang up from the weeds and uttered the words that would echo in my mind for many moons: "David's cursed!"

A feeling of dread came over me. Though I tried to act unaffected. "What are the chances that stuff's even real?"

Sam burst out laughing. "What are the chances you'd hit a sparrow dead on?"

"Sam's got a point," Harvey said. "I couldn't pitch that if my life depended on it!"

"See? Not even Harvey could do that," Dominic said. "Ha! Leave it to you to kill one of God's innocent creatures."

I swallowed hard. "Nah, it was just an accident. That cursed stuff ain't real."

"Real or not," Sam said, "I wouldn't wanna be the one to find out."

Harvey spit on the ground. "Ain't that the gospel truth!"

The Lockhart brothers agreed it was probably not a good idea to be "hanging out with such a bag egg."

"Time for us to skidoo," Dominic said. "Before we catch David's curse."

"Ha ha!"

They took off down the road together, looking back now and again. Amid the crowing and the cackling, I picked out the one word that could be heard distinctly: *Cursed*.

And how could I not be cursed? I wanted nothing more than for Dominic to eat humble pie. But no! Kingsley had to go and get thrashed instead!

As if I was contagious, I turned to Carl out of consideration. Carl patted me on the back and said, "I'd better head home."

Thankfully, Daryl stayed behind. The one thing I was grateful for was Daryl Mitchell. He had been my best friend since I was eight. The two of us had gotten into a little scuffle over Alice Stratton one year. It turned out Alice didn't like either of us anyway, so it worked out in the end. We became best friends.

Daryl was tall and slender. His dark hair was parted and combed over, his little ears protruding from his slim face. He rarely smiled, and he usually looked serious. But he was not ill-tempered in the least. He was just Daryl.

I grabbed my bicycle, and the two of us ambled down the street together.

"Can something really be cursed?" I wondered. "I know they say the Slater house is cursed, but how can all that stuff be real?"

"I don't know," Daryl said. "My uncle says the Slater house is positively cursed. Lester Harrison says so, too, and even swore on his grandmother's grave. And you remember that big rain we got a couple years ago when Cherry Creek overflowed and uncovered those bones. Seems like a cursed place to me."

"I know! How did those bones even get there?"

"Lester says the Slater woman buried her victims right there on her own property."

"Man alive! I'm glad she doesn't live there anymore. Knowing me, I'd probably be one of them. It's just not fair. Why does Dominic seem to be the kind of guy protected from curses?"

As troubled as I was about my newfound misfortune, my heart was simultaneously plotting revenge. With such ill-will toward Dominic, I decided he needed to be utterly humbled.

Chapter 4

Throughout the remainder of the week, I continued to wrestle with the belief that I was ruined. I had sought an opportunity to talk with my parents, but I couldn't manage to find an open door. Or rather, I couldn't find the gumption to bring up the subject—I had a hunch what my parents would say. I could envision my father's carefree reaction and the reluctance to take my point seriously. I could hear my mother's insistence that it was all "horsefeathers." But none of that could suppress the eerie feeling I had inside.

Saturday morning arrived. My spirit still had no rest. I resolved to break open that door no matter what and obtain my parents' counsel on the matter.

Our family was seated at the dining room table while Andrew was in the kitchen preparing breakfast for us all. Dad was in his summer suit and had finished with his usual Bible reading. He placed the little ribbon inside the old black book and closed it, then he took up the day-old newspaper in his hands.

At last, breakfast was ready. Andrew divvied up the eggs and hash browns then joined us at the table. Dad put the paper aside and handed me his reading glasses. "Do me a favor, Son. Put my cheaters over on the end table, please."

"Yes, sir. There we go."

"Thanks, David." Dad took Mom's hand and bowed his head. "Let's pray—Father, we just want to say thank you for the food we're about to eat. Now we ask you to be with us throughout the day. Thank you for loving us. Amen."

"Amen."

"And thank you for making this, Andrew," Dad added. "It sure looks delicious."

"You can say that again," Evelyn said. "Thanks, Andy."

Andrew nodded.

"Before I forget, David," Dad said, stirring his coffee, "there's a new washbasin in the wagon. I forgot to bring it in last night. Go ahead and fetch it after breakfast. We'll use that for bathing from now on. It's a little bigger than the last one, so I reckon it'll take a few more trips to fill it."

"Yeppers," I said.

"Luckily for us," Evelyn said, "Andy changed out the piston rod on the pump, so we won't have to bathe in the creek like last weekend."

"That's right," I said. "Thanks a million, Andrew."

"Uh-huh."

"I can't tell you how much I appreciate that," Dad said. "I've been so busy at the shop, I really didn't know when I'd have a chance to get to it."

After a moment of silence, Evelyn said, "I hear the new rubber company is gonna be opening up in just a couple weeks."

"That's what I hear," Dad said.

"Nothing wrong with that. More jobs for the county."

"More jobs is right. And decent paying ones, too. I know we're doing great as well. We're manufacturing so much millwork now, and we're shipping it out to Indianapolis *and* Louisville. I've never been so busy trying to handle orders. In fact, I pulled some strings these last couple weeks and was able to get Stephen Thomas a new job working with me."

Evelyn clapped her hands. "That's fabulous, Dad!"

"Sure is. I think he's gonna do very well. The young man's got a promising future, no doubt."

"Did you hear that, Evelyn?" I said. "Istvan's got a future. And one which you'd like to be a part of, I'm sure."

My sister kicked me from under the table. "For the last time, David, I don't—like—Stephen! And stop calling him Istvan."

"Why? That's his real name—Istvan Tamas." I mimicked the accent. "Besides, what does it matter to you seeing you don't even like him?"

"I don't!"

"Then why do you get mad whenever I call him by his real name?"

"Because he likes to be called Stephen Thomas, that's why."

Dad scraped his food together. "And I think David likes to be teasing his sister."

"That's for sure," Evelyn said.

"I was just pointing out the truth," I said. "What can I say? Evelyn likes Stephen, and it's obvious as the color in her face."

"If my face is red, it's because I'm a little warm is all. You read into things too much."

"I didn't read into things when you dropped your schoolbag on purpose the other day."

Evelyn glared at me. "What are you talking about, David?"

"You dumped your things on purpose, hoping Stephen would come over and pick it up for you."

"Evelyn, dear!" Mom cried. "You're as red as a rose!"

"I'm mad. David's making up stories again."

"You're the one making up stories," I said. "I overheard you and Beth talking about ways to get a guy's attention, and you rather liked

Beth's idea of dropping something deliberately. That's how I know what I'm talking about because you said so yourself. Ha!"

"Can you please tell him to knock it off. He's being rather annoying."

"Alright, alright," Dad said. "That's enough, David. One ought not to be going about aggravating people on purpose."

"Thank you," Evelyn said.

Mom turned to Dad. "Now back to what you were saying, dear—Mikklos and Csilla have got to be proud of Stephen!"

"They're pleased as punch," Dad said. "He said his parents couldn't be any happier."

"Well, good for him. And I'm glad you get to pass on your woodworking skills."

"We can use the help, that's for sure. We're busy as all get-out. Man alive! The whole town is busy. I mean business is doing real good right now."

"It seems Avondale's becoming quite the booming town," I said.

"You can say that again," Mom said. "It seems there's more and more of those machines lined up along the curbs, too."

Dad sipped his coffee. "Well, it's certainly no South Bend or Canton."

"Well, no," I said. "But at least it's big enough to be considered a town. The way I see it, Belfast is hardly a town. It's just a name and has nothing. But Avondale's got a grocery store, a bank, a barber shop, and plenty of factories. What do we have?"

"Each other," Evelyn said, turning her nose up at me.

"You're absolutely right, honey," Mom said.

My sister smirked at me and then looked away. "And we've got less crashes, that's what we have. Did you hear about that awful crash down in Johnstown?

"I know," Dad said. "Just read about that a few minutes ago. All I can say is the youngster better thank his guardian angel—or *angels* I should say! Probably wore 'em all out on that one mishap alone."

"Why? What happened?" Mom said.

"The guy was going too fast and lost control," Evelyn explained. "And I mean completely. The car turned turtle."

Mom put her hands over her heart. "Oh, my stars!"

"Walked away with only a broken arm. Can you believe it?"

"How's that even possible?"

"You got me. But he's a mighty blessed man, that's for sure."

I resented my sister for having uttered the word *blessed*. It was the contrast to being cursed. However, it reminded me I needed to push the issue that weighed heavily on me.

Dad tapped his finger on the edge of my plate. "Another young person thinking that death is something that happens to other people. I hope you're paying attention."

"Wait a minute here," I said. "Of course, I'm paying attention. To begin with, we don't even own a car—"

"So what?" Evelyn said. "You don't have to be driving a horseless carriage to do something stupid."

I gulped. My sister couldn't have been more spot-on. "Well, n-no...But all I'm saying is if I ever drive a car, I'm not gonna go zipping like a madman down some winding road till I crash the blasted thing. Besides, you're the dumb Dora who's gonna end up colliding into a telephone pole like Fisher did."

"My, my!" Mom cried. "Aren't we a little prickly this morning, calling your sister names like that! And what she said is the truth. One doesn't have to be a fool to play the fool, you know."

Dad placed his hand on my shoulder. "Not to mention they're called *accidents* for a reason—they weren't supposed to happen. Just looking out for you is all."

Andrew wasn't the only one staring down at his plate now. I tried to finish my breakfast.

"You probably read about the Knights of Columbus, too, huh Dad?" Evelyn said.

"I sure did," Dad said. "I suspect the Kluxers got their hands on it. Just like they did with St. John's over in Chesterfield. Burnt the whole thing to the ground."

"And no marvel," Mom cried. "Not when you've got the devil quoting scripture for his own purpose."

"Speaking of scripture," I said, picking at the last bit of my hash browns. "Is it possible for a child of God to be cursed?" I said it as offhandedly as I could.

"Of course, not," Mom said. "I mean God's child could do something that requires his chastening hand, but that's entirely different from being cursed."

"What made you ask?" Dad said, brushing some crumbs from his suit.

"Well, me and some of the boys were walking home from school this past week, and we thought we'd have a little rock throwing contest—"

"Yes, that's right!" Evelyn chimed in. "Beth and I heard all about it. Serves you right. You'll think twice next time—"

I gave Evelyn's foot a kick. "Let me tell my story—please!"

She held her cup of coffee to her lips with both hands, smirking. "Go ahead, Davey."

"As I was saying…" I turned back to Dad, with an eye on my sister. "…Me, Daryl, and some of the other guys were having a rock throwing contest to see how good our aim is."

"So how good's your aim?" Dad asked.

"Not so good," I said.

"Well, I wouldn't let it bother you none. I wouldn't go so far as to say we're cursed, but us Hayeses never did have a good arm."

"Yes, but mine's *really* bad."

"Nah, that's nothing to bother your pretty little head about. I couldn't hit the broad side of the barn from ten feet away."

"Well, apparently I can hit...just not the right target."

Mom slapped her hands down on the table. "Don't tell me you busted a window!"

Evelyn giggled.

I gave her another kick. "No. I missed the—I mean I didn't hit any windows."

"My stars!" Mom said. "I could just see you knocking a window out of someone's new Ford or something."

"No, no. Nothing like that."

Dad wiped his mouth with his handkerchief. "So then what d'ya hit that's got you having kittens?"

I took a deep breath and blurted it out: "A bird."

"A bird?"

"Well, not just any old bird."

Mom held her hand over her heart. "You hit a songbird!"

"No, Mom. I didn't hit a songbird."

"It was someone's cockatiel, wasn't it?"

"It wasn't a pet."

Dad squinted hard. "Then out with it, Son. What on earth did you hit?"

"A sparrow."

Evelyn almost spewed out her coffee.

"A sparrow?" Dad cried.

"Yes. I nailed it dead."

Mom burst out laughing. "How did you manage that?"

"I have no idea."

Andrew looked up from his plate—the first time he had at the table. "How's that even possible?"

"I don't know," I said. "That's the problem. That's why I must be cursed."

"Who said anything about being cursed?" Dad asked.

"Some of the guys. They said if you kill a sparrow, that means you're cursed. Even Daryl seems to think it's bad luck."

"Horsefeathers!" Mom said.

Dad chuckled. "Son, believe nothing of what you hear and only half of what you see. You should know better than that."

"Well, that's what they said, and I've got this dreadful feeling about it."

"Well, it's enough to make a stuffed bird laugh," Mom said, scraping out the pan.

"A stuffed sparrow even," Evelyn said, laughing.

I glared at her.

"I've heard that sort of thing before," Dad said. "It's all rubbish, Son."

"So you don't think I'm cursed?"

"How can you be cursed if you have God's blessing?" Mom asked.

I held my hands up. "How can I be sure I have God's blessing?"

"Well, you know the Lord, don't you?"

I rolled my eyes. "Yes...but he's never given me any sign or anything. In fact, if there's any sign at all, it's that stupid sparrow. There's no way I should've hit that thing. But leave it to me!"

Evelyn slapped her cup down. "Try killing two birds with one stone next time. Ha ha!"

"Real funny," I said dryly.

Mom chuckled. "You have to admit, it sort of is, David. So don't be a grouch. And sparrows aren't stupid, by the way, so stop saying that.

"And God's child doesn't need a sign," Evelyn chimed in. "Nor should you be seeking one. You've got his word."

"Evelyn's got a point," Dad said. "And from where I stand, if there's any sign here at all, maybe it's God reminding you of his sacrifice."

"What do you mean?" I said.

"Well, Jesus said two sparrows were sold for a farthing and that not one of them would fall to the ground without the Father. So he's aware of every little thing, even the death of this sparrow that's got you so worked up. But my point is, under the Old Testament system, one sparrow had to die while the other one was set free by the priest."

"Why's the Old Testament so strange?" I said.

"Well, it showed the future death and resurrection of Christ. So maybe God's just trying to remind you what he's already done for you."

It dawned on me that, while I shouldn't have been throwing rocks in the first place, Christ *did* come to die for the very things I shouldn't have done! That gave me some comfort.

"That's wonderful," Evelyn cried. "We're like the sparrow that gets to live and go free!"

As soon as Evelyn uttered those words, Andrew muttered something under his breath and got up from the table and went upstairs.

The conversation ended there. I got up and cleared the table.

The moment I finished my chores, I went upstairs to our room. My brother lay on his back with his hands behind his head, staring at the ceiling. I debated whether to ask him the burning question, but I couldn't bring myself to do it. I went over to my dresser and opened the top drawer, pretending to be occupied about something. I grabbed the round identification tag my brother had given me when he returned from France. I had read the tag a hundred times before, but something about it captivated me.

ANDREW HAYES
PVT.
3RD INF.
U.S.A.

I thought about the years gone by when my brother was fun and spirited, when he was lighthearted like Dad and full of life. Like when he'd pick me up and launch me to the ceiling and call me "little brother." Or when he'd wrestle me to the ground and tickle me and give me a "knuckle twist." Or when he'd take me to the swimming hole where we'd swing from the rope. Or when he'd tell me a story or a funny joke or read me a portion of *The Jungle Book* before bed. Or when he'd hide the little strawberry glass ornament for me to find at Christmas. There were so many memorable moments I treasured in my mind. My brother was such a joy to be around.

Now, if Andrew ever happened to smile, even that was tinged with sadness.

I knew why the tag captivated me. It signified the reason for my brother's change. It was the link between the brother I knew as a little boy and the one who returned home. It held the secrets of a now twenty-six-year-old man. What he had seen. What he had lived through. Andrew never talked about the War, and no one thought it wise to bring it up. All my family knew were two words: "shell shock."

I gave the tag one last read then tucked it back into the drawer and closed it up. I sat down on the edge of my bed and observed my disheveled brother as he lay there on his bed with his eyes open.

I hesitated once more. I finally concluded it wouldn't hurt to ask a simple question.

"What do you think, Andrew?" At least I got that much out.

"About what?" he mumbled.

"About what we were talking about at the table. Do you think someone can be cursed?"

He squirmed a bit and tried to get comfortable. Then he folded his hands over his chest and closed his eyes. He took a deep breath and said, "You're asking the wrong person."

I didn't know what else to say. I got up and left the room.

Chapter 5

Thankfully, October came around and helped distract my mind. There was something magical about the changing leaves, especially the rich shades of orange and red that adorned the maple trees. To me, the falling leaves were nature's confetti, the added blessing of their sweet-scented spices filling the air. Without a doubt, crunchy leaves and warm weather were the best combination. Then add fresh apple cider and the smell of evening fires. There was just something special about fall that reached down into the depths of my soul. I cherished each day before it morphed into winter.

My most treasured memory that autumn is the delightful time my family had at the Sawyer farm one day. The Sawyers lived a half mile up the road, and they invited us over for "some good food and fellowship." It couldn't have been a more perfect day. The air was comfortably warm, the sky was bright blue, and the patches of clouds were fluffy.

The Sawyers were a genuine, down-to-earth family. Mr. Sawyer was a tall, broad-shouldered farmer with a huge head and a huge set of hands and a heart that matched them both. He was a lighthearted fellow who enjoyed a good laugh. Mrs. Sawyer was a whole foot shorter than her husband. She had these deep-set eyes that made her look glum in her tasks, but as soon as you engaged her in conversation, she beamed all of a sudden and became the kindest soul you'd ever met. I took a liking to Mrs. Sawyer the day I saw her grab an old Winchester and shoot a deer over a hundred yards away!

Pete and Erma had five children: four sons and one girl. Nathan was the oldest. He had short, wavy locks and was about the same height as his mom. Give him an apple and a book, and he was as happy as can be. He was a hard worker, but he had no interest in farm life. Irvin was the next oldest. He was even taller than his father. Unlike Nathan, Irvin wanted to keep the farming tradition. Allen was a short fellow who had survived a "nervous fever" when he was little. It took him a long time to put his sentences together. Sometimes he said things twice; sometimes he abandoned the part altogether. Wayne looked like his mom; he had the same serious look that turned to sunshine the moment you talked to him. And then there was Ann, the youngest of them all. She was "a little church bell"— always chattering about something, always "shining around" with her billows of hair all pinned up.

As soon as the wagon pulled into the yard, we were greeted by the Sawyer boys storming out of the house like a herd of hippopotamuses in bib overalls. Ann was right on their heels, lightly flickering about in her plain dress while her parents lagged behind. Soon enough, our moms were hugging, our dads were shaking hands, and they were all jabbering about life, marriage, and the "donkeywork" of raising children. "But children are a heritage of the Lord," Mrs. Sawyer added humorously. "I just keep telling myself that." Mom chuckled, nodding in agreement, which compelled Evelyn to claim she was a "perfectly proper child." Mom just rolled her eyes and cried, "Horsefeathers!"

Andrew did his best to greet everyone and eventually found his place on the porch swing. He had that faraway look in his eye. The rest of us boys wasted no time at all and started on our hike.

We crossed the brook by the carved-up elm tree and scaled the ridge, up to where a small number of gravestones stood hunched over, hiding amid some trees. We arrived at a small grove, whereupon each of us picked out an apple we could sink our teeth into. The crunchy bites and chomping provided the background music to Nathan's story about William Tell and how he used a crossbow to shoot an apple off his son's head—"from a great distance," he said. Wayne tossed his core at him, insisting the story wasn't true. Irvin said it was "something only Mom could manage," to which Allen firmly nodded and said, "Yep." Nathan accused Wayne of being a "killjoy," then pitched the remains of his apple back at him. That incited a game of dodgeball, only we were lobbing rotten apples and chewed-up cores at one another.

As usual, I couldn't hit anything on purpose if my life depended on it—which directed my train of thought to something else I had hit by accident! Irvin came up to me afterward and patted me on the back. "Goodness gracious!" he said. "I had you right in my sights when you were fixed on Wayne. That chunk whizzed right past your face. Ha! God must have a hedge of protection around you." I was certainly no George Washington who survived despite having two horses shot from under him and several bullets pierce his coat—but never were such words more welcome!

We dispensed with the apples and returned to the house to throw the football around instead. We arranged a little game. A game of two-hand touch since none of us wanted the displeasure of being tackled by Irvin. Each of us tried to make the spectacular play as best we could with Ann darting in and out of our game, despite the objections from her older brothers. She finally succeeded at nabbing the ball and took off with it through the yard, her pinned-up hair rising and falling like the raging sea. One would have thought her the greatest running back as she evaded the tackles of her brothers.

Irvin cornered her between the barn and the grain storage. She surrendered the football, but it was too late. He caught her by the arm and carried her all the way to the pond where, despite all her kicking and screaming, she was unceremoniously "baptized." Ann climbed out of the water and marched back to the house, asserting that she had been "baptized the year before," and that what her "mean brother" did was "blasphemous." Which gave the rest of us a good laugh!

After mealtime, we gathered around the biggest bonfire I had ever seen. While we were on our hike, Andrew had gone out and collected all the deadwood he could find from the nearby woods and constructed a gigantic teepee. The flame must've been twenty feet high, and it illuminated the yard like daytime. "Andy's gonna turn the whole world to ashes before the Lord even returns," Evelyn said. Mr. Sawyer slapped his knee and laughed uproariously. Mrs. Sawyer shook her head and said, "Goodness gracious! Get a hold of yourself, Pete." And just about the time he did, Mom had to go and say, "Erma's gonna haul you over the coals if you don't knock it off." Mr. Sawyer took one good look at the glowing embers and cried, "Well, that seems like a cruel and unusual punishment, don't ya think?" Then he lost it all over again.

Andrew stood there with his arms folded, clearly pleased. It was one of the rare times my brother's face beamed with joy.

Mrs. Sawyer dished out slices of apple pie. Upon being "thoroughly filled from top to bottom," Mr. Sawyer brought his guitar out and played for us. Irvin pulled out his harmonica as well, and the rest of us joined in on the chorus, singing and clapping our hands. Mrs. Sawyer took Mom's arm, and the two of them danced around the fire while Allen cheered them on.

At last, we tired ourselves out with all the merriment. Not to mention all the dessert and cider that had settled in our bellies. Each one of us took a seat on the benches, entranced by a more subdued fire now. The mood became reflective, and it was at this time Mr. Sawyer tuned up his guitar one more time and began to sing *The Old Rugged Cross*. Others joined in, including my mother and my sister who were sitting close by. The sweet tone of their voices reached down into my heart. I couldn't have been more grateful; it was the first time in a few months I had felt peace in my soul.

Chapter 6

The old house was clad in wooden strips of siding, gray and weather-beaten. The front door was centered, but high off the ground about six feet or so, and it was hemmed in by a large porch. One had to brave the steps at the right corner of the house to reach the door. On the left corner of the house was a rounded spire with bay windows. It towered beyond the porch roof, up to the second story, and added to the house's spooky influence.

Daryl and I looked both ways, then slipped into the driveway, which was nothing more than a stone pathway overtaken by weeds. Daryl moseyed through the yard, while I climbed the porch to have a peek inside. A whiff of decay and mustiness wafted up through the floorboards as I peered through the window. The place looked even more dismal and dirty than the last time. The plasterwork of the ceiling had broken off around the chandelier, leaving fragments littered across the floor. A thick layer of dust blanketed the rickety sofa. Cobwebs shrouded the candleholders on the wall and dangled from the corners of the molding around the entryway into the living room.

Daryl snapped me out of my trance. "David, come here! Look at this!"

I hurried off the porch. "What is it?"

"There's another one!" Daryl poked at the ground with a stick.

To my shock, another skeleton had surfaced in the yard. You could make out the spine and part of the ribcage. Daryl scraped away the muck from between the ribs with the stick.

"This place is definitely cursed," I said. "You can feel it in the air—and now this!"

"Wait till my uncle hears about this one," Daryl said. "God only knows how many more bodies she buried around here!"

"Pshh! No wonder she skipped town. Probably ran out of room."

"Well, thank goodness she's gone, that's all I can say. I mean can you imagine if she still lived here, knowing she's right around the corner from where you sleep at night?"

"It wouldn't be much better for me. This road begins at Healy, not far from—man alive! Do you realize we're both connected by Snake Hollow Road?"

"You just figured that out?"

"No, I mean we're connected in a weird way by this house. A house people say is haunted."

"My uncle says it is. He says the woman was engaged to be married, but that the man deserted her on the day of her wedding, never to be seen again. She went mad as a March hare and started offering up sacrifices to put a curse on him. Lester Harrison says she appears in her wedding dress at night to guard the graves of her victims."

I shuddered. "The thought is enough to make someone's blood run cold. Thank heavens she's gone. At least we don't have to worry about her since she only visits this place at night." That's when it occurred to me; something I had been mulling over for weeks. "I got a grand idea!"

"What's that?" Daryl said.

"Let's get Dominic to come up here and then we'll scare him half to death!"

"How would we do that?"

"You know how he loves Evelyn—he'd do *anything* for Evelyn. Well, let's get her to dare him to come up to the Slater house in the middle of the night. Then we'll scare him. It'll be hilarious to see him scream like a little girl!"

"You're telling me you'd come here at night to brave a ghost? I don't think so. You'd be the one running scared."

"Not if we go together. Besides, I don't really believe a ghost actually comes back at night."

"Well, neither do I, but it's too farfetched of a plan."

"Not really. Think about it. What better way to get even for all the things Dominic's done to us over the years? When has he ever gotten what's coming to him? Never, Daryl. Never!"

"I know, I know. Trust me, I'd love to see him shaking in his shoes, and I'd pay a large sum to make it happen, but—"

"That's just it, Daryl. This wouldn't cost you a penny. It's free! All we have to do is get him here!"

Daryl shook his head. "How would that work? He'd knock your face in as soon as he realized you set him up. I don't care *how* much he loves your sister, that would be a dance with death."

"We'll make it look like we had nothing to do with it. If anything, it'll look like Evelyn set him up, and there's no way he'd lay a finger on her. His little heart would be crushed. And honestly, Daryl, I think he likes my sister way too much to fight me."

"If you say so. But what if he chickens out?"

"His heart would still be crushed. He'd feel so unworthy of my sister, and we'd have something to make fun of him with."

Daryl raised one eyebrow. "You can make fun of him. Not me."

"Fine. We won't make fun of him—I mean not to his face anyhow. But he'd still be embarrassed, and it'd be so much fun just to see him that way. And listen, if he does go through with it—which I happen to think he would—then we'll have Evelyn hide out near the porch or something and scream like a banshee. He'd be scared out of his mind! I'm telling you, Daryl, it would work!"

Daryl rubbed his forehead. "And when would we do this?"

"Well, that'll be the next thing to figure out, but we'll—no, I got it! Halloween is coming up. That would be the perfect night to do it!"

Daryl's eyes lit up. "Halloween *would* be perfect!"

"So you're in?"

"I'll give it some thought."

"What for? What other kinda plan you gonna come up with that even comes close to this?"

"I don't know, but I'm sure we can think of something."

"Listen to yourself. You mean to tell me you never tried thinking of ways to get back at him?"

"No, I have."

"Exactly. And whatever came of it? Nothing. And you wanna know why? Because there's nothing as perfect as this plan. I'm telling you, Daryl. Nothing!"

Daryl finally shook my hand. "It's a done deal. I'm not gonna lie; there's not much more I'd love to see than for Dominic to tuck his tail. Now it's up to you talk Evelyn into it."

I was determined to get with Evelyn that very night. At bedtime, I went over and stood in the doorway. She was beside her bed, reading under the lamplight.

She looked up at me. "Oh, wouldn't you love to live in Green Gables? Just ponder that, Davey."

"May I come in?" I said.

"Sure. What's on your mind?—Obviously not Green Gables."

"I need a favor. Er, I mean I have an idea, and it requires a little help from you."

"With what?"

I closed the door behind me. "Well, you know how Dominic is...um...well, the way he's always mistreating others..."

"That sounds about right."

"...and browbeating everybody. You know, just how proud he is."

She nodded. "He thinks the sun comes up just to hear him crow—I get it."

"Exactly! Well, it's time he gets what he deserves. And since he's smitten with you, you're the perfect person for my plan."

She winced. "I don't like the sound of this already."

"Well, hold on. Don't answer yet. Just let me explain."

"Alright then. I'm listening."

"So Daryl and I gotta get Dominic to go with us to the Slater house on Halloween night—"

"Nope. Tell it to Sweeny."

"No, I'm serious."

"Good heavens, Davey! That place is—"

"Shh!"

"Sorry," she whispered. "That place is scary enough, let alone in the dark on Halloween. You gotta be kidding me."

"Please, Evelyn. The only way he would go with us is if you came along. That's the only way this whole thing would work."

She shut her book. "Oh, so there's more?"

"Well, let me finish."

"You've got two minutes. Then I need my beauty sleep."

"So the plan is for you to dare Dominic to, let's say, sit on the Slater porch all by himself. If he turns you down, then his heart is broken since he's rejected Your Majesty's wish. If he does accept the dare, then this is where you come in again—"

"You mean I've got more than one part?"

"One more *little* part. Once he sits down on the porch, you'll scream."

"You want me to scream?"

"Yes! It'll scare him for sure. You gotta help me, Evelyn."

She shook her head. "This is outlandish. You mean to tell me your head concocted this batty idea? There's something wrong with you, Davey."

"Evelyn, he's got it coming to him. You gotta help me, or Dominic will always get away with it. Don't you get it? He will always—get—away—with it."

She buried her head in her hands. "I don't know. I'll need some time to think about this one. I just can't believe you sometimes."

"Fair enough. Just think about it. Alright?"

"I'll *think* about it."

"That's right...Just think about it...Now goodnight."

I left the room and started down the hallway. I turned back one more time and peeked my head into her room. "It would mean a lot to me...."

"Good night, David!"

"Alright, alright. Goodnight."

Chapter 7

You can imagine how surprised I was when Evelyn approached me the next morning and said, "I'm game." I picked her up and told her she was "the bestest sister in the world." She seemed even more thrilled now about the scheme than I was. After breakfast, she came out back while I was splitting logs and took me aside. "Just so you know, Davey, Mom and Dad are gonna be out of town Halloween night. They're spending the weekend with the Swansons out in Carlton. What we need to do is host a party at our house the night of the scare. Then we'll all walk to the Slater house afterward. It makes perfect sense, Davey. The Halloween party would set the mood for the entire evening!"

The plan couldn't have worked out any better. All I needed to do was get Dominic to commit to coming to our house Halloween night. And like I had suspected, a mere mention of Evelyn's name did the trick!

The next couple weeks were the longest weeks of my life. I was like a little child waiting for Christmas—except I was waiting for Halloween. Nevertheless, I survived, and Halloween arrived.

It was midday. Dad was getting the horses ready, whistling a tune he made up as he went along. Mom was finishing up her preparations while singing *Great Is Thy Faithfulness*, her new favorite song. Getting together with Dan and Sara Swanson was a yearly tradition. Their friendship went back from the time when they were youngsters.

Andrew and I loaded up their belongings. When all was ready, I said goodbye to Chester and Checkers, our beloved horses. They had beautifully spotted coats and black manes. Their chests were charcoal gray, and the bulk of their bodies was white with spots on their hindquarters. Chester's legs were all white, whereas Checkers looked like he wore gray stockings. I loved petting the soft spot between their nostrils while watching their mouths fidget.

Dad escorted Mom to the carriage and gave her a hand boarding.

"Alright, my dear ones," Dad said. "Don't go burning the house down now."

"Don't worry," Evelyn said. "We will."

"I'm sure you will. Now remember, Andrew's in charge. He'll take you both behind the workshop if he needs to."

"Phonus-balonus!" Evelyn said. "I'm seventeen. I don't have to listen to Andy."

"That's what you think," Dad said teasingly.

Evelyn pointed to herself. "I'm in charge around here."

"Well, you can be in charge, but that ain't gonna stop Andrew from taking you out back if you misbehave."

"I'll take Andy out back, and I'll give him a paddling he'll never forget."

Mom chuckled. "You do that. Just be safe—and David, don't go waking snakes."

I gave Evelyn a quick look. "Yes, ma'am. Anything you say."

"Love you all."

"Alright, take care—Yah!"

The horses took off, and Mom blew us all one last kiss. "See you in a couple days."

"Lord willing and the creek don't rise," Evelyn hollered back.

About an hour later, Beth Harrison showed up at the house. Beth was Evelyn's best friend. I took Evelyn aside in the kitchen and asked her what was going on. She informed me Beth was there to help with the decorating as well as with the screaming later. I thought it all too convenient since Beth had a crush on Daryl. I was not happy with my sister, and I felt she was simply doing Beth a favor. "And now is not the time for favors," I said. Nevertheless, Evelyn assured me the plan would work out "even more fabulously with Beth's participation."

I went into the living room where Beth was seated and welcomed her. She tilted her head to the side, presenting her dimpled smile. She always smiled like she was hiding her bottom row of teeth. In any case, I felt the secret was safe with Beth, and I became fond of the idea as the evening drew near.

Evelyn and Beth did a fantastic job with the decorating. The dining room table was covered with an orange and black tablecloth that had scary pumpkins and witches printed all over. Orange streamers draped from each corner of the room and joined a cut-out paper pumpkin that hung from the center of the ceiling. Little skeletons also dangled here and there from above. Most impressive of all was the large jack-o-lantern that occupied the center of the table. It had a sinister grin that seemed to foreshadow an unfortunate event.

At about six o' clock, there came a knock at the front door.

"C'mon in, Daryl. Good to see you, Dominic. I'm so glad you fellas could make it. We've got things ready."

"Thanks, David," Daryl said.

Dominic patted me on the shoulder and peeked around the room. "It's gonna be a rare old time, David. I can tell already. Anybody else here?"

"Yeppers. Beth's here. She's in the kitchen."

"Oh...is, um, your sister here?"

"Oh, yes. Yes, Evelyn's here—Hey, ladies, our guests are here!"

Evelyn and Beth entered the living room, full of welcoming smiles.

Evelyn shook Dominic's hand. "Good evening, Dominic. May I take your coat?"

He blushed. And Dominic never blushed. "Um, sure. Thank you, Evelyn."

"Hi, Daryl," Beth said bashfully. "May I take yours?"

"Thanks," Daryl said. "But I think I'm gonna keep mine on."

"Oh, sure. Well, let me show you to your seat."

Daryl glanced at me and then followed Beth into the dining room. He knew Beth adored him, and it made him feel uncomfortable. I leaned in and whispered, "Not my doing!"

"This is Daryl's seat, right, Evelyn?" Beth asked.

"Yep. That's his," Evelyn said. "And then you're sitting right across from him."

Daryl hesitated. He closed his eyes for a second then took his seat.

"And then you sit here, David," Evelyn said. "Right next to Daryl. Dominic can sit here on the end, and I'll sit across from you." Which happened to be next to Dominic who seemed rather pleased!

"Where's Andrew?" Dominic asked.

"Oh, he's upstairs," I said.

"Is he gonna join us?"

"Probably not. He's busy painting right now."

"One of the rooms?"

"Oh, no. He paints pictures. It's his hobby. He really enjoys it. Does a pretty darn good job, too."

"I see. I haven't seen your brother in ages. Does he work?"

"He does."

"Where?"

"Um, usually here around the house. He helps us out."

"Whew! I'd get cabin-fever."

I tried to change the subject. "Didn't the ladies do a great job with all the decorations?"

"They sure did!"

Evelyn lit the candle inside the jack-o-lantern.

"Ha ha! This jack-o-lantern is incredible," Dominic said. "Who did this?"

"Evelyn did."

He gazed at my sister. "Wow! You're quite the little sculptor."

Evelyn gave him the brightest smile.

The fire flickered about the room, the skeletons danced to the rising heat, and Dominic's eyes glowed with delight.

Just then, Evelyn placed three cups on the table. She filled one with milk, one with vinegar, and one with water. "Now each of you gentlemen must pick your cup of fate. Once you are blindfolded, you will reach for one of the cups. The first cup you touch is the one you dip your finger in. If it's milk, that means you'll have a happy married life. If it's water, you'll have a blessed, single life. And if you dip your finger in the vinegar, that means you'll have a sour spouse. So who will go first?"

Dominic shot his hand up.

"Alright, Dominic. That's the spirit!"

Evelyn blindfolded him, which he clearly enjoyed. He then felt around for a cup. He touched one and dipped his finger in and tasted it.

Milk.

"Ha ha!" Dominic had a grin that rivaled the jack-o-lantern. He poked me in the ribs. "Looks like I'm gonna be happily married."

The thought made me sick to my stomach. I knew he was dreaming about my sister.

Next, Beth blindfolded Daryl and mixed up the cups. Daryl reached his hand out and touched one.

Vinegar.

"Well, that settles it," Daryl said lightheartedly. "I guess I'm destined for a sour woman."

I overheard Beth whisper to Evelyn, "I'm not sour!"

Finally, my turn. Evelyn blindfolded me and mixed up the cups. My hand grazed a rim, so I dipped my finger in.

Water.

Evelyn snickered. "Fabulous! You each picked something different. It looks like you're gonna have a blessed, single life, Davey."

"What's so blessed about being single?" I said, sulking.

Dominic sneered. "If I didn't know any better, I'd say you're cursed."

I wanted to punch him in the mouth!

"Speaking of being cursed," Evelyn said, "you all know how the Slater house is cursed, with all the bodies buried there and all."

Dominic folded his arms. "My dad says that property's an old Quaker burial ground."

"It's a frightening place of the dead is what it is!" Evelyn cried. She leaned in so that the jack-o-lantern lit up her face, and she talked in a spooky voice. "A woman once lived there—a woman engaged to be married. They say she wore that ring proudly on her finger…But the man she loved with all her heart betrayed her the very day of their wedding! He abandoned her. And he skipped town, never to be seen again…They say she sank into the depths of despair and fled to the tombs, wailing and howling like the madman of Gadara…But with the passing of days, sorrow turned to anger. Anger turned to fury. Until her soul turned utterly black. Black as a witch's cat. Black as the moonless night…They say she lurked in the shadows to slay the innocent ones. Anyone she thought was false-hearted like her lover…She offered these sacrifices to put a curse on the one who betrayed her…They say the house is now haunted. That

59

she appears in her wedding dress at night to guard the graves of her victims." She gave one last menacing laugh and said, "The end."

Dominic smacked the table. "That was a terrific ghost story!"

"Glory be!" Beth said, clapping her hands. "Whatta ya say we all go up to the Slater house tonight? Wouldn't that be so fun, especially on Halloween night?"

"Oh, Beth!" Evelyn cried. "Let's do it! It'll be a memory. Whatta ya guys say?"

"Sounds like a great idea," I said, looking over at Daryl.

"Me, too," Daryl said. "I've got a hankering for something hair-raising."

"How about you, Dominic?" Evelyn said.

"Sure. If that's what ya'll want. As long as I'm home by ten."

"Isn't this just the bee's knees?" Evelyn said. "Oh, I almost forgot! This would be the perfect time to sign these." She handed out a sheet of paper to each of us guys.

I scowled. "What's this?"

"It's a Halloween will," Evelyn said. "There's no telling what might happen tonight."

I read the paper.

If the Witch of Snake Hollow Road should take my soul tonight on this 31st day of October 1924, I, David Millard Hayes, leave all my possessions and personal property to be divided between Beth Harrison and Evelyn Hayes. Signed:

"What are you waiting for?" Beth said. "You gentlemen have to sign it."

"I'm not leaving my stuff to you two," I said.

"You ain't got nothing to leave anyway, Davey, so don't be a wet blanket," Evelyn said. "Now we can't leave until all of you sign it."

"What are you afraid of?" Dominic said, signing the paper.

I rolled my eyes. "Nothing. Gimme the stupid pen."

Daryl glanced at me then scribbled his name across the paper.

I did the same. "There. You happy?"

Evelyn snatched the paper out of my hand. "You never know, it might be curtains for you tonight."

"What about you ladies?" Daryl asked. "Why don't *you* need a will?"

"Dominic will keep us safe," Evelyn said. "Won't you, Dominic?"

Dominic grinned at me. "You betcher."

Evelyn lit the lamp. "Then let us be going. I'll be right back down; I'm gonna let Andrew know we're leaving."

We all got up from the table and grabbed our things.

I was in such deep thought buttoning my jacket when Dominic came up from behind and startled me. His hand was on my shoulder. With beady eyes, he said, "Ready, Davey? 'Cause there's no telling what might happen tonight!" His expression gave me the heebie-jeebies. I turned about and headed for the door.

Evelyn came back downstairs, and we all ventured out into the dark.

We started down the road. The night sky looked ominous, the way the moon peeked out from behind the clouds and scowled at me. Even the wind whispered a ghost story.

We veered down Snake Hollow Road, which felt even gloomier. The lofty trees obstructed the moonlight, and the scrawnier trees looked like skeletons coming to beset us. Evelyn had done a tremendous job setting the mood for the night. Too good of a job, in fact. As much as I hated to admit it, I felt safer with Dominic there. We all kept close as we trudged down the old dirt road together, hanging onto every crackle and random sound around us.

Everyone was jittery. Except Dominic. He chattered and snickered with the girls.

At last, we arrived at the Slater property. The house was nestled in trees, which enhanced its ghostly impression. The lantern helped light our path, but it did little to illuminate the overall prospect. We huddled together and inched our way up the old driveway.

Evelyn and Beth strayed into the yard. "Look!" Beth said. "Here's where that body was buried." Evelyn dangled the lantern over the area. The skull was exposed and seemed to mock our adventure.

"There's another one over there, too," Daryl said. "Me and David found it one day."

"Good heavens!" Evelyn cried. "I'm not going any farther then."

"Me neither," Beth said. "This place is too scary. We're likely to trip over bones."

"Only a man would go up to that house," Evelyn said.

"Nah, it's not that big of a deal," I said. I couldn't believe I said it. Not to mention how foolish I felt, since my own sister knew I was feigning bravery!

"Listen to you, David," Dominic sneered. "You know you ain't got the guts to go up there."

"Well, what about that porch?" Beth chimed in. "Has anyone gone up there before?"

"I don't think it's *ever* been done," Evelyn said. "Only the bravest of the brave would climb that awful thing."

"I'd do it," Dominic said.

"My stars!" Evelyn cried. "You would do that?"

"Sure, I would. I mean I don't need to prove I'm brave or anything, but I can do it. And if *I* can do it, then surely David can, too. Right, David?"

I gulped. "Sure."

"How long do I need to stay up there?" Dominic asked.

"I'd say at least twenty seconds," Evelyn said. "Wouldn't you, Beth?"

"At least."

"Alright," Dominic said. "I'll do it for *thirty* seconds. Here goes." He went ahead by himself. Evelyn and Beth handed me the lamp and wandered off according to plan. I could barely make out Dominic's silhouette as he climbed the porch. "I'm here," he hollered. "Let me know when thirty seconds is up."

"Sounds good, Dominic," I answered back.

All of a sudden, Evelyn and Beth came rushing back like two ghosts in the night, almost enough to make me scream. Evelyn gripped my arm. "Davey!" she gasped. "I just saw something move up there."

"You can't be serious!" I said.

"I saw it, too!" Beth said. "Oh, I'm not feeling right about this."

"Where?"

"Over there," Evelyn said.

Nothing but darkness.

"Davey, I'm about to scream for real," Evelyn said.

"We should go!" Beth said.

"Hey!" Dominic shouted. "What's going on down there? That's more than thirty seconds."

"You can come down now, Dominic," Beth hollered.

Dominic came back, his face beaming in the lamplight. He thumped me on the back. "Now it's your turn, Davey."

Terror struck my brain. Shadows were swooping everywhere.

"You're not scared, are you?" Dominic said.

"No," I said, shaking.

"Then let's see it. Are you a real man or what?"

What on earth is going on?

Dominic burst out laughing. "He looks like he saw a ghost."

"Enough, Dominic," I said. "The girls just saw something up there."

"As you would expect," Dominic said. "The house is haunted, remember? But I did it. Now let's see if you can do it."

I don't know how, but I managed to put one foot in front of the other and started creeping my way toward the porch.

"Look at Davey go!" Dominic cried. "At a snail's gallop! Ha ha!"

There was no way out of it. I could not be outdone by Dominic again. I would never live it down.

The girls are just imagining things! They're just being panicky!

I reached the porch. My heart pounded in my chest. My head felt woozy. My hands were clammy.

The sooner you get on that porch, the sooner this whole thing's done with!

I lugged up the stairs, one step at a time, trying to peer through the darkness.

I reached the top.

I was about to announce my arrival when something in the far corner growled at me. I heard it scratching across the floorboards. It came scurrying after me.

"David! Run!"

I screamed and leaped off the porch, tripping over who-knows-what and tumbling on my arm. I heard a snap. With no time to think, I sprang up and darted toward the others, the girls still screaming at the top of their lungs and urging me on. We fled the property and ran up the road, looking back to see if it was chasing after us.

"What the dickens just happened?" Daryl cried. "What—just—happened?"

"I don't know!" Dominic said. "But those stories are no joke! That place is haunted alright!"

"Let's just keep moving," Evelyn said, looking back.

"Ah!" I groaned. "It hurts so bad now."

"What hurts?" Evelyn said.

"My arm," I said. "It's broken."

"It's *what*?" Evelyn said. She rushed over with the lantern. "Oh, my stars! Beth, come look at this. His arm is broken!—Davey, I'm so sorry!"

Chapter 8

Evelyn and I told our parents the same thing we had told Dr. Thompson when he set my arm—that I had tripped and fallen "off the porch." Which was true, nonetheless.

I was more troubled now than ever before. *How did I end up on that blasted porch? And how did Dominic get away with it...again?* As much as I had confidence in my parents' knowledge of the scriptures as well as their insight into life, I concluded they were missing a piece to the spiritual puzzle. All things considered, my parents still knew more than most, I thought, but they must've been mistaken on this point.

I'm cursed! Simple as that!

Needless to say, I couldn't play baseball in a cast. However, my arm eventually healed, and the year wrapped up with nothing sensational to write about. The holidays were as delightful as usual, another year come and gone. It's strange looking back knowing Hitler was released from prison that very Christmas Eve after being locked up for high treason. Little did any of us know what lay ahead! A darling lesson of life!

For now, it was 1925. The year Ford presented the Model T Roadster Pickup. The year the frisbee was invented. The year Charlie Chaplin's film *The Gold Rush* hit the movie houses. The year the Tri-

State Tornado tore a path of destruction through Missouri, Illinois, and even into Indiana, killing almost seven hundred people.

It was likewise the year my mother became ill. We thought she had the flu; she had a high fever and felt queasy, and her body ached all over. She seemed to recover in less than a week, but a couple days later, she grew pale and was confined to her bed again. Dr. Thompson visited our home. On one hand, he was encouraged to see my mother was not jaundiced. On the other hand, he was perplexed. He told her to drink plenty of water and to eat as much soup as she could handle despite not having an appetite. So Andrew cooked up plenty of chicken soup, which seemed to agree with her best. At least she was getting nourishment.

While my mother was confined to her bed, rumor began to churn about an upcoming trial. What would commonly be known as the Scopes Monkey Trial. John Thomas Scopes was a substitute teacher who allegedly broke the law of Tennessee which stated it was "unlawful for any person" in a school funded by the State "to teach any theory that denies the story of the Divine Creation of man as taught in the Bible, and to teach instead that man has descended from a lower order of animals." He had been indicted in May.

Thank heavens the trial was to be held in July. I didn't have to be preoccupied with school. Apart from my daily responsibilities, I was free to listen to the radio broadcast and consume all the newspaper accounts. In fact, Daryl's parents had bought a new radio—another reason I was envious of him. (I couldn't wait for the day the Hayes house had electricity!)

William Jennings Bryan was one of the premier leaders of the Democratic Party in those days, and he was to be part of the prosecution team. I felt confident he would be the champion for all of us who believed the biblical account of creation. However, defending Scopes and evolution was the famous defense lawyer and agnostic, Clarence Darrow. I'll never forget the first time I saw a picture of him; he looked fierce and daunting to me. There were other men on the defense team, but Darrow was the one who left an indelible impression on me.

Friday. The first day of the trial. I was eager to hear Bryan speak, but I didn't realize all the preliminaries that had to take place. The court opened with prayer, and the judge called the case. Then the outside counsel and the defense team were introduced. The judge read the charge to the grand jury and followed with a reading of Genesis 1. After that, the selection of the jury took place, and that took up the remainder of the day.

Monday. I returned to Daryl's. Lucy shuffled her way to the door, on her crutches.

"Hello, David."

"Hey, Lucy. You gonna listen to the trial today?"

"Not really. Daddy says it should be a simple trial, but that it's gonna be made into a great debate. He says the whole thing's a setup by the ACLU. Besides, I got a new book.

"Really? Whatcha reading?"

"*Little Women.* Mattie Hall gave it to me as a gift. Isn't that sweet of her?"

"That was very nice of her to do that."

She shifted her weight on her crutches, trying to get comfortable. "Yep. She wrote a very kind note to me, too. Right inside the cover. Says she thinks of me and prays for me."

"That sounds like Mattie. She's a good friend."

"Yep."

"Well, speaking of a good friend, is your brother home?"

"He sure is. Come in."

"Thank you."

"You're very welcome."

I followed her into the house and went into the living room where Daryl was already seated near the radio.

"Anything good?" I asked, taking a seat.

"Not really," Daryl said. "The jurors have been sworn in, and they just read the indictment. But nothing too exciting, just part of the process."

"I guess so. I didn't realize it would be so drawn out."

I didn't understand much; it seemed too confusing. Daryl, however, seemed to grasp every bit of what was coming across the radio.

Later on, I asked, "So what's going on now?"

"Um, the defense wants the case canceled," Daryl explained. "That's what they're asking for."

"How can they ask for that? Scopes broke the law."

"Well, they're arguing the law is unconstitutional."

"What?"

"Well, the law's a bit unfair, and the defense is quoting other laws to prove it."

"How could there be laws to prove *that*?"

"For one, there's a Tennessee law that says places of education should value science."

"But they *do* value science."

"I'm not sure they do as much as they should."

"What do you mean? I'm sure the students learn science. Just like us."

"Well, some science, but not all science."

"But evolution's not science."

"Yes, it is."

"What? You think evolution's science?"

"I do."

I was astonished. I had known Daryl for years; he had never defended evolution before. We attended different churches, but I had always felt we believed much the same way, and I could remember him saying so.

"You really believe that evolution stuff?" I asked.

He stared at the radio. "I do."

"How long?"

"Well, I've actually been thinking about some things for quite a while now."

"Wow. You never told me that."

He shrugged his shoulders. "Meh, I figured it would just come up on its own sometime. I guess this was the time."

"But there's no proof of evolution."

"Yes, there is."

"Where?"

"Charles Darwin documented evolutionary changes in his book. He showed how all sorts of things could have come about through a common ancestry."

"You read Darwin's book?"

"Well, not the whole thing, but I remember it in biology. And my uncle's got a copy."

"I didn't think anybody actually believed that silly diagram."

This time, he looked right at me with one eyebrow raised.

I leaned back in my chair, completely incredulous. I tried to change the subject. "So the defense thinks the law's unfair, huh?"

"Yep. And now they're saying that there are two different accounts of creation in Genesis."

"Two? What do *they* know?"

"Well, there are two accounts. You didn't know that?"

I scowled.

"If you read the first two chapters of Genesis," Daryl continued, "the second chapter clearly presents a different story than the one in the first chapter. I've read it myself."

There was nothing I could say. I had never gotten that impression in the past when I went through Genesis, but it was something I'd have to examine for myself. I took a deep breath and pretended to listen to the commotion on the radio. In truth, I was brooding over all that had just transpired between Daryl and me. The bottom had fallen out of my heart.

I decided to head home. I got up and shook Daryl's hand and thanked him for having me over. He gave me a hearty smile, which he rarely did, and he told me I was welcome to come back the next day.

As soon as I got home, I headed straight to my bedroom and grabbed my Bible. I perused the first two chapters in Genesis.

I heaved a sigh. It seemed Daryl was right.

How can anyone trust the rest of the Bible?

Andrew was sitting next to me with a brush in hand, working on his painting.

"What do you think, Andrew?"

"About what?"

"About evolution."

He faintly chuckled. "Been following the Monkey trial?"

"A little bit...Do you believe God created Adam and Eve?"

"I suppose."

"Daryl says there's proof of changes."

Andrew paused for a moment and turned to the picture frame on the shelf. It was our departed sister, June. She was nineteen years old when she died from the Spanish Flu, just a few months before my brother returned from the War. Another aspect of his grief. (I was only nine when she passed away, but I'll never forget the times she'd take me outside and play our game of counting birds. Or when she'd read me a story or help me with my homework. I miss her very much.) Andrew straightened the picture and took up his brush again. "Things do change, that's for sure," he muttered.

I wanted badly to talk to my father, but he was working late. I couldn't ask Evelyn because she was still out galivanting with Beth.

My mother was resting, and I couldn't find it in my heart to disrupt her.

I went to bed early that night, feeling more cursed than ever. I couldn't even pray for my mom as I usually did at bedtime.

What's the use in praying anyways?

Chapter 9

The next morning, I went outside to help my sister gather the eggs. "Have you heard there are two different creation accounts in Genesis?"

She stood up and smacked me on the arm. "Phonus-balonus! What have you been reading?"

"That's what the defense lawyers are saying in the Monkey trial. Daryl says so, too."

"I'm gonna have a little talk with Daryl. That's a twice-told tale, Davey. The accounts are one and the same."

"But I read them myself. They're different."

"Don't be silly. You're just reading what someone else already told you. The first chapter is about the entire order of creation. It's all given in the right order. The second chapter concentrates on finding the right mate for Adam, which is on the same day God had already made all the land animals—none of which proved right for Adam, of course." She smirked. "That's why God gave him a woman. Ponder that, Davey!"

I set the basket down. "Please forgive me, Evelyn. I gotta take care of something." I scrambled through the brood of chickens and hurried out of the coop.

Evelyn hollered back, "Someone needs to pay better attention in Sunday School!"

I ran into the house and up to my bedroom and grabbed my Bible. I sat down on the bed and read the two chapters all over again. A smile stole across my face. I tossed my Bible down on the dresser and rushed back downstairs.

My sister had just returned from outside. "Evelyn, you're the greatest!" I gave her the biggest hug then hurried out the door.

I hopped on my bicycle and rode to Daryl's. As soon as he opened the door, I bombarded him with the lesson Evelyn had shared with me.

He shrugged his shoulders and offered me a coke.

Deflated again, I didn't say much more to Daryl. We just spent the time playing chess, mostly in silence, apart from the trial airing in the background.

Again, no speech from Bryan.

Wednesday. The effort to "quash" the case, based on the objections raised on Monday, were overruled. The case was to move on, and the jury was called. The defendant pleaded not guilty, and the defense alleged that Scopes hadn't gone against the Bible account of creation; that there were Christians who weren't like the "fundamentalists."

"What are fundamentalists?" I asked.

"People like you and the Klan," Daryl said. He said it in such a matter-of-fact way.

I flinched. "What? I'm not like the Klan."

"Well, what I mean is, um, your family believes in the so-called fundamentals of the Bible. You know, like the virgin birth, the deity of Christ's, the resurrection of Christ, and so forth. It so happens the Ku Klux Klan believes like you do, that's all—I mean my own family does, too. Not me, but *they* do. I was just trying to explain, that's all."

I shook my head. "I just can't believe you said that...."

"I told you, David. You and my family both believe the Bible. It's just that modernists like me don't believe the Bible the way you and the Klan do. That's all I meant."

I couldn't tell if there was something different about Daryl, or whether I was just suddenly made aware of the difference. I couldn't say he was being unkind, but he seemed so plainspoken now, and I wasn't used to that. Nevertheless, I dropped the argument, and we continued to listen to the broadcast.

Again, no speech from Bryan.

Dad called on me to help run the bandsaw at the lumber yard on Thursday and Friday. Production was in high gear, and they needed some extra help until they could get caught up. I was glad to be able to make a little extra money, but it frustrated me to no end that I missed the trial both days.

By the time Monday rolled around, I couldn't take it anymore. I wanted nothing more than to hear Bryan speak with Daryl right beside me. I wasn't good at putting things into words, and I was sure if Daryl heard it from someone more eloquent than me, he would be convinced. I returned to his house, and we resumed our chess playing while listening to the radio.

I captured his pawn with my knight. "Check."

Daryl sat up straight and seemed not to hear me. "The part you've been waiting for, David. The judge just announced Bryan's name."

"Thank heavens!" I said. I dumped the pieces into the box.

"What are you doing?"

"I'm getting ready to hear Bryan speak."

"Well, you didn't have to put the game away."

"Oh, I'm sorry. I was just excited."

Daryl shook his head. "It's your loss. You were putting all the pressure on me."

"I didn't lose."

"Well, it's a draw. Which is a win for me as far as I'm concerned 'cause I was losing anyway. But whatever. Have it your way."

"I'm sorry. I wasn't thinking."

We both sat back in our chairs and listened. I couldn't contain the smile on my face.

Daryl glanced at me and chuckled. "You really like this guy, don't you?"

"Yeppers. He's a great spokesperson."

Here I had been anxious for Bryan to speak, yet when he finally did, I couldn't understand much of what he said. I still felt proud of his testimony though. I could pick out enough to tell that he scoffed at the idea of evolution, and every now and again, Bryan's witty comments drew laughter from the courtroom, which made me snicker inside.

I glanced over at Daryl. He was unmoved by it all.

Then the unexpected twist came.

The defense called William Jennings Bryan to the stand!

The chief prosecutor did not like the idea at all, but Bryan insisted it would be fine. He said he would go along with it providing that, in turn, Darrow and the other lawyers would also take the stand. To which they agreed.

Hence, the examination began.

"Do you claim," Darrow asked, "that everything in the Bible should be literally interpreted?"

"I believe everything in the Bible should be accepted as it is given there," Bryan replied. "Some of the Bible is given illustratively. For instance: 'Ye are the salt of the earth.' I would not insist that man was actually salt, or that he had flesh of salt, but it is used in the sense of salt as saving God's people."

"But when you read that Jonah swallowed the whale—or that the whale swallowed Jonah—excuse me please—how do you literally interpret that?"

"When I read that a big fish swallowed Jonah—it does not say whale."

"Doesn't it? Are you sure?"

My heart sank. I clearly remembered Evelyn showing me before how the Bible said "great fish" in one place and "whale" in another. It was a sincere mistake on Bryan's part, but I suddenly felt nervous about Darrow's line of attack.

"That is my recollection of it," Bryan answered. "A big fish, and I believe it, and I believe in a God who can make a whale and can make a man and make both do what he pleases."

"Mr. Bryan, doesn't the New Testament say whale?"

"I am not sure. My impression is that it says fish; but it does not make so much difference; I merely called your attention to where it says fish—it does not say whale."

"But in the New Testament it says whale, doesn't it?"

"That may be true; I cannot remember in my own mind what I read about it."

"Now, you say, the big fish swallowed Jonah, and he there remained how long—three days—and then he spewed him upon the land. You believe that the big fish was made to swallow Jonah?"

"I am not prepared to say that; the Bible merely says it was done."

"You don't know whether it was the ordinary run of fish, or made for that purpose?"

"You may guess; you evolutionists guess."

"But when we do guess, we have a sense to guess right."

"But do not do it often."

"You are not prepared to say whether that fish was made especially to swallow a man or not?"

"The Bible doesn't say, so I am not prepared to say."

"You don't know whether that was fixed up specially for the purpose?"

76

"No, the Bible doesn't say."

"But do you believe he made them—that he made such a fish and that it was big enough to swallow Jonah?"

"Yes, sir. Let me add: One miracle is just as easy to believe as another."

Bryan continued to give his responses to the questions Darrow put forth. At one point, the crowd in attendance cheered for Bryan.

"Great applause from the bleachers," Darrow said.

"From those whom you call 'yokels,'" Bryan replied.

"I have never called them yokels."

"That is the ignorance of Tennessee, the bigotry," Bryan explained, intending to convey how Darrow really felt about them.

"You mean who are applauding you?"

"Those are the people whom you insult."

"You insult every man of science and learning in the world because he does not believe in your fool religion."

Both the court and outside counsel objected to the heated exchange.

Still, Bryan remained on the stand.

Darrow proceeded to question him about the age of the earth and about where Cain got his wife. Then he asked him about the days of creation, whether they were literal days or not.

"Does the statement," Darrow asked, "'The morning and the evening were the first day,' and 'The morning and the evening were the second day,' mean anything to you?"

"I do not think it necessarily means a twenty-four-hour day," Bryan replied.

"You do not?"

"No."

"What do you consider it to be?"

Bryan answered saying the word "day" could also "describe a period."

Darrow smelled blood and went in for the kill. "Then, when the Bible said, for instance, 'and God called the firmament heaven. And the evening and the morning were the second day,' that does not necessarily mean twenty-four hours?"

"I do not think it necessarily does," Bryan said.

"Do you think it does or does not?" Darrow pressed.

"I know a great many think so."

"What do you think?"

"I do not think it does."

"You think those were not literal days?"

"I do not think they were twenty-four-hour days."

That's when Daryl got up and slapped his hands down on the radio. "Good gracious, David! Even Bryan admits the Bible shouldn't be interpreted literally!"

I slumped into my chair. The feeling of triumph I had felt over Bryan vanished away. It was gone.

Completely gone.

Salvation's just a fairytale! I'm so cursed!

It mattered nothing to me that Scopes was found guilty the next day and fined. In my mind, Darrow won, and Bryan lost. And that was certainly the impression one got from the newspapers.

Chapter 10

I had finished mowing the lawn and was moping around the front yard when Dad came out onto the porch and waved me on. "Come hither, Son. I've got some woodwork in the shop, and I need a hand loading it up."

"Yes, sir."

I grabbed the push-reel mower and followed him back.

He showed me the hefty cabinet he had made. We both took an end and lifted it up, then we shuffled our way to the wagon. As soon as we got it loaded, we covered the cabinet with a sheet and strapped it down so it wouldn't bounce around or get chipped.

"Coming with me?" Dad asked.

"Where ya headed?" I said.

"Up to Hideaway Hills. There's a gentleman there who's new to the area, just moved here with his family. I ran into him at the barbershop a month or so ago. He found out I did custom work on the side, so he went ahead and ordered this."

"Sure. I'll go with you."

Dad smiled, then he smacked me on the back. "Well, I'm glad to hear that because it really wasn't an option anyway."

I hitched up the horses and went inside to say goodbye to Mom. "I'll see you later, Mother," I said, stepping into the bedroom. "Love you." I tucked in the sheets around her and covered her legs with her favorite stars and stripes blanket. Mom smiled at me. "Thank you, David. I love you, too. I've been praying for you." I forced a smile in return, then I left the room. I could barely refrain from crying. I had been neglecting to pray for my mom, and here was my sick mom praying for me!

I left the house and waited in the wagon for Dad.

Before long, he came out and hopped aboard. "Ready, Son?" he said, taking up the reigns.

I wiped any trace of a tear from my face. "Ready as I'll ever be."

"Alright then—Yah!"

We took off down the dirt road into town, then traveled up Ludwig right past Daryl's, out the other side of town, northward. Crossing the Seymour River, we continued to weave our way down the county road. The episodes of the past week flashed through my mind—like the way the roadside zipped by as I stared across my shoulder. I pondered all that had occurred between Daryl and me. I tried to muster the strength to seek out my father's mindset on some matters, but the sound of the wagon wheels careening down the road kept me spellbound.

Dad leaned over and tugged on the shoulder. "Pretty funny what Mrs. Goodwin blurted out last Sunday, huh? That lady's sure got a knack at making waggish remarks. Pastor should've known better than to call on her with a Bible question. Ha! You ask her a question, and she'll give you an answer you'll never forget."

I nodded. "She never disappoints, that's for sure."

"No, she doesn't. And she's got a long history, that woman. I remember her way back when we first added on to the sanctuary. Mr. Porter was our choir director then, and he was calling on people to tell him their favorite song. So Mr. Goodwin raises his hand and says, '*I Love to Tell the Story.*' Well, Mrs. Goodwin yells out, 'It's 'cause Elmer's nothing but a talebearer!' Ha! The congregation was in fits and stitches. And then Pastor, who's pretty nimble-witted himself,

80

yells back, 'Now don't be telling any tales, Marjorie.' And of course, she just laughs in her usual rowdy manner."

"I've seen her speak her mind once or twice."

"Ha! That reminds me of the time Joe Simmons came back to church. Now you could tell the moment he walked through the doors he had an axe to grind with Pastor Richardson. Well, there's a group of us still chatting after the service, and we're all making our way to the front door, along with Pastor and Simmons. Pastor keeps trying to lighten up the mood and put out all of Simmons's little fires, but you could tell Simmons wasn't having any of it. When ole Joe reaches the door, he says to Pastor right then and there, real loud for all to hear, "I know one thing, your sermons ain't what they used to be!" Well, Mrs. Goodwin turns and says, "Don't listen to a word he says, Pastor! He's just saying what we was already thinking!"

"She said that, huh?"

"She sure did. Well, you know how good-natured Pastor is; he just laughs and laughs, even though he's the butt of the joke. But leave it to ole Joe to turn a pair of long trousers inside out. He thinks he's just been reprimanded by Mrs. Goodwin, and so he yells at her, "Well, don't get mad at me for having the guts to speak my mind. Shame on you!" And then he storms out of the church. I mean your mother and I lost it. We all laughed so hard we were crying, and we just kept saying, 'Shame on you, Marjorie! Shame on you for never speaking your mind!' Ha ha!"

"Leave it to Mrs. Goodwin," I said. "She'll make anybody laugh." I regretted that statement as soon as it came out of my mouth. Not only was I *not* laughing, but I could hardly force a smile. I suddenly felt silly.

We jostled around in the wagon for another minute or so when Dad pushed the issue. "You've been quiet," he said. "Not just since we left home, but I mean this past week. What's eating you?"

I shrugged my shoulders. "I don't know."

"Bushwa! You've had the mullygrubs for days. Who do you think you're kidding?"

"I got some things on my mind is all."

"No kidding. Let's hear it."

"Well, hear me out, alright?"

"I'm listening."

I took a deep breath and made the best of it. "We're fundamentalists, right?"

"Sure."

"Well, Daryl says the Klan are fundamentalists, too."

Dad scowled. "Well, I reckon robins and ravens are both birds...."

"What do you mean?"

"I mean we're still different. Different as can be from where I stand."

"Well, Daryl says we sing out of the same hymnbook."

Dad chuckled. "I see Daryl's got you flustered. What's got into him?"

"I don't know...but something's happened though. He's different now."

"Well, you can't say you believe the Bible while going about breaking it."

"But even you and Pastor say that we all break it."

"True. But what I mean is, the Klan goes around terrifying people, trying to force things to be the way they want. Jesus said the violent take the kingdom of God by force—and that's not a compliment. No, we preach the word—whether it's in season or not, we must still preach the word—but we live by example. We don't put a pistol to someone's head, you see. That's what I mean by breaking it."

"I see...It just seems like times are changing."

"Yep. They are."

"You know, all this evolution stuff now."

"I hear ya."

I looked away and watched the trees rush by. "Do you think America will be here, say, in the next hundred years?"

"Only God knows," Dad said. He gave it more thought. "I would say there will probably be an America. Now whether she's the same country that was founded, only God knows. To tell you the truth, I'm surprised she's made it *this* long."

"Really? I'm surprised you say that."

"Absolutely, Son. It's nothing short of a miracle."

I mulled over what my father had said. Then I began to go over the main points of America's history in my mind.

"Do you think the Bible will ever die out?" I asked.

"No," Dad said. "Well, maybe in this country, I don't know. Who can say? But it will live on somewhere somehow. That much I can tell you."

"Even with this battle between science and religion?"

"What do you mean? There's ain't no such battle, Son."

"How can you say that? That's what the Monkey Trial was all about."

"Well, don't get me wrong. There's a battle alright, but not between science and religion. It's more like a battle between religion and religion."

"How's that?"

"All that evolution malarkey, it isn't science. It's faith. What they imagine might have happened. What they hope happened or will happen." Dad turned to me and shook his finger. "Then they mock us for our sacred books because they were written by men, yet they've got their own stack of books just as well. Don't let them kid ya."

"But Daryl says the size of certain birds has changed over time. Even the shape of their beaks."

"Oh, those kinds of changes? Well, that's the way God made 'em. But it's still a beak, right? It's still a bird, right? And that much we can say with certainty!"

I thought about it for a moment. "I see what you're saying."

"I mean take, for instance, all the dogs that folks own in this county," Dad said. "They're as different as chalk and cheese. Now how do you think we got so many different dogs? Well, they came from other dogs that came from other dogs, and they just kept changing little by little over the years. God didn't create all these sorts of dogs, and Noah didn't have to house every sort of dog in that big boat. He just needed one kind. And to this very day, all these creatures in this world are all still having pups and litters and whatnot, 'after their kind'—that's how Moses put it."

Just then, we pulled up to a Colonial style two-story house with a stunning wrap-around porch adorned with hanging flowerpots. Nearby the back patio was a little bench that invited you to have a seat and take in the scenic view of the vale below. Parked in the driveway was a Rolls-Royce.

"Whoa!" I said. "A brand-new Silver Ghost! This is the place?"

"This is it," Dad said. "It's a beauty isn't it?"

"Man alive!"

Dad applied the brake. "Go ahead and give 'em a knock while I get this woodwork unstrapped."

"Yes, sir."

I strolled up the walkway hemmed in by brick borders and flowerbeds and shrubberies. Passing by the lamp post, I climbed the few steps and availed myself of the decorative doorknocker.

I was soon greeted by the most beautiful girl I had ever seen. She was about my age. Her dark hair was parted on one side and flowed down to her shoulders, perfectly crimped and wavy. Her brown eyes gleamed, and her long lashes summoned me to get closer. Her eyebrows seemed perfectly drawn, and her lips were small and delicate.

"May I help you?" the girl asked.

"Um, y-yes. My dad and I are here to deliver the buffet cabinet?"

"Of course. Let me get Daddy."

She disappeared into the house.

A few moments later, the man stepped outside, accompanied by his beautiful daughter. He wore a pin-striped suit and a crisp white shirt and tie. "Howdy, Mr. Hayes." He tipped his hat.

"Hello there, Mr. Pearce," Dad replied. "I've brought the goods."

"Well, let's take a look at this thing. Whatta we got?—Wow! You did a fine job, Mr. Hayes. I knew you would after seeing those pictures—Jewel, go get your mother. She'll wanna come see this."

"I'm very pleased with it myself," Dad said. "There's just something about the red oak and dark stain finish. And then I added these extra drawers here." He pulled one out. "Pretty fancy, huh?"

"It's fabulous. I just love the finish and the adornments around the edges over here."

"Oh! I can't wait to see this," Mrs. Pearce cried, hurrying out of the house. She had her long dress bunched up in her hand so that she could bustle freely.

"Mr. Hayes, this is my wife, Rosa, and my daughter, Jewel—This is Mr. Hayes."

"Nice to meet you, sir."

"Nice to meet you, too."

"And who's this young gentleman?" Mr. Pearce asked.

"I'm David."

"Well, David, it's a pleasure to meet you, young man."

"Same here, sir," I said. Then I turned to Mrs. Pearce. "Nice to meet you as well."

It was all I could do to make eye contact with their daughter. She spun to the side, flaunting her white lace dress, and gave me the warmest smile.

"I absolutely love the buffet," Mrs. Pearce said. "I can't wait to see it in the house."

Dad tapped my arm. "Wanna give me a hand here?"

I hopped up and glided it to the edge.

Mr. Pearce took over from there and helped Dad carry the cabinet into the house, Mrs. Pearce following close behind.

"So, David," Jewel said, "do you attend the Avondale school?"

"Yes," I said. "Will you be going this year?"

"Of course." She twirled her hair with her finger. "I guess that means we'll be seeing each other then."

"You're right."

"How old are you?"

"Sixteen."

"Says you! *I'm* sixteen."

"What a coincidence," I said. I tried to think of something else to say. "So where you from?"

"Carroll. Daddy made a lot of money there as a salesman, but he got tired of traveling all around the country. He bought this fancy house and property. Paid for it all in cash. Now him and Momma can relax he says. He's a banker now in town, but Daddy says we don't really need the money."

"Oh! Well, that's good for your folks...It's a very nice house."

"Daddy says the whole upstairs is mine."

"Really?" I observed her closely as she looked the other way. "So what's your favorite subject?"

"Um…" She pondered the question, holding her finger to her lips. "...Hollywood!" She blurted it out and laughed.

I was taken aback.

"Just kidding," she said, touching me on the arm. "Though I absolutely love theaters and performances and all that sort of thing. Aw! It's so romantic. Momma and Daddy would take me to the movie palace in Carroll—it's so sad Avondale doesn't have a movie palace." She pouted.

"No," I said. "But we do have a regular movie house though."

"Do you ever go?"

"Not much," I said. "My folks say it's a petting pantry."

"Ooh!" She swayed, pivoting on her heel. "So what's *your* favorite subject?"

"Um, I do like plays," I said. "I mean, in general. Our school doesn't have any classes like that or anything, but I sort of like arithmetic."

She giggled. "Well, I sort of like *you*." Then she gasped. "I can't believe I just said that. I meant you seem like a nice guy."

A warm feeling came over me. "I, uh, I know what you meant."

She shifted to the side again, gently lifting a shoulder. "Do you think I'd make a great actress?"

"Well, I don't see why not."

"But then again, those movie actresses are all so pretty, aren't they?"

"Um, sure. I think they're good-looking."

"But you really think I'd make a great actress, huh?"

"Yep."

"Says you!" She clasped her hands over her heart and looked up at the sky. "Ahh! I could only dream of living the life of Mary Pickford...or Gloria Swanson...or Lillian Gish." She turned back to me. "They're so lucky, you know. They have the perfect life."

"I'm not sure they have a per—"

"Daddy says I'm the most beautiful girl in the world. Pshh! I don't know where Daddy gets his silly ideas from. But do tell, David. Do you ever see yourself as an actor?"

"Not really. It seems kinda strange when you really think about it."

"Then don't!" She pouted again. Then her eyes lit up as she pointed her finger at me. "But I see a little Valentino inside *you*. And believe you me, he's quite the sheik."

Just then, the door opened, and our parents came back outside.

"…I mean what else could you say?" Mrs. Pearce cried. "They're a match made in heaven."

Without thinking, I glanced over at Jewel.

Our eyes met.

I quickly looked away out of embarrassment.

"They sure are," Dad said. "Looks great along that one wall, right in between those sconces; and it perfectly complements both the mural and the dining room set."

"Well, I cannot thank you enough, Mr. Hayes," Mr. Pearce said.

Dad shook his hand. "Well, you certainly have already, and I thank you for the business. Now you folks take care of yourselves."

"You, too," Mrs. Pearce said. "Thank you so much. Like I said, exquisite work."

"You're welcome—Ready, David?"

"Yes, sir." I turned to Jewel. "Well, nice to meet you. I guess I'll see you in school."

Her eyelashes fluttered. "You will."

I boarded the wagon.

Dad took up the reigns and waved goodbye. "Take care now—Yah!"

The wheels started to roll. I waved one last time.

Jewel waved back, posing in her white lace dress.

My heart was smitten. I wanted nothing more now than for the new schoolyear to begin.

Why does it have to be the middle of summer?

*   *   *

Next week, it was all over the front page of the newspaper: *WM. J. BRYAN DIES SUDDENLY.* Bryan had just attended church that Sunday in Dayton, Tennessee, the very town the trial had been held. He took a nap and then died in his sleep.

Why did God let this happen? How's this even fair?

Nevertheless, as befuddled as I was, my befuddlement was soon swallowed up by the contemplation of that angel of beauty known as Jewel Pearce!

Chapter 11

The dog days of summer dragged on eternally. Never had someone shown interest in me. At least not one whom I was interested in as well. Though it was more like being under a spell. It was the first time I longed for the schoolyear to get underway. I slogged through those days like a mountaineer carrying weight on his back. Except the weight I carried was in my infatuated heart. But thank goodness I was finally approaching the summit. It was tail end of August and that signaled the opening of the county fair. It was the last hurrah of the summer before school started back up, and I was looking forward to it with great anticipation.

Aunt Mary had a home in Avondale, which was conveniently situated alongside the fairgrounds, right across the street. It was our yearly tradition to spend some time with her then walk over to the fair together.

Mom wasn't well enough to attend the fair, but she wanted badly to come along for the ride to get some fresh air and to see my aunt. Mom had begun to show signs of improvement about midway through July. Her appetite returned, and her face didn't look so pale. Over the next couple weeks, Mom was sitting up on the side of the bed. Within a few more days, she was able to stand by the window for a little while before lying back down. Halfway through August, Mom was out of bed. She still couldn't do anything around the house, but it was uplifting just to see her sitting in her chair in the living room.

Andrew came out to help me hitch up Checkers to the carriage.

"You coming with us, Andrew?" I said, arranging the bridle.

"Nah. I think I'm gonna stay back and clean the stalls out. They're a bit past due. Then I'll probably do some painting or something."

"But it won't be the same without you. Why don't you come?"

"I appreciate that, little brother, but I really do need to pick the stalls and get some fresh bedding down. Besides, I sort of like the quiet. Helps clear my mind."

"I understand. But we'll miss you."

Andrew patted me on the back. "Here, I'll take the collar. I got the rest."

"You sure?"

"Yep."

"Alright, let me just tighten up the throat lash here and then he's all yours. There we go. That should about do it—You're such a good boy, Checkers." I caressed his neck. Then I took a handful of grain and molasses and let him eat it out my hand.

I went to the pump and washed up, then headed back into the house to finish getting ready. I put on my gray dress slacks and my blue and white striped shirt, as well as my bowtie. I polished up my brown shoes, put those on, then styled my hair.

All was set to go.

Andrew accompanied Mom to the carriage and gave her a hand stepping up. The rest of us boarded and then bid Andrew a good afternoon.

As soon as we arrived at Aunt Mary's, I unhitched Checkers and let him graze in the backyard. I closed the gate and returned to the front of the house just as Aunt Mary stepped out. "You're here!"

"Hello, Aunt Mary."

"David, you're so handsome, and you're getting so tall. Either that, or I'm getting even shorter, which is probably the case. But it is so good to see you—And Evelyn, look at you! You grow prettier with each passing month! Come here, you two!" She showered us with hugs and kisses.

Dad tipped his hat. "Good afternoon, Mary."

"Hello, Millard." She gave him a hug. "How's my brother?"

"I'm hale and hearty. Can't complain."

Aunt Mary smiled. "Oh, good. 'Cause I wouldn't listen."

"Come again?" Dad said, putting his hand to his ear.

"I said, 'Good, 'cause I wouldn't'—stop that, Millard!" She smacked him. "I fall for it every time!"

Dad chuckled.

"Oh, Doris!" Aunt Mary cried. "I'm so glad you could make it."

"I'm glad, too," Mom said, taking hold of Dad. "It was such a wonderful ride into town, and it feels good to get some fresh air. I've been so stir-crazy, you know."

"Aw! You poor thing. How've you been feeling?"

"Better. Much better. Still tuckered out though."

"I hope you're not doing too much, Doris."

"Pshh! I've been as busy as a hibernating bear."

"Ha ha! Well, good. So long as you're taking care of yourself. It's a bit hot right now though, isn't it?"

"I'm a little warm," Mom said, fanning herself. "But I'll be fine."

"Well, I've got *just* the thing for you. Here, come in. You all make yourself at home."

Aunt Mary led the way into the house.

I loved my aunt's house. It had electricity and running water just like Daryl's. My aunt had a bathroom with her very own bathtub and toilet, and next to the kitchen stood a washing machine, which was the envy of my mother. Mom never knew what it was like to have a washing machine, a vacuum cleaner, or kitchen appliances.

"Here, Doris," Aunt Mary said. "Come in the parlor. You just make yourself comfortable. This chair is for you, and I've got the fan facing it right over here. Go ahead, take a load off your feet."

Mom sat down and breathed a sigh of relief. "This is heavenly. What I would give to have one of these electric fans!—See? We need to move into town, Millard."

"It's tempting," Dad said. "If they'd just run that line to Ashford like they've been yakking about for the last two years, then we could have a fan of our own. I know Pete and Erma wouldn't object to having power, especially with the farm."

"It feels so good," Mom said. "Thank you, Mary."

"You're welcome. Now you just take it easy. I see you've got your book. Good."

Mom chuckled. "I probably won't do much more than stare at the cover, so I'm not sure why I bothered. It's good intentions anyhow."

"Well, that's quite alright. I'm just delighted you could make it."

We all grabbed a seat in the living room. Aunt Mary served us sweet tea then proceeded to talk our ears off about Nancy Hill's "unrivaled gardening" and how "even Elanor Parker herself," who ran a nursery of her own, said that Nancy's roses were "the best this side of the Mississippi." This led to a mention of Mollie Carter's new "pet duck," simply because it had been discovered under some hydrangeas. Evidently, it had a bum leg, and Miss Carter "took that poor animal into her heart." Which reminded my aunt of Henry Burton who, intending to pay Miss Beatrice Hart a compliment, insulted her when he said the young men were drawn to her "like flies on manure."

We all laughed.

"Speaking of manure," Aunt Mary said, "wait till you see the Belgian draft horses at the fair this year. Oh, they are of a beautiful chestnut color, and they are the most submissive creatures you'll ever meet on God's green earth, despite being so huge. I'm telling you, they've got these gorgeous heads and brawny legs, and they're—"

The commotion outside disrupted my aunt's train of thought. She looked out the window.

"Oh, the Klan parade..." My aunt cranked her neck to have a peek up the street. "...and it looks like there's more of them this year."

I got up to get a look for myself. The Klansmen were arrayed in their usual white garb and pointed hats. Their faces were masked as they marched down Fair Avenue, right past my aunt's house. Two of them supported a sign that read: "One God. One Country. One Flag."

"They look so spooky," Evelyn said. "Somehow I don't see Jesus dressed in those things."

"Ain't that the gospel truth," Aunt Mary said. "Probably a shoddy knockoff of the white robes of heaven, I suppose. Though the Bible says nothing about wearing disguises and going around looking like ghosts."

"A bunch a jiggery-pokery!" Mom cried. "Not to mention they got their hands full with all those scandals."

"Their cloaks will fall off soon enough," Dad said. "I think they are already."

The parade ended.

"Shall we head over to the fairgrounds now?" Aunt Mary said.

"Sounds like a plan to me," Dad said. "Ready, youngsters?"

"I think I'm just gonna stay back with Mom," Evelyn said.

"No, no," Mom said. "I'll not have any of it. I want you to go and have a good time."

"But I don't want you to be alone."

"I'll be fine, Evelyn. My book will keep me company and so will this fan. I've never been more comfortable. Now go along."

"If you say so."

"I do so say. Now have fun."

"Bye, Mother," I said. "We'll see you in a little bit."

"Alright, David. Enjoy the fair."

Dad kissed Mom. "See ya, snookums. I love you."

"Love you, too, dear."

Aunt Mary opened the door. "The house is all yours, Doris. There's plenty of tea and refreshments in the kitchen, so help yourself."

"Thank you, Mary. You're too kind."

We left the house and crossed the street together. We passed underneath the gateway that read: "Sidon County Fair." The enormous barn shelter rose from the center of the fairgrounds, where all the livestock were kept. It was one of the few permanent structures that reminded you all year round of the good times gone by. Booths were set up, full of merchandises to be sold or traded. Food stands advertised barbecued meats, candy apples, and funnel cakes; their aromas wafting through the air. The magic show and the lion tamer lured passersby to surrender their tickets to gain private admission. People lined up to try the balloon and dart game or the horseshoe pitching contest, and crowds gathered around the Ferris wheel.

Red and white striped tents were pitched here and there, one tent displaying all sorts of farm implements and tools. It drew in Dad every time. He always promised to be "only a minute," yet he always took fifteen or twenty. Not that I disliked farm tools, but I wasn't charmed by them like my father. It was the perfect moment to break away and grab a bag of fairy floss. I told my sister I'd be right back.

As I waded through the crowds, I heard someone call my name. I looked around.

"Over here, David!"

It was Mr. Foster. He was waving his hand vigorously.

Now what?

Lawrence Foster was our local barber. His hair was white and combed back, and his eyes were blue and penetrative. He had a square face with a tiny chin along with a bushy mustache that covered his mouth entirely.

"Good afternoon, Mr. Foster."

"Good afternoon, David. I was just passing through and I thought to myself, 'Now that young man is the spit and image of David Hayes.' And lo and behold, it's David Hayes." He leaned in. "Now let's be clear, I'm not here for all these amusements and distractions. Strictly business." He held up a bag. "Keller & Company always has outstanding deals on razors and creams and whatnot. Anyways, what is a young man like you doing wandering through this wilderness?"

"Well, I'm here with—"

"I almost said *worldliness*. Then again, I would not have been wide of the mark, to be sure. If you ask me, I'd say we're surrounded by a bunch of sabbath-breakers. But you didn't ask, so I'll just keep my sentiments to myself. Ehem. But are you here alone?"

"No, Dad's over there checking out the farm stuff. Aunt Mary and Evelyn are with him as well. I ran over here to grab some fairy floss."

"Your mom still not feeling well?"

"Mom's actually doing much better, but she stayed back at my aunt's. She's still not quite right."

Mr. Foster got in close. "I'll tell you what you need." He placed his hand on my shoulders and looked me square in the eyes. "Faith! That's what you need, David. You need faith."

"I have faith, Mr. Foster."

"Yes, but you need the sort of Holy Spirit power and divine healing that our dear—Sister—Annie—preaches—about!" He emphasized the last words by thumping on my shoulder like it was his pulpit. Evidently, I couldn't hide my bewilderment. Mr. Foster stepped back and cried, "Surely your pastor has mentioned the great evangelist, Annie Henderson?"

"Oh!" I said. "I've read about her in the papers."

"Pshh! I would hope so, young man. It would be a sad testament of our times if you knew Barnum and Bailey and not the name of Henderson."

"But I do believe, Mr. Foster, and I've prayed for my mom. I believe God can heal my mom. In fact, he—"

"Let's be clear, David—look right here!" He snapped his fingers. "You must believe God *will* heal your mother. You see the difference?"

I didn't know what to say.

Mr. Foster got in close again. "Listen to me. Do you believe that God *will* heal your mother?" I remained fixed on his piercing eyes. "In my humble opinion, you do not," he said. "I can tell. Anyways, give it some thought. It's no accident we had this little meeting. God bless you."

Just like that, he walked away.

I took a deep breath and got in line. I bought some fairy floss, then returned to the others as quickly as I could.

"We were about to leave you," Dad said, shaking his finger.

"Don't worry, David," Evelyn said. "Aunt Mary and I were about to leave Dad. We've had enough of these farm tools for one day."

"You got that right," Aunt Mary said.

"Now hold your horses," Dad said, putting his arm around Evelyn. "If I'm not mistaken, I've gotten stuck at some home decoration workshops once or twice."

"I got held up by Mr. Foster," I explained. "But I hotfooted it back as best I could."

Dad chuckled. "That sounds like Lawrence. What did he have to say this time?"

"Um, nothing much. He was just saying hello."

"Wow. Surprise, surprise."

We left the tent and wandered down the various lanes and footpaths while Evelyn and I savored the sugary clumps that melted in our mouths.

Just then, a motor started up. A plane with double stacked wings took off in a nearby field. It circled around a few times, then it did a flyover. The stuntman coiled through the air and flew upside down. Then he soared to the sky, only to stall out and plunge to the ground. We waited breathlessly as he pulled up at the last second.

"Phew!" Dad cried. "What a spectacle!"

"That was a beauty!" I said.

"You're not kidding," Dad said. "Almost as beautiful as your mother!"

Dad always said that, and it never ceased to draw a smile.

"Who would've ever thought, just thirty years ago?" Evelyn said.

Aunt Mary shook her head. "What would possess someone to get in one of those things and do all that craziness up there?"

"Who knows?" Evelyn said. "It makes you wonder if we'll ever travel through the air, as normal as a car or a bus."

"Heck no!" Dad said. "Airplanes are for wars and fairs. I don't see us belonging up there."

"Me neither," I said.

Little did we know.

From there, we passed by the carnival tent and the swings and made our way to the carousel.

"Whatta ya know?" Dad hollered. "It's the Pearce family!"

"Fancy meeting you here!" Mrs. Pearce cried.

"I know, I know," Dad said, tipping his hat. "How do you do, Mr. Pearce."

"I'm doing very well. Thank you, sir."

"I'd like you to meet my sister, Mary—Mary, these folks are new to the area."

"Well, I'm delighted to meet your acquaintance."

"Let me tell you," Mr. Pearce said, "your brother does excellent work."

"Good heavens!" Mrs. Pearce cried. "He made us a fabulous buffet. I've got all my special china and dishes stored in it now, and I just love it."

"Millard is very good at what he does," Aunt Mary said. "He made me my own dining room set. Goes perfectly with the hutch."

"It must be handy having him in the family," Mrs. Pearce said.

"It sure is!"

"Well, you folks enjoying the fair?" Dad asked.

"Oh, we're having a rare old time," Mrs. Pearce said. "Aren't you, Jewel?"

"Of course," Jewel said. She eyed me.

"So where ya'll headed?" Dad asked.

"We're about to ride the roundabout," Mr. Pearce said.

"That's just where we're headed."

"Whatta ya know?" Aunt Mary said. "Great minds think alike."

"Hey, I never thought of that," Dad said, poking my aunt in the side.

"Oh, stop your kidding, Millard."

"Well, what are we waiting for then?" Dad said. "Let's take a ride on the roundabout."

We all sauntered over and got in line.

I looked back. Our eyes met. I smiled back at her.

The gate opened, and we hustled to find a good seat. I wanted to sit near her, but I was too uneasy to arrange it.

"You riding a horse, Evelyn?" I asked.

"I'm gonna ride the teacup," she said.

"That's no fun. It doesn't go up and down like the other animals."

"I know. But I think it's adorable."

"Fine. I'll ride with you."

"Promise me you won't whirl us around?"

"That's the point of the teacup."

"I know, but I wanna just sit and enjoy it. Now promise me you won't whirl us around."

"I won't, I promise."

"You better not."

"Better not promise?"

"You know what I mean, Davey."

We sat across from one another.

Where'd she go?

"Glory be!" Evelyn cried, jumping up. "Sorry, Davey. Change of plans."

"Thanks for stepping on my shoes!"

"I'm sorry! The girl just hopped off the rabbit, and it's the cat's meow!"

"That doesn't even make sense!" I hollered back.

Just then, Jewel came wandering around, still trying to find an open seat. She glanced at the available spot across from me, then she looked over the carousel again.

"Jewel!" Mrs. Pearce cried. "You're holding everybody up."

"I'm *trying*, Mama!"

"You're too picky," Mr. Pearce said. "You should've just sat down somewhere."

"Fine!" she said, stepping into the teacup. "I'll sit here."

Next thing I knew, the here and now changed into a magical motion picture starring the angel of beauty! The band organ began to play, and the carousel began to move.

"Whatta ya say, David?" Jewel asked. "Should we give this thing a whirl?"

I smiled. "Before my sister upped and moved, she made me promise not to spin it."

"Of course. But I'm not your sister."

She grabbed the wheel and turned it.

Each turn was aided by the motion of the carousel and gained momentum.

The teacup began to spin out of control. I came crashing into Jewel's side.

We burst into laughter.

We whirled around and around, pressed up against the barrier together.

"Woohoo!"

"This is incredible! Ha ha!"

It was a swirling vision of rounding boards and galloping cranks, scenic panels and mirrors, the animation of horses and wildlife. Then I focused on the face right beside me. An attractive face. With eyes that glistened.

In a little while, the carousel began to wind down.

The ride was approaching a stop. I felt embarrassed; I was still snuggled against her, shoulder to shoulder, so I returned to the opposite side.

"You don't wanna be next to me?" Jewel said.

"No, nothing like that," I said.

She giggled. Then she leaned in and whispered, "Do tell, do you think I'm pretty?"

How could I say 'no'? It seemed rather insulting. Not to mention I felt warm and comfy inside at the very thought of telling her the truth. "Yes," I said.

She sat up straight and put her hand over her mouth.

As if she were surprised by my remark.

Chapter 12

I finished at the lumber yard one afternoon and stopped by the grocery store to grab a soda. I handed Mr. Cooper my nickel and headed outside. I used the iron armrest of the bench to pop the cap off my bottle. I looked out from behind the lamppost and spotted Daryl coming out of Trottman's. I hadn't talked to Daryl since the Monkey Trial, and I wasn't in the mood to talk to him now. I slipped back into the hollow of the grocery store entry, hoping he wouldn't see me.

He's bound to come this way.

I went back inside and stood by the spice rack next to the window. A few seconds later, Daryl walked by.

Just then, the door opened, and someone walked in.

"Hey, David."

I turned around. "Oh, Daryl. Whatcha been up to?"

"Not much. I just got back from my uncle's about a week ago. The one out in Clarksville. I've been staying at his place for the last month, helping out at the saddlery. Made some money. It was a nice change of things, but it feels good to be back." He held up a piece of paper. "My mom gave me a list of things to pick up for her. You know how that goes."

"Nothing like being an errand boy."

"Especially when your bicycle has a flat. I put off patching it before I left for my uncle's and then forget all about it. I could kick myself. But I promised her I'd get these before she comes home."

"That's a bummer. Here, why don't you grab your things and then I'll give you a ride back. You can ride the handlebars the way we used to do."

"Sure. That would be great. I won't keep you. I just gotta get a bag of flour, sugar, and a can of baking soda."

"No problem. Take your time."

Daryl rang the bell on the counter.

Mr. Cooper came out from the back room, and Daryl handed him his list. "I'll take two soft pretzels, too," Daryl said.

"Fantastic." Mr. Cooper fetched the items and handed Daryl the pretzels.

"Here you go, David," Daryl said. "One's for you."

"Gee, thanks," I said. "Hard to say *no* to one of these."

Daryl bagged the items and completed the purchase. Then we stepped outside.

"Mmm!" I said. "They sure know how to make a good pretzel."

"That's for sure," Daryl said. "The dough's perfectly browned, and then the right amount of salt."

"The fair had some good pretzels. Did you get a chance to see the fair at all since you've been back?"

"I did. I went with my family Tuesday. We had a good time. I made sure to ride the Ferris wheel with Lucy. It's her favorite. Something we do each year. How about you?"

"I went with my dad, my sister, and my aunt. Got to see the stuntman fly the plane."

"You're so lucky! He wasn't flying the day we went. I bet that was the best part of the fair."

"Close. I also got to ride the carousel…." I couldn't hold back the grin.

Daryl raised his one eyebrow. "You think the carousel's better than the plane?"

I grabbed my bicycle from against the lamppost. "Here, let's hop on. I'll explain."

Daryl finished his last bite and wiped his mouth. "When the train's ready to depart, you better be on board." He climbed up and sat himself on the handlebars, facing forward. "So what was so funny?"

"Well, it's not anything funny funny," I said, pedaling up the sidewalk. "It's just that I got to ride the teacup with the most beautiful girl ever."

"Your dad let you? Everybody knows the teacup's for lovers."

"I know, I know," I said. "It just happened to work out that way. Her name is Jewel. She just moved here. I met her over the summer, right after the Monkey Trial."

"Really?"

"Yeppers. Wait till you see her, Daryl. She's gonna be in our class. It was killing me not being able to see her till then, but then I got to see her at the fair. Can you believe it?"

"A little good luck, huh?"

"You can say that again."

"Sounds like you're really stuck on her."

"Can't say I'm not."

"I'd say so. I haven't seen you this giddy since the days you crushed on Alice Stratton."

"Wait till you see her, Daryl. You'll understand. She's even better looking than Alice."

"C'mon now!"

"No, I'm dead serious. Jewel makes Alice look like a toad."

"What? I don't believe you."

"Alright, fair enough. Alice is pretty, I'll give you that, but—"

"She's more than pretty."

"Fine, so she's really pretty, but Jewel is absolutely gorgeous. I mean this girl's a knockout."

"I guess I'll find out soon enough with school being right around the corner—not that I wanna talk about that. I mean where did the summer go?"

"What do you mean? It was slower than molasses going uphill in January."

"You're crazy. It feels like it was just Independence Day."

"Ha! That was years ago."

"Pshh! That girl's broken your sense of time."

I chuckled. "Well, I can't say you're wrong."

We turned down Ludwig and pedaled toward his house.

"I hear your mom's doing a lot better," Daryl said.

"Yes," I said. "Mom's on the upswing. Thanks to everyone praying and all. She's still not doing any cooking or cleaning, but at least she's not cooped up in the bedroom all day long."

"That's true. Well, I'm glad to hear that."

"I appreciate it. I really believe she's gonna mend completely."

"I sure hope so."

We arrived at Daryl's house.

Daryl hopped off the bicycle. "Thanks for the ride, David.

"You're welcome. Take care now."

"Um, before you go, I need to tell you something. It's something I just found out."

"Sure," I said. "What's on your mind?"

"Well, it's about your sister...."

"Evelyn?"

"Yes…Well, this was supposed to be top secret. But Beth broke it to me—you know how Beth likes me. I think she thought it would help win me over or something. But anyways, Beth told me all about it."

"About what?"

"To be honest, it's about Evelyn *and* Beth. You see, last year when we all went up to the Slater house on Halloween…well, it was a setup."

"A setup?"

"Yes."

"I knew it!"

"And you remember that ghost on the porch? Well, that was Lester."

"Beth's older brother?"

"Yes, it was Lester on that porch, and it was your sister's idea. She got Beth in on it, then the two of them got Lester in on it, too. You were set up, David."

"But why would Evelyn do that to me?"

"To get even with you."

"For what?"

"Listen, I hate to tell you this, but she told Beth she vowed to get even with you for scaring her. I guess you jumped out of the outhouse or something?"

I was floored. I could not picture Evelyn ever making such a vow. Then to follow through with such a plan of revenge. "Are you sure, Daryl?"

"Trust me, David. Beth was telling the truth. When you went to her about your plan to scare Dominic, Evelyn found the opportunity she had been looking for. The only reason her and Beth kept quiet about it is because you broke your arm."

I placed my hands to my head. "Man alive!"

"Listen," Daryl said, "I'm your friend. And I couldn't keep something like that from my friend."

"Well, I appreciate it," I said. "I appreciate you telling me the scoop."

I bid Daryl a good evening and rode my bicycle straight home.

I went into the house and marched upstairs then knocked on Evelyn's door.

"Come in."

I closed the door behind me. "I found out about the whole thing."

"About what thing?" Evelyn said.

"What you and Beth did last Halloween. It was you."

"Oh, Davey! I'm so sorry! You have no idea how badly I felt about that night. Especially after you broke your arm. There was no way I could tell you; I was the one to blame for your broken arm."

"How could you do that to me, Evelyn?"

"Davey, I was just getting even. You know how weary I was with the way you kept scaring me. You wouldn't stop. You kept jumping out of this corner, jumping out of that corner. And then when you jumped out at me from the outhouse, that was it. I swore I was gonna scare you so bad, you'd never do it again. But I never meant for you to break your arm. I'm sorry, Davey!"

I stood there by the door, dumbfounded. I never knew my sister was capable of contriving such a plot. On one hand, I was upset; on the other, I was impressed. "Well, I guess I deserved it." I took a deep breath. "You're lucky I love you. Though I've got to hand it to you, I don't think I could ever top that. From here on, I won't even *think* about scaring you."

To be honest, I felt relieved. While the thought of ghosts and curses had lost its influence over the summer, still, the mystery of that Halloween night lingered in the back of my mind. At least that part was put to rest. Now, as for the skeletons surfacing on the property, they refused to be put to rest, and they still raised their own questions.

Chapter 13

The first day of school. I went downstairs and found Mom at the stove. It had been months since I last saw her doing anything of the sort.

"Making yourself some breakfast, Mother?"

"No."

"Then who's it for?"

"You and Evelyn."

"Mom, I appreciate it, but I think we're big enough to be making our own breakfast."

"Who ever said you weren't?"

"Well, you need to take it easy."

"Horsefeathers! It's not your funeral, so you just get ready for school, and I'll call you as soon as it's ready."

I saluted her. "Yes, ma'am!"

I ran upstairs and finished getting dressed.

Mom's healed!

Evelyn and I rode our bicycles to school that day. As we wheeled through town, I spotted Daryl at the corner of Broad and Mill. "I'll meet you there, Evelyn. I'm gonna talk with Daryl—Daryl! Wait up!"

I raced up to him. "I've got good news!"

"What's the word?" Daryl said.

"You won't believe it. My mom is healed! I mean—truly—healed!"

"That's wonderful."

"Isn't God good?"

"It's real good. I'm so happy for you."

"I mean our family prayed and prayed and prayed. I knew God would do it, and I believed he would do it."

"Some good news for a change. Now let's pray we have a good first day of school, right? I still can't believe summer's over."

"I'm actually looking forward to school—hey, that was Jewel! There's only one Silver Ghost in this county that I know of! I'll catch up with you later."

I sped down the street as fast as I could, trying to meet up with her as she got dropped off. I arrived in time and met her on the walkway. "Hey, Jewel!" I pulled up alongside and slid off the bicycle.

"What's the hurry?" Jewel cried. "Did ya miss me?"

"I did. I did miss you, but you gotta hear this: My mom's been ill this entire summer, and she's finally back to her old self."

"Says you!"

"Yes. And I've been praying so hard for a miracle."

"Of course."

"I had to believe God would heal my mother. That's the trick."

"Anything you say. Just be sure to pray for me while you're at it. 'Cause I'd love a trip to California and a house in Beverly Hills, right next door to Mary Pickford. And believe you me, if you don't think I'd tell the world about the prayers of David Hayes, then by golly, you're mistaken!"

I leaned my bicycle against the tree. "Here, I'll show you to the main door, and we'll head upstairs together. That way you don't have to walk in all by yourself."

"Thank you, Davey."

I opened the door for her, then I escorted her to the classroom. I introduced her to Mr. Wagner and took my seat.

Before long, class started. Mr. Wagner welcomed us back and said he hoped we all had a great summer. Then he introduced the new student.

We all clapped for her.

While he proceeded to review the classroom rules, I noticed Dominic eyeballing the back of the room.

I turned. Jewel was sitting comfortably in her chair with her legs crossed, smirking at Dominic and playing with her hair.

For crying out loud!

Like a match to a parched field, jealousy ignited, bursting into flames. Dominic had left me alone for the better part of the year, ever since that memorable scare, and I had done my best to keep my distance. But in a flash, I resented him all over again. I could discern by the look on his face that he had a newfound desire. And that's when it struck me: Evelyn no longer stood between me and Dominic.

It's over!

From that point on, Jewel hardly acknowledged my presence. Whenever I said something to her, she snapped a quick response and moved on by. As if our sweet introduction over the summer never happened.

A few weeks later, Jewel surprised me when she approached me under the tree during recess. "So what's this I hear about a haunted house?"

I put my book down. "You mean the Slater house?"

"Yes, that's it."

"Oh, it's just an old abandoned house. They say it's cursed now."

"That's what I've been told. That some sort of witch haunts the place at night in her wedding dress. Dominic says you were chased off the porch and broke your arm."

110

"Yes, I did break my arm."

"You must be really brave, David."

"I don't know about that, I just—"

"Believe you me, I know a brave man when I see one."

"It's nothing really. Dominic stood on that porch as well, you know."

"Of course. Dominic's brave, too. The only thing braver than what you two did is if someone were to go inside that house. Now *that* person would be the bravest of all!"

I shrugged. "I could if I wanted to, but I really don't have a need to."

"Says you! You would do that?"

"If I really needed to, but I don't see the—"

"Believe you me, if some brave fella brought me back something special from that house, now that would be something out of a movie! I could just marry him and smother him in kisses!"

That was all I needed to hear.

I was thrilled to know my sister's ghost story had been entirely made up. It gave me an advantage now. There were no ghosts. There was nothing to be scared about. And it was the perfect opportunity.

However, my initial enthusiasm began to wane upon further consideration.

What about those skeletons? What am I gonna do?

And then it dawned on me—

Who says I have to do it at night? I'll do it during the daytime. With Daryl's help!

* * *

We climbed the porch together.

"I'm not so sure about this now," Daryl said. "This place wreaks of mildew and worms."

111

"You can't back out now," I cried. "You said you'd help an old friend out."

Daryl huffed. "I know what I said. But this is breaking and entering, in case you didn't know."

"The place is abandoned."

"Um, if my memory serves me right, weren't you the one who had a problem throwing rocks at an old abandoned building once? My, how we've changed in our old age!"

"So I've lightened up a bit. Besides, we're not breaking windows, so what's the harm?"

"What's the harm? You're breaking into a house. It's against the law!"

"Listen, Daryl, I've got to do this for Jewel. This is the perfect way to prove myself to her."

"Pshh! You're starting to worry me, you know."

"Someday you'll understand."

"I hope I never do. It's a sickness."

"You'll be smitten."

"I'll never be smitten."

"Don't be so sure about that."

Daryl rolled his eyes. "Anyways, what's in it for me?"

"I'll make it up to you," I said. "Besides, you were never here."

"Ha! Like that's gonna help me."

"No, I'm serious. I give you my word."

"Whatever."

I tried the handle of the front door. It was locked. I rattled the door. It was sealed shut. "How do we get in without making it obvious?"

"Try the windows," Daryl said.

"I think I will."

"It's a good thing I'm not here to help you, huh?"

"Cheer up." Try as I might, none of the windows would budge. "If I do it any harder, the glass is gonna break. We'll have to try the other windows. Come with me."

We left the porch and went around. The bay windows were way above our heads, so we kept on. The only other window was about four feet from the ground on the side of the house.

"Here, Daryl. Put your hands together like this and hoist me up."

"What?"

"Just do it. Make a stirrup with your hands. It'll work, trust me."

"Sure. With me doing the work...*Trust me.*"

"Why do you mock? C'mon. Where's your spirit? It'll be worth it."

Daryl exhaled. "How the dickens did I even get talked into this?"

"'Cause I'm your friend, that's why. Now c'mon. We can't just sit here."

Daryl spit on the ground and muttered something under his breath. He crouched down and coupled his hands together. "Let's go!"

I stepped in. He lifted me up.

"Dash it all!" I said. "I think this one's locked, too."

"You're too heavy," Daryl said.

"Wait! It just budged. Try lifting me up a little more."

"You can't be serious!"

"That way I can—hey, the latch busted off!"

"Alright, I gotta set you down."

We took a break. Daryl inspected his hands. "I should've brought gloves."

I looked up at the window. "Well, at least it opened a tad. You ready?"

"What, for jail?"

"Don't be so glum. We're almost there."

Daryl rolled his eyes. "Easy for you to say." He got into position and put his hands together. "What are you waiting for? My back's gonna be as sore as my hands."

I stepped in. He took a deep breath and lifted me up.

"Alright, hold it there!" I kept banging on the frame. "It opened up!" I got my grip from inside the frame and tried pulling myself up. "Can you lift me up any higher? Yep, like that...almost...just…a little—yippee!"

I was in the house.

I leaned over the frame and grabbed Daryl's hands and helped pull him up.

We were both in the house.

"Can you believe it?" I whispered. "Who would've thought?"

"I don't like this," Daryl whispered back. "Find what you need and let's get out of here."

"Well, let's see. I need something unmistakable...something that would prove I was here...."

The room was filled with clutter: A rinky-dink dresser with a missing drawer, boxes of old newspapers, a lap desk, a globe, a couple suitcases, and a pair of boots.

"Nothing to write home about here," I said. "I wonder what's in here."

We entered the living room. There was the old couch and chairs, all coated in dust.

"Can't fit these in my pocket," I said.

I entered the family room. I tried stepping around the plaster bits on the floor, then I made my way into the kitchen. I spotted a mouse in the corner by the dish cupboard. It scurried across the floor and hid behind the cast iron wood burning stove. I picked up a potato masher from the table and looked it over. "This is too big to bring to school, and there's nothing special about it." I peeked into the scullery then returned to the family room.

I went back around and walked to the foot of the stairs. "Do I dare?"

"You're crazy," Daryl muttered.

"Will you come up with me?"

"Sure. But why are we whispering?"

We both laughed.

It echoed throughout the room, adding to the spookiness.

We covered our mouths. Then we started up the stairs together, the steps creaking beneath our weight.

We reached the top and peeked in the rooms. The two smaller rooms were empty; however, the master bedroom was still furnished. There was a four-post bed, a couple end tables, and an old princess vanity dresser in the corner next to the walk-in closet.

As I approached the vanity, something in the closet caught my eye.

"Daryl, you're not gonna believe this!"

"What is it?"

A wedding dress hung in the closet.

"Oh, wow! There must be some truth to the story," Daryl said. "Even before Evelyn told us that ghost story—"

"Hush! Don't say that word! Not right now."

"What word, *ghost?*"

"Stop it!"

"Don't be silly. There's no such thing as ghosts, ghosts, ghosts, ghosts."

I glared at him.

"Anyways," Daryl continued, "even before Evelyn told us that *story*, I had heard Faye was engaged to be married."

"Whatever. I need to find something and get the heck out of here."

"You do that, and I'll keep on the lookout by the window."

I opened the top drawer of the vanity dresser. It was loaded with books. I opened the bottom drawer and found the same.

"What's with all the books?" I said. "Who stuffs books in a dresser?"

"She liked to read, I guess," Daryl said.

I reached in and pulled a stack out. "Let's see...*The Old Curiosity Shop.* Mom loved that. *Emerson's Works.* Boring. *The Booted Cat.* Hmm, seems interesting. *To Have and to Hold.* Pshh! She was definitely interested in marriage."

"Sounds like someone else I know," Daryl muttered.

"Easy now. Just 'cause you wanna live footloose and fancy free—hey, this one's got *Faye Slater* penciled in on the first page. This is it! This is my gift for Jewel! There'll be no way to deny I was here."

"Good," Daryl said. "Now let's get going."

"Now what's this? A crumpled-up piece of fabric." It was stuffed behind the books. I tried wrenching it out of the drawer. As soon as I got a bunch of it through, I let go of it. I felt like I had just contaminated a crime scene. "There's blood!" I cried.

"What are you talking about?" Daryl said. "Oh, my goodness! That *does* look like blood."

Daryl yanked the rest out. And that's when it fell out onto the floor.

"What's that?" I said.

Daryl picked it up. "It's a necklace."

"What's a necklace doing wrapped up in a bloody rag?"

Daryl held it up to the light of the window. "Yep. That's blood, alright."

"What in Sam Hill is going on with this place, Daryl? We've got bodies in the yard, and now there's blood in the house. Let's get out of here!"

"But what should we do with this?"

"I don't know. Who cares?"

"You don't wanna give it to Jewel?"

"Are you kidding me? I ain't touching that. Stuff it back in the drawer. I'm done with this place. I got what I needed, now let's skidoo."

Daryl dropped the necklace in the cloth and stuffed the whole thing back into the drawer then slammed it shut. "Yuck, I need to wash my hands."

"I need to get out here!" I hollered back, halfway down the stairs already.

Chapter 14

Jewel stopped by my desk on the way back from sharpening her pencil. She leaned in and whispered in my ear. "I visited the haunted house."

I looked up. It was the cutest expression. Her eyes twinkled, and she seemed thrilled to tell me all about her experience. I came close to telling her I had something to give her, but I hesitated just long enough for her return to her desk.

I glanced over at Daryl. He had obviously been watching the whole time. He had a smirk on his face, and he shook his head before going back to his work.

I couldn't wait to give Jewel the book. My infatuation with her kept me from acknowledging any wrongdoing. I was proud of my accomplishment. In my mind, it was the perfect gift, the most thoughtful gift I could've given her. No different than had I purchased it from Sears and Roebuck or McMurray's.

I searched all day long for an opportunity, yet I couldn't find a suitable moment. The difficult part was getting the two of us alone. I didn't want anybody finding out about my little escapade.

At last, school let out. I left the building and walked languidly down the front steps. Then I caught a glimpse of her beneath the tree by the road: the angel of beauty, all by herself, waiting for a ride.

I jogged up to her at a leisurely pace, trying to act as calm as possible. "Hey there, Jewel. So you got to see the Slater place, huh?"

"Oh, my! Yes, I've been wanting to tell you, Davey. I went and saw it last Friday!"

"So you went up by yourself?"

"Oh, no! I heard enough about that place. I wasn't gonna go there all alone. No way. Betty Quinn showed me."

"So whatdya think?"

"Let me tell you, that house is perfectly creepy. Just walking by the road was enough to give me the chills. But then Betty grabs me by the hand and practically drags me into the yard and shows me this scary skeleton coming up through the ground. Now what is going on with that place? That is something frightening!"

"And that's just one. There's more."

"You can't be serious!"

"I am. I've seen it myself."

"Believe you me, that place holds some dark, dark secrets."

I looked down momentarily. "Trust me, I know." My heart pounded in my chest. I tried to stay calm and just do it. The thought of wasting a perfect opportunity prodded me. "Anyways, I wanted you to have this."

"What's this?" Jewel cried.

"Just a little something I picked up at the Slater house."

"You did it? You went inside?"

"Yep."

"Says you!"

"I did. And let me tell you, this here is quite a humdinger. Open it up; look what's written at the top of the first page."

"Faye Slater."

"See, that's the name of the woman who used to live there."

"Davey! I can't believe you!"

"It was her own copy," I explained. "It's proof I was there. I wouldn't lie to you."

"I just can't believe you did it. You're so brave and fearless. Why, this book is hotsy-totsy!"

I couldn't have been more pleased. She held the book close to her heart. It was a perfectly good moment. Like being in a dream.

Unluckily for me, I got a wakeup call. "Don't take any wooden nickels!" someone shouted.

We turned around. It was Dominic.

"What's that David just gave you?" Dominic asked, catching up to us.

"It's a gift!" Jewel said. "For me."

"Who woulda thought?" Dominic said. "Davey-Boy on the make with Miss Pearce."

I blushed.

"It's something he got from the Slater house," Jewel said.

Dominic took it from her hand. "Let me see. *To Have and to Hold.* Whoa! Looks like someone wants your last name to be Hayes. I'd watch out for this twerp if I were you. He'll lead you down the garden path."

"That book happens to have Faye's name in it," I said.

"So what?" Dominic said. "You still wanna marry Miss Pearce. Just say it."

Jewel chuckled. "David's a brave soul for going in that haunted house."

"Ha! That's what ole Davey-Boy wants you to think," Dominic said. "That house ain't haunted. Right, David? Lester Harrison told me your sister set you up. Your very—own—sister!"

Jewel gasped. "A setup? Do tell!"

I rolled my eyes. "It's a long story."

"Lester rushed him on the Slater porch," Dominic said. "And ole Davey-Boy screamed like a little schoolgirl and jumped right off and broke his arm—like the cursed boy that he is!"

"Knock it off, Dominic," I said.

"It's true." Dominic touched her. "Be careful his curse don't rub off on you."

"What curse?" Jewel asked.

He pretended to whisper: "Well, let's just say he killed a sparrow once."

Jewel pursed her lips. "Aw! Poor thing."

"With a rock!" Dominic added, in his normal tone of voice. "Nailed it from fifty feet away."

"It was an accident," I said. "I was trying to hit a window."

Dominic got in my face. "I don't give a hoot in hell's hollow what you were tryin' to hit. You killed that innocent bird."

"That *is* bad luck, David," Jewel said.

Dominic shoved me backwards. "Cursed, cursed, cursed. You know, if I told my dad you were breaking into houses, he'd have you arrested." He crossed his arms. "But since I'm such a nice guy, I probably won't say nothing."

"I wasn't doing any harm," I said. "And I didn't break anything either. I was just getting this book."

"You weren't just getting a book," Dominic said. "You stole that book." He got closer yet. "From a house you broke into."

"Gimme the stupid book then," I cried, snatching it out of Jewel's hand. "I'll return it myself."

"That's *my* book!" Jewel said, crossing her arms.

"Well, I'm taking it back."

She pouted.

"Yep, you take it back," Dominic said. "Like a good little delinquent."

"I'm not a delinquent."

"Sure you are...just like your brother."

"Leave my brother out of this!"

"Easy there, tiger. It's not my fault your brother sits home all day doing nothing but painting pretty little pictures."

"My brother's back to work! And he helps around the house!"

Dominic snickered. "A housekeeper who paints pictures. Whoop-de-doo!"

I shoved Dominic as hard as I could. "You're not gonna talk about Andrew that way!"

"You wanna come at me? Let's go!" He bounced right back, snapping jabs at my face. "Let's go Davey-Boy! You wanna show off for your Jewel? Huh, cursed boy?" He caught me in the mouth and kept coming at me.

I shuffled backwards and returned a feeble punch.

He caught me in the mouth again.

"Fine, Dominic!" I said. "You got what you wanted!"

He cocked his fist back. "Come again?"

"You win! Alright? I said it: You win! Now leave me the heck alone!"

"That's what I thought. You're so lucky 'cause I was gonna pop you in the beezer next."

"I hate you," I said, touching my lip.

There was blood on my fingers.

I glanced at Jewel then looked away.

Just then, a Rolls-Royce pulled up alongside the curb. Jewel waved goodbye to Dominic and got in. She rolled the window down and batted her eyes before taking off down the road.

I picked up the book I had dropped during the scuffle and started for home.

I don't give a rip! I'll lie about the whole darn thing!

I paused by the side of the road. I looked both ways. I grit my teeth and hurled it into the woods as hard as I could. "I hate you!"

Chapter 15

I was lying in bed, staring at the ceiling, when I heard Andrew knock on Mom's door.

"Who is it?"

"It's Andrew."

"What do you need, honey?"

"I was just checking on you. You doing alright, Mom? You haven't come out all day."

"Oh, I'm doing fine."

"It's just that you hardly came out yesterday either."

"I said I'm fine."

"Well, it's getting late and I was starting to worry. That's all."

"What time is it?"

"It's almost mealtime."

"My stars! Your father should be home soon. I'll be down in just a minute."

Evelyn came into the hallway. "Good heavens! I got so distracted with all my homework. I'll get supper started, Andy."

"Don't worry about it, sis. I got this—No, Mom. I was just checking on you. You take it easy. I'll go ahead and start cooking something up."

"No, I'm coming right now."

"I'm cooking tonight, and you can't stop me." Andrew proceeded downstairs.

Mom eventually stepped out into the hallway. She smoothed out her dress and wiped her forehead. She reached out to feel the wall with her fingertips as she made her way to the staircase.

I stepped out from my bedroom doorway to accompany her.

"Oh, I didn't see you there, David. You coming down?"

"I am. Here, we'll walk together."

She gripped the railing and walked cautiously down. "Don't mind me. I've just come down with something, and it's got me all tuckered out."

"You're fine, Mother."

Once we arrived at the bottom, I moved off to the side and motioned for her to go first.

"Why, thank you, David. You're such a gentleman. Now let's see if your brother listened to his mother."

We went into the kitchen. Andrew was at the stove with a smile on his face, stirring the pot. "I told you you couldn't stop me."

"You should do as you are told," Mom said. "I'm still your mother, and I'm not afraid to give you a good spanking. I don't care *how* old you are." She made as if she were going to hit him on the backside with the wooden spoon, then she shrugged. "Fine. If you wanna cook, cook. You're right, I'm not gonna stop you."

Andrew took the spoon from her. "You got it."

Mom gave him a light smack on the face. "And *you'll* get it. So don't push it now."

Evelyn stole the spoon from Andrew and swatted him.

"Whatdya do that for?" Andrew cried.

"Because I could," Evelyn answered back.

"You're lucky I'm making supper, or I'd take you outside and douse you under the pump."

"Wouldn't be the first time you did that."

"C'mon now. That was years ago."

"I know. I'm just teasing. I learned never to sprinkle water in your face after that."

Then she swatted him again.

"Ouch! That really hurt!"

"It's meant to," Evelyn said. "Anyways, how've the meetings been going?"

"Just like that? You swat me, then demand an answer to your question?"

"That's right. I just wanted to know how the meetings have been?"

"Good."

"That's it? Good? That's all you're gonna tell me?"

"Yep."

"Well, I'd say so. You've been meeting with Pastor two and three times a week now. I would assume it's good. But I was curious about what you two have been talking about...."

"My stars!" Mom said. "You're so nosy, Evelyn. It's not your funeral."

"I'm not being nosy. I was just being curious."

"Well, that's your problem," Andrew said. "You shouldn't be curious."

"Stay out of this, Andy?"

"What do you mean *stay out of this?* You're the one who came to *me.*"

"What's so wrong with being curious?"

"First of all," Mom chimed in, "curiosity killed the cat."

"And satisfaction brought him back. So there!" Evelyn made a face.

"*So there!*" Andrew said, mockingly.

"I didn't say it like that."

"Yes, you did."

She smacked him again with the spoon.

"You're asking for it, Evelyn."

"Whatever." She made another face then proceeded to set the table. "So you like your new job at the upholstery shop?"

"Yep."

"I know you had already learned a lot from Dad, but it sounds like Mr. Bradford's really taken you under his wing, huh?"

"He has."

"So how's it been going?"

"Good."

"Good? That's all you're gonna keep saying?"

"Yep."

"That's it! I've had enough! We're going in circles!" She rushed back into the kitchen and smacked him again.

"We're *about* to go in circles!" Andrew said, tossing the ladle down. He rushed Evelyn and threw her over his shoulder and twirled her around the kitchen.

"Andy! Alright, alright!"

"Yee-haw!"

They spun around and around and around.

"Andy, I'm getting dizzy! I'm getting dizzy!—Andy, my skirt's going up!"

"That's your fault," Andrew said, setting her down. He went over to the sink and leaned on the edge. "Whew!"

"You alright?" Mom asked.

"I'm fine. I just can't handle spinning anymore, that's all."

Evelyn grabbed the spoon and swatted him again. "And that's *your* fault!" she said, fleeing the room. "That'll teach you a lesson to go picking me up." She took cover on the other side of the table.

"You can't hide."

"Be nice to me. I'm your little sister."

"I am nice to you. Why do you think I'm making you supper?"

Andrew took the pan out of the oven and set it on the table. He brought the pot out as well, and the three of us took our seats.

Mom poured the drinks. "Your father said he'd be home by now."

"I know," Evelyn said. "I wonder what's keeping him?" She gripped her fork like a hunting knife.

Andrew took his apron off and hung it up. "Who knows? One thing I do know is smelling all this good food has got me hungry."

"Man alive!" I said. "My stomach's growling. I'm about to dig in."

"And eat without Dad?" Evelyn cried.

I scowled. "If he doesn't show up in the next five minutes, then yes!"

Evelyn giggled. "I just wanted to see if you'd tell the truth."

"Pshh! I'm as honest as Abe Lincoln."

"Phonus-balonus! Don't go dragging Lincoln's name through the mud."

I put my hand to my heart and stuck my nose up. "If Mr. Lincoln were here, why, he'd tip his stovepipe hat to me."

Evelyn rolled her eyes. "Tell it to Sweeney!"

"Listen to you! Like you're any more honest than me."

"I am."

"Ha!"

"I am, though."

"No, you're real funny. That's what you are."

Mom peered over her glasses at the both of us. "Listen to the two of you now. I mean *seriously*."

"But it's true, Mother. This is the same Evelyn who once told me that Alice Stratton liked me—"

"She didn't *loathe* you, right?"

"Let me finish, please! You know very well what someone thinks when you go and tell them that so-and-so *likes* them—Now not only

127

was that a lie, Mother, but she knew I was stuck on Alice. I mean that's not just being dishonest, that's downright vicious."

"Oh, please," Evelyn said.

"So what happened?" Mom asked.

"Well, I believed what she said to me—'cause I never would've thought I had to second guess my own blood sister who happens to be my older sister, which means she's supposed to be a good example to follow—"

"Oh, please."

"Anyways, I never thought I should've doubted her when she said something to me so matter-of-factly and so honest-looking—"

"Cut to the chase," Mom cried. "What happened?"

"I was about to tell you—I wrote Alice a letter."

Mom burst out laughing.

"It's not funny. My heart was crushed. Evelyn knew I liked her."

"I know, I know," Mom said. "It's not really funny...except that it is. Ha! That was a good laugh. I needed that. Thank you."

I rolled my eyes. "Don't thank me. Thank, Evelyn. She's the one who lied to her little brother, so that you could have a good laugh, I guess. Oh well. At least Honest Abe would defend me if he were here...even if my own mother won't."

"Oh, brother! Would you like a little cheese with that whine?" Mom got up and covered the pot and stuck the pan back in the oven to keep supper warm. "We'll give your father ten more minutes. If he's not back by then, we'll go ahead without him."

Andrew leaned his head back and closed his eyes. "Father, where are you?"

I glanced over at Mom to see if she was looking.

"David Millard Hayes!" Evelyn cried, smacking me on the hand. "Shame on you!"

"What did he do?" Mom asked.

"He tried stealing a piece of cornbread," Evelyn said. "And yet he was here just a moment ago beating his gums about how honest he is!"

"You little thief!" Mom said.

I cringed at those words.

I'm more than a thief. I'm a housebreaker!

Rouge began to bark, which snapped me out of my gloomy thoughts. "What is it, girl?"

She ran into the parlor and continued barking.

A car could be heard coming up the road. The person laid on the horn.

"Now is that really called-for to go around beeping like that?" Mom cried, shaking her head. "I mean, what an ignoramus! Those machines make such a racket down our road now. It wasn't even a few years ago, and you would've *never* heard this kinda thing."

The horn blared in our front yard now.

Evelyn ran to the living room window. "It's Dad!"

"What do you mean?" Mom said.

"Come see! He drove a car home."

I darted through the room and opened the front door. Sure enough, there was my father sitting in a car, with the happiest look on his face. "Where'd ya get the wheels?"

"From Bellman's."

"Holy smokes!—Hey, Dad bought a new car!"

"Well, new to us anyhow," Dad said. "It's a '22 Model T."

Mom came outside with the rest of us. She made her way across the porch with some difficulty. "My stars! Our very first car, Millard."

"That's right, snookums. Be careful there—Andrew, give your mother a hand, would ya?"

Andrew came up and took hold of Mom's arm and tried to help her along.

"I'm fine, I'm fine," Mom said, holding onto the railing. "I just got a little light in the head from the excitement is all. I mean no one told me we were getting a new car, for goodness' sake."

"I wanted it to be a surprise," Dad said.

"Well, it's a dilly of a surprise, I'll tell you what!"

"Whatta ya think, Andy?" Evelyn said. "Isn't it the cat's meow?"

"It's wonderful. It's a good-looking Touring. Enough room for everyone."

"What about poor Chester and Checkers?" Mom said.

"We'll be using them less, no doubt," Dad said. "But they're not going anywhere. They're part of the family."

"I just can't believe we own one of these machines now," Mom said, wiping her forehead.

"Well, you better believe it," Andrew said, placing his arm around her.

Dad honked the horn one more time. "That's the dinner buzzer. That means it's time to head in. I'm starved."

"Whatta you mean it's *time*?" Evelyn said. "It's *been* time. We've been waiting and waiting for you so we could start. Mom gave you a few minutes to get here or we were gonna eat without you."

"Is that right?" Dad said, straightening out his hat.

I nodded. "You cut it close."

He turned the car off and got out, then he closed the door and gave Mom a kiss on the cheek. "You would eat without me, Doris?"

"I just assumed your boss kept you over, or that you were busy about a project or something and forgot all about the time. If my memory serves me correctly, you've done that once or twice before."

"And little did you know I was held up at Bellman's to buy us our very first automobile. Took a little longer than what I had thought." He helped Mom up the steps. "How ya feeling by the way? You still don't seem right?"

"See?" Evelyn cried. "Andy was right. Mom's not feeling well."

"Oh, stop it," Mom said. "It wouldn't be wrong to say I've had my better days, but this too shall pass. I'm just a little tired is all. But that doesn't mean we need to be going about making mountains out of molehills. My stars!"

"I'm not gonna lie," Andrew said. "You got me a little worried."

Mom nudged Dad with her elbow. "See what you did? You got a big mouth, Millard!"

Chapter 16

I had finished hanging the clothes on the line to dry when the horse and buggy pulled into the front yard. I emptied the dirty water out of the basin and set the washboard against the pump, then I scurried around the house.

It was Dr. Thompson. He was in his customary wool suit coat and scarf tie, and he was carrying his leather medical bag. He was a slender man with a trimmed mustache that curved slightly on the ends, and he had a mellow manner that matched the thoughtful expression on his face. His hairline receded from his forehead, but he had plenty of white hair otherwise. He was about to knock on the door when I stepped onto the porch.

"Good morning, Dr. Thompson."

"Howdy, David. Your father had arranged for me to stop by this morning...."

"Sure thing. Here, I'll get the door for you."

"Thank you, sir."

He went inside and set his bag down, then stood there submissively by the door, with his hands folded in front of him.

"I'll be right back," I said. "I'll go and get Dad for you."

I went upstairs and gave a little knock on my parents' door.

"Yes?" Dad said.

"Um, Dr. Thompson's here. He's right downstairs."

"Oh, good. Thank you, Son. Go ahead and send him up."

"Yes, sir."

I returned downstairs to the living room. "My dad says you're welcome to come up."

He nodded his head and followed me upstairs. I showed him to the room and announced his arrival.

"Dr. Thompson," Dad said. "Come on in."

Dr. Thompson nodded and entered the bedroom. "Good morning, Mrs. Hayes."

"Hello, doctor," Mom said. "Eh-hem. Thanks for coming by— excuse me. I must have a frog in my throat."

"Not a problem, ma'am. Let's see if we can figure out what's going on here, shall we?"

Dad turned to me from inside the doorway. "We shouldn't be long. As soon as we're done here, I still plan on heading up to the Sawyers, so don't go anywhere. That's if you're still interested in coming along."

"No, I'd like to," I said. "I haven't seen Irvin and the boys in a while. I'll be in my room. Just give me a knock when you're ready."

"Alright. Will do." He closed the door behind him.

I went to my room and sat down on the edge of my bed and began to wonder what it was they were talking about. After a few minutes, the spark of curiosity ignited a fire of interest in me.

I stood to my feet and opened the door slowly to stifle any squeaky protests of the hinges. Once it was open far enough, I stretched my head out into the hallway. I could hear the low rumbling of the men's voices through the walls, but I couldn't make out anything they were saying.

I left my room. I tiptoed down the hallway, pausing now and then to test my hearing.

Still, nothing.

I tiptoed further and paused once more to listen in. This time, I could pick out a few words here and there, but not enough to provide me with any clues.

I inched my way closer yet, until I was about five feet from my parents' bedroom door. That's when I distinctly heard my mom say she had "found a lump." I also thought I heard someone shuffling by the door. I tiptoed back as quickly as possible, with the longest strides I could manage, as if I had the legs of a giraffe and the feet of a cat.

It wasn't the close call I had imagined. About five minutes later, my parents' bedroom door opened.

"Thanks again, Dr. Thompson," Dad said.

"Yes, sir. I'll be back in a few days for a checkup. Until then, we'll be praying."

"That's right. Thank you. Here, I'll show you to the door."

"Oh, no need to bother yourself with that. I'll be just fine. Good day now."

"You too. Take care, doctor."

Dad remained in the room with Mom for a few more minutes before finally heading out. He tapped on my door. "Ready, Son?"

I stepped out into the hallway. "Sure. I'm just gonna say goodbye to Mom real quick." I went in and kissed her on the forehead. "I'll see you in the evening, Mother. Hope you feel better." Mom reached out and touched my hand. "Thank you, David."

I left the room and headed to the staircase. Dad put his arm around me. "Let's lend the Sawyers a helping hand, shall we?"

I smiled. "Let's do it."

Dad went out back to fetch his box of tools. He stepped out of the workshop and turned to my sister who was at the chicken coop. "We'll be gone for a bit, Evelyn. Doing some work at the Sawyers. So just check on Mom now and then. Make sure she's got a full glass of water and plenty of apple slices."

"Will do."

"Thanks, honey."

As we approached the car, Dad set his toolbox down and pointed to the crank on the front. "Make sure the key's off before you go priming the engine or that thing could buck like a bronco." Dad pulled the choke out and cranked it a few times. "Now that there's fuel up in the cylinders, you come over here." I walked over to the driver door; Dad showed me the lever on the floor. "Make sure your handbrake is engaged so the car doesn't roll on ya. Then set the spark and throttle levers here on the column to about there, and then turn the key on—now it's ready to start." He walked me back to the front of the car. "Only use your left hand when you give it the final crank because the engine rotates in this direction. You don't wanna end up like ole Hammermeister?"

"Why? What happened?"

"Well, he went to go drive his first car off the lot and told Bellman he didn't need no help starting it up. Turns out he was so sure about what he was doing that he grabbed hold of that crank with his right hand and then wham! That thing kicked back so fast it broke his wrist."

"Man alive!"

Dad winked. "It's a mistake you make only once. Now you can grab hold of the fender with your right, like this, to give you better leverage. Then give the crank a good turn." The engine started right up. "Just like that. Not too bad, huh?"

Dad set the toolbox in the back seat and then hopped in. He adjusted the spark to smooth out the engine, then off we went, sputtering down the road.

As soon as we pulled into the yard, the Sawyer boys came running out of the barn, clad in their muddy overalls. "The Hayeses got a horseless carriage!"

135

Ann sprang out of the house in her ragtag dress and leaped off the porch, evidently in no need of steps. She galloped through the yard like a wild horse. Her billows of hair refused to be tamed, despite being pinned up. "Hurray for David and his dad! Hurray for David and his dad!"

"Now that is what I call a warm welcome," Dad said, giving her a hug. "How are you youngsters doing?"

"Swell."

Mr. and Mrs. Sawyer were on their way, walking hand-in-hand from the barn. "Look what the cat dragged in!" Mr. Sawyer hollered.

"Ha! Must've been a mighty big cat to be dragging that," Nathan said, pointing to the car.

"When d'ya get it, Mr. Hayes?" Wayne asked.

"Just this week."

"It's a beauty."

"Well, thank you. It's certainly no Rolls-Royce, but it's no hayburner either."

"Nah," Irvin said. "You don't need all the fuss and feathers. Just as long as it gets you down the road. And like you said, it's good on gas, so who cares?"

Allen tapped me. "Are y-you gonna d-dr—?"

"Am I gonna drive it?"

"Drive, yep."

"That's my plan," I said, glancing over at Dad. "I suppose if I can't drive that car to town, that car will end up driving me to drink!"

"Ha ha! That is f-funny."

Mr. Sawyer came up and shook Dad's hand. "Moving up in the world, I see."

"A little bit," Dad said. "Not as much as Irvin, though. Man alive! If this boy gets any taller, he's gonna have to duck just to get through the doorway."

Mr. Sawyer burst into laughter.

"Oh, my. Not already," Mrs. Sawyer said. She nudged her husband. "They just got here, Pete. Keep your hands on the reigns."

"I don't plan to, Erma," Mr. Sawyer said, trying to catch his breath. "I've already done let go of 'em. The man is funny as all getout. Ha ha! Helps blow away the cobwebs!"

Dad smirked. "You heard the man, Erma...For Pete's sake!"

Mr. Sawyer shook with laughter. "*For Pete's sake!*—get it? Ha ha!"

Now all of us were laughing.

Mrs. Sawyer turned to Dad and smiled. "He sure doesn't waste no time having a good laugh, just in case you couldn't tell. I'm sure you'll be entertained this whole afternoon. Thanks for coming, Millard. We really appreciate the work you've done with that mantelpiece."

"Not a problem," Dad said. "I brought my right-hand man with me to help finish it up."

Mrs. Sawyer gave me a hug. "Well, good. Thank you, David. It's so good to see you."

"You're welcome, ma'am."

Mr. Sawyer shook my hand. "What can I say? You gotta make the best of your time. Right, David?"

"I think so."

"See? Even David agrees you gotta have a good laugh now and then."

Mrs. Sawyer chuckled. "*Now and then*—not as soon as company gets here. You couldn't even wait half an hour."

"Why wait? If something's funny, it's funny. It don't matter what time of the day it is."

"Or year, for that matter—You wanna know what he did this past spring?"

"C'mon, Erma. How many times you gonna bring that up?"

"You mind your laughing, and I'll mind my bringing up— Anyways, he took the scythe and hacked all my merrybells to death because he mistook them for weeds. So he says. And then he found the whole thing to be rather amusing."

"First of all," Mr. Sawyer said, "it was a sea of green; you couldn't make out any yellow it was so overtaken by weeds. And then it finally dawned on me: I had done turned a flower bed into a grave, so I couldn't help but laugh. What can I say? Ha!"

"See? He still thinks it's funny. The problem wasn't that it was an accident, the problem was that he laughed at me when I said I could cry."

"That's my point," he said, slapping his knee. "In my mind, I had done turned it into a grave, and then you go and tell me you're gonna cry. People cry at graves, ya know! And you even said so yourself, that your merrybells were all 'dead.' Ha ha! That's what you said. And then you had to take it further, telling me what I did was 'grounds for divorce'—I mean she actually said those words to me, so that *really* made me laugh!"

"Like you weren't really laughing already—He found the whole thing to be amusing. And he knows I'd never leave him. But you wanna know what he did?—Go ahead, Pete. Why don't you tell 'em what you did?"

Mr. Sawyer's face lit up. "Well, seeing that she said it was grounds for divorce, I handed her my cup of coffee and said, 'Now there's grounds for canoodling!' And I grabbed her and smooched her right then and there, even though she was mad as a wet hen. Ha ha!"

Mrs. Sawyer smiled. "He's crazy, let me tell you. And he's bad enough all by himself. But then when you two get together, I'm tellin' ya—Ann, get out of there!"

We all turned. Ann was in the car, pretending to be driving.

Dad chuckled. "Oh, she's fine."

"I'm telling ya," Mrs. Sawyer said, "that girl's a live wire. I wonder where she gets that from, huh, Pete?"

"Well, don't look at me," Mr. Sawyer said. "You've been known to generate a little current yourself, especially when our lips meet. Ha ha!"

"Peter Sawyer! I don't know about you sometimes. Now tell her to get out."

"Don't you worry. Irvin knows what to do in these sorts of situations."

"Honestly," Dad said. "She ain't gonna hurt nothing."

"That's what you think," Irvin said. "Trust me, she'll manage."

"I heard that, Irvin," Ann shouted.

"Good," Irvin said. "Then get out like Momma said."

She stuck her tongue out. "You can't make me."

Irvin ran over and plucked her out of the car. "You wanna bet?"

She kicked and flailed around. "Put me down! Put me down!"

"Nope," Irvin said. "Not until you settle down."

"I won't settle down."

"Then I won't set you down."

"Next time I'll just run. I'm faster than you."

"Next time you'll just do what you're told. Besides, I'm stronger than you, and I'll hold you till sunset. Or better yet, I'll baptize you in that pond again!"

"Fine! Fine!"

"You gonna settle down?"

She scowled. "I said *fine*. I'm settled, aren't I?"

"Just making sure."

As soon as her feet touched the ground, she smacked him. "Meany!"

"That's enough, Ann," Mr. Sawyer said. "Stay out of Mr. Hayes's car and don't go smacking folks on the caboose. Ha ha! I don't know why, but whenever I hear that word, it makes me laugh—*caboose!*"

Mr. Sawyer was hilarious to observe, and Ann was just cute and comical. Truly, more playful than spiteful.

While we were all cackling and cutting up, Dad caught my attention. He squinted his eyes and seemed distracted. "Hey, Pete," he said, pointing to the storehouse. "Who's that?"

There was a boy about my age. He was hurling hay bales up to the loft.

"Oh, that's Silas," Mr. Sawyer said. "He's the new addition to the family. Erma and I told him to come join us when we were coming out to greet ya'll. He said he was just gonna finish up with the cattle, but the boy don't know when to stop."

"He's a real blessing to have around," Mrs. Sawyer said. "He's such a tremendous helper."

"Where d'ya find him?" Dad asked.

"My sister," Mr. Sawyer said. "She spoke to me about him. From what I've been told, he'd been at the orphanage down in Lyon for some years. Well, it so happened it closed, and he needed a place to live, so my sister took him in till she could find him a new home. She got a hold of me and said he had a wonderful spirit and assured me he'd be a great help to the farm. We got the space n' all, so it's really worked out for the both of us. And let me tell you, the boy's fit as a fiddle and as strong as an ox. Just watch him toss them bales."

"I see that!" Dad said, raising his brow.

Mr. Sawyer nudged Dad. "He's got a grip like a machinist's vise. No lie! Wait till he shakes your hand—Hey, Silas!" He waved his hand. "Come join us!"

"We have to give him orders to stop working," Mrs. Sawyer said. "Otherwise he won't."

Silas jogged over. "Yes, sir?"

"I want you to meet some dear friends of ours."

"Oh, I promise I was planning on coming over to say hello, but I got distracted when I saw them bales. I wasn't meaning to be rude."

"That's quite alright," Mrs. Sawyer said. "Silas, this is Mr. Hayes—and this is David. They live just up the road. Good friends of ours."

Silas smiled and shook my hand. "A pleasure to meet you, David."

"Same here."

He shook Dad's hand. "A pleasure to meet you, Mr. Hayes."

"Nice to meet you, young man. You must be a hard-working fellow with a grip like that."

Silas beamed.

"What did I tell you?" Mr. Sawyer said.

"Silas here is the real McCoy," Mrs. Sawyer said. "He was our guest of honor for maybe a day or two, but he quickly became one of the bunch."

Silas raised his eyebrows. "I guess I'm just as crazy as they are, so I fit right in. Except for the color of my skin. Ha!"

We all chuckled.

"Why don't you take a break, Silas?" Mrs. Sawyer said. "We're gonna cobble up a meal and have a bite to eat, then we can finish up with those bales."

"Yes, ma'am. Sounds good to me."

"Ya know, Nathan's been teaching Silas how to read and write," Mrs. Sawyer said. "And he's catching on fast, too. Aren't you, Silas?"

He smiled. "I sure am. Why, I can read just about every letter of the alphabet now!"

Mr. Sawyer clapped his hands. "Ha ha! You're stringing them letters together pretty good though. Before long, you'll be writing like Shakespeare."

"Silas doesn't have a last name," Nathan said. "So we'll just have to call him Silas Shakespeare."

"Kinda has a ring to it," Ann said.

141

"You all can call me anything you like," Silas said. "Just don't call me late for mealtime!"

"Oh, no," Wayne said, shaking his head. "Anything but that."

Allen tugged on my arm. "N-Nathan is a, a, good tea—yep!"

"You're right, Allen," Silas said. "Nathan's a *great* teacher. I owe it to him."

Allen smiled. "S-Silas is a g-good stu—student."

Silas put his hand on Allen's shoulder. "And Allen is a good friend."

"N-No," Allen said. "B-Brother."

"A brother? Wow!"

"Yep!"

"And you can take that to the bank," Nathan said. "Allen's as honest as the day is long."

"Holy mackerel!" Silas said, putting his hand on my shoulder. "The Sawyers sure are good to me, David."

Without warning, Irvin tossed the football at Silas. The ball fumbled around in his fingertips, but he got hold of it and held it close.

"Terrific!" Wayne said. "Silas has good hands, David. Wait till you see this—Show him your hands, Silas."

Silas held out his hands, grinning.

"You know what I mean," Wayne cried.

Silas chuckled.

Irvin ran over and crouched down before him. "He may have good hands, but I've got good cover."

"Nah, Silas can cut like a cheetah."

"But he can't escape these long legs and height."

Allen stood by his older brother and proudly smiled. "Yep."

"I bet he can," Wayne said.

"Not today," Irvin added.

Allen looked up. "Not today. Yep."

"We'll see," Wayne said. "Ready...hike!"

Silas took off through the yard with Irvin in close pursuit. Wayne got into his ready stance and looked for an opening.

Without warning, Allen charged Wayne, yelling and waving his hands like a madman.

"What are you doing?" Wayne cried, skirting the tackle. He surveyed the yard. Irvin had Silas well covered, so he hesitated. Then right about the time he signaled for Silas to cut the other way, Allen came charging after him again.

"Here, David!" Wayne cried. "Quick!" He tossed me the ball as Allen plowed into him, taking him to the ground.

I had no time to think.

"Over here, David!"

Silas cut back to the left, waving his hand. I lobbed the ball as hard as I could, probably the most awkward-looking pass I had thrown in my life. It wobbled through the air and dropped just enough over Irvin's reach, right into Silas's hands.

"Touchdown!" Wayne cried, getting up from the ground. "Oh, my goodness!"

"Way to go!"

"Ha! He caught it!"

Ann skipped through the yard. "Irvin got beat! Irvin got beat!"

Irvin shook his head. "Holy smokes! That was a perfect throw."

Nathan and Allen grinned at me.

"Don't look at me," I said. "Silas is the one who caught it."

"But you're the one who threw it!" Nathan cried.

Ann was still skipping about. "Hurray for David and Silas!"

I looked back at Silas. "Great catch!"

Silas jogged up to me, smiling from ear to ear, and patted me on the back. "We make a good team. No one gets past Irvin the Great. No one except us!"

That was my first encounter with Silas. Little did I know how the Lord had led our paths to cross.

Chapter 17

Lucy shuffled her way to the door.

"Good afternoon, David."

"And good afternoon to you, Lucy. Is your brother home?"

"He sure is. Come in and make yourself at home."

"Thank you."

I followed her into the house, then I called up to Daryl from the bottom of the stairs.

He popped out of his room. "Hey, whatcha up to?"

"You wanna come with me and grab a coke? It's on me."

"Sure. I was just trying to finish up on some homework that's due Monday. It gets away from you fast. You know how that goes. But a coke does sound refreshing."

"You sure? Don't let me keep you from your schoolwork."

"No. I'll be fine. I've got most of it out of the way already. Besides, I should give my mind a break."

"Sounds good."

Daryl sat down at the top of the stairs and slipped on his shoes. "Did you hear about what happened to Earl Bennett?"

"Ole Glad Rags? No, what happened?"

"Well, he's been following Alice Stratton around town. No matter where she went, Bennett just happened to be somewhere around. All gussied up, of course."

"Seriously?"

"Dead serious. If she came out of Trottman's, he was there sitting on the bench. If she came out of Edwards, he happened to be crossing the street, wanting to talk to her."

"Ha! Glad Rags has got some guts."

Daryl tied his laces. "Well, it gets better. She was walking down Highland back to her house one evening when she spotted someone peeking from behind that giant oak tree. You know, the one on ole Howard's property?"

"Sure."

"Well, she got the jitters and started picking up the pace. Next thing she knows, she hears these footsteps. She looks back, and Bennett's hot on her trail. She, being scared and all, just stopped right there and asked him why he was following her. She said he acted like he didn't know what she was talking about and told her he was just heading up to Bellman's for supper. So now Alice is just plain mad and tells him he's not her type."

"Ha! So then what?"

"Well, he gets mad back at her and says she's nothing but a canceled stamp and then walks off."

"Earl Bennett said *that* to Alice Stratton?"

Daryl grinned. "Yep. And guess what? She went home and told Roy."

"Uh-oh. That's not good."

"Nope. He tracked Bennett down one night and dragged him behind the gas station where they stack all those tires and threw him headfirst in the wastebin."

"Are you serious?"

"Then he told him if he ever hounded his sister again, he was gonna cancel his Christmas. That's exactly how he put it, too."

"Man alive!"

Daryl grabbed his flannel jacket and started down the stairs. "Bennett won't so much as look at her now."

"Pretty smart of him."

"Pshh! If brains were leather, he wouldn't have enough to saddle a June bug. I mean, c'mon. How was trailing Roy's sister ever a good idea?"

"True."

We left the house and walked down to Brackman's and picked up a couple bottles of orange soda. Then we made our way to the nearest bench, right outside Foster's Barbershop, and sat down.

I took a sip. "Ha! I still can't get over that."

"Oh, about Bennett?" Daryl said.

"Yes. I can easily picture Roy doing something like that. Then he says he's gonna cancel his Christmas. Ha ha!"

"Oh, I know. I'll never forget when Turner was stupid enough to throw a punch at Roy. Roy slapped him upside the head so hard that Turner's head bounced off Mr. Wagner's filing cabinet like a basketball. That was it. Turner put his hand to his head and just walked away."

"I wish Roy would teach Dominic a lesson. Why couldn't Roy be a few years younger?"

"I know."

Just then, Mr. Foster stepped outside. "Hello, gentlemen. Ahh, what a gorgeous day that the Lord hath made. We will rejoice and be glad in it."

Daryl raised his bottle. "Yes, sir. Goes along perfectly with some soda, too."

"I see," Mr. Foster said. "So you gentlemen coming in for a haircut?"

"Oh, we're just chitchatting," I said.

"Frittering away time, to be sure," Mr. Foster said, twitching his mustache. "You know, idle hands are the devil's workshop."

Daryl stood up from the bench, shaking his head. "We're actually going now."

"Hope I'm not driving you away. No, no. You're both welcome to come in and get a haircut. In my humble opinion, you both need one. But anyways, I was simply taken by surprise to find both the Hayes boy *and* the Mitchell boy loitering, that's all."

I stood to my feet as well. "I'll be back in a week. My last haircut should hold out till then."

"Well, aren't you gonna tell me how your mother's been before you go running off? It seems she made quite the recovery, right?"

"Yes, sir," I said. "Mom got better."

Mr. Foster stroked his bushy mustache. "So it turns out you had the faith that Sister Annie preaches about. I'd have to say, I'm very pleased."

"I suppose."

"Well, let's not just suppose. God healed your mother, didn't he?"

Daryl tapped me on the arm. "We should be going, David."

"Just a second—Yes, God did heal her."

"Then let's be clear, God rewards that kind of faith. Look at what Sister Annie went through just a few months ago. Why, many had given her up for dead! I—mean—dead! Turns out she was kidnapped. Yet the Lord preserved her all the way through, and now her ministry will bring even more glory to God!"

"I hate to say this, Mr. Foster, but Mom is ill again."

"Is she, though?"

"Yes, sir."

"Hmm." He stroked his mustache again. "Ehem. Well, I had almost said I'm sorry to hear that, but what is this but yet another opportunity for God to show himself faithful? Why, this is but the Red Sea that must needs part before the power of the Almighty!"

Mr. Foster stepped forward and stuck his finger in my chest. "Do you believe, David, that God—will—heal—her—again?"

"I do," I said, regaining my balance. "Now if you'll excuse me, sir, Daryl and I must be going. Good day."

"Alright, alright. Good day, Mr. Hayes. Good day, Mr. Mitchell."

We left the barbershop and continued up the street. I could tell Daryl was upset.

"You don't care for Mr. Foster, do you?" I asked.

"Pshh! The man's rude," Daryl said. "And his smugness is about as thick as his mustache."

I tried not to laugh. "I admit he can be a little overbearing, but I think he's a good man overall."

"A good man? Nah! I mean what business does he have getting in your face and pushing you like that? It's so stinkin' rude!"

"That's just his way…I don't take it personal."

"Well, you should—the way he talks about your mom like that! Like you can just *believe* your mom into health. Such bunkum!"

"But I did, Daryl. I did believe. I prayed for my mom's healing, and she was healed."

"Pshh! Then why's she sick again?" He turned to me and took a deep breath. "Listen, I'm sorry. I don't mean to be rude like Foster…but seriously, David, what kind of healing is that?"

"I don't know. That's just the way life is, I suppose. All I know is you'll see, Daryl. You'll see what I mean. I believe with all my heart my mom's gonna be made better again."

We turned down W. Breckenridge and cut through the park. I knew I was on delicate ground, but I ventured to pick up where I had left off.

"Look around, Daryl. I mean how did this all get here? If God has the power to create everything we see, then I believe he has the power to heal."

"I do look around. That's the problem, David. I do look around! *My* eyes are wide open. I look around, and what do I see? I see suffering! I see misery! I see your dead sister, June. I look around and see my little sister limping around on crutches with her buckled legs! That's what I see! So why the heck did God let my sister get Polio? Huh, David? Tell me! Why did your God who's so powerful—so loving—so merciful—that's what they taught us in Sunday School, right? If he's so stinkin' loving and kind, then why the heck did he let—"

Daryl burst into tears.

"What Daryl? Why did he let what?"

He buried his face in his hands. "Why did he let that happen to me?"

"Let what happen?"

He wouldn't say.

"Daryl. Let *what* happen to you?"

"Never mind!"

"I'm your friend. You gotta tell me."

"I don't wanna talk about it!"

I just stood there. What was I to say?

At length, he regained control of himself. "I'm sorry, David." He sat down on the park bench and wiped his face with his sleeve. "If you wouldn't mind, I'd like to be alone."

"You don't need to apologize," I said. "I'll let you be…I'm really sorry if I made you upset. I meant well."

"No, you're fine…I just got steamed up…and I'm a little embarrassed is all."

"Alright…Well, there's nothing to be embarrassed about…Just take it easy…I'll talk to you later."

I headed home in a somber mood, chucking rocks at trees on the side of the road.

What just happened?

Chapter 18

I had gone over my conversation with Daryl a million times in my mind, wondering what I should or shouldn't have said. At last, I approached the foot of my driveway. Dad and Pastor Richardson stepped out of the house.

"...I reckon the rest is up to him," Dad said, glancing up at the sky. "I appreciate your time, sir."

Pastor Richardson didn't say anything. He placed his hand on Dad's shoulder and stood there with the most compassionate expression on his face, slightly nodding his head. He gave him a final pat and parted ways.

We met on the porch steps. "Take care, Pastor," I said.

He patted my shoulder. "You, too, David. Good to see you."

I went into the house with Dad. "Pastor stop by again to see Andrew?"

"Um, yes," Dad said. "He did see Andrew. But he was actually here visiting with Mom for the most part."

"Did he pray with Mom?"

"As a matter of fact, he did." He turned to me. "Listen, Son...um, I already talked with your brother and your sister—I thought you would've been here, too, otherwise I would've told you as well—"

"Oh, I'm sorry. I headed into town to get with Daryl. I wasn't planning on it at first, but I did finish up all my chores before I left the house."

"No, that's fine. That's just fine…but I told your brother and your sister that Pastor was coming over, and they wanted to know why, of course. And seeing the reason for him coming over and all, I thought it was time to tell you just how sick your mother has been."

"I know, Dad. But I believe God's gonna heal her. And thankfully we have a pastor who cares enough to come over and pray with her, right?"

"Your right, Son. He did come over and pray for her…and he anointed her with oil, just like James instructs us to do—"

"For healing, right?"

"Yes."

"Well, there you go. Pastor believes as much as me that God's gonna make Mom better."

Dad looked down at the floor for a moment and cleared his throat. "As I was saying, I thought it was time to tell you just how sick your mother is…Um, like I told Andrew and Evelyn, Mom has cancer."

I heard what my father said to me, but the announcement did not seem real at all. "Then we'll keep praying for her."

Dad put his arm around me. "That's right, Son. We'll keep praying."

"Can I see Mom right now?"

"You sure can. I think she'd love that."

I made my way slowly up the stairs, gazing blankly at each step. *No wonder! This is for Daryl! Daryl's gonna see!*

I paused at the top of the stairs. I decided to stop by my bedroom to look up the passage of scripture Dad had referenced.

I went in and closed the door behind me. Andrew lay on his bed and appeared to be sleeping. I grabbed my Bible from the dresser top and thumbed through the entire Book of James until I arrived at the verses.

Is any sick among you? let him call for the elders of the church; and let them pray over him, anointing him with oil in the name of the Lord: And the prayer of faith shall save the sick, and the Lord shall raise him up; and if he have committed sins, they shall be forgiven him.

I gazed at the verses for several minutes. I read them again. And again.

"Whatcha up to?" Andrew muttered.

I flinched. "Oh, nothing. Just reading."

My brother's eyes were still closed. "Whatcha reading?"

"Oh, just some verses on healing. I'm actually about to visit with Mom."

"I see."

With a feeling of certainty in my heart, I closed my Bible, set it back down on the dresser, then left the room.

"Come in," Mom said faintly.

She was sitting up against the wall with a pillow propped behind her back, her feet covered with her stars and stripes blanket. She had clearly lost more weight, and her skin was tinged with yellow.

I sat down on the chair beside her. "I love you, Mom."

"And I love *you*." She reached out and touched me on the arm. She shifted around a bit, trying to get more comfortable. "Do you know why I named you David?" she asked, straightening out her blankets.

"How come?" I said.

"Because King David was the youngest of Jesse's family, and I knew in my heart you were to be my last. That's why I named you David."

I smiled. "You knew?"

"I sure did," she said, turning to me. Then she leaned her head back and folded her hands across her lap and stared off into the distance. "My, how the time has flown by...It seems like it was just yesterday I swaddled you in those wraps I had sewn. I stitched the letter 'D' on all of them before you were even born." She chuckled. "I mean your name was beginning with 'D' one way or the other, whether you were a girl or a boy! Now I knew in my heart I was having a boy—I can't explain it, but I knew—so I was settled on 'David.' But your father wasn't so sure about it. He said, 'I know you think you know, but what if it's not a boy, then what? You've got all these swaddling blankets with a 'D' on them now.' And I said, 'Then she'll have to be Deborah or Delilah.' Ha! Your father jerked his head and squinted his eyes at me. 'Well, it's not gonna be Delilah, I can tell you that much!' he said. Then he walked away. Turns out, I was right anyhow."

She paused to catch her breath.

"My oh my, let me tell you, you were the cutest little bundle—your dark eyes all wide open and looking right at me as you listened to me so intently as I talked to you...after you had stopped screaming, that is. My stars, did you scream! You screamed and screamed and screamed...but then I got you all wrapped up and comfy, and I cradled you in my arms and spoke to you softly. And you snuggled right down and listened to me."

I smirked. "Of course, Mother. I was your best-behaved child. I always listened to you."

"Horsefeathers! You mean listen like the time I told you to stay away from the creek, and you snuck down anyway to go meddling with that beehive? Pshh! You must've gotten stung a dozen times. I'll never forget that."

"I was merely fetching honey for our family."

"Fetching honey! Those weren't no honeybees. I don't know who you're trying to kid."

"I didn't know any better. I was just trying to help."

154

"Listen to you. Telling more tales…How about the time I sent you to your room, huh? This very room, in fact. It was your bedroom then. And what did you do? Why, you climbed out the window and onto the roof and then got down to the ground only God knows how—"

"I used the post, I slid down."

"I'm sure you did. And then I'm in the kitchen doing some cooking and whatnot, and I just happened to glance out the window. Goodness gracious, I see a boy who looks just like you, and he goes running around the side of the workshop. And I thought to myself, 'What in the world is going on? That boy can't be my David; I just sent him to his room but twenty minutes ago, and I know for sure he didn't come down those stairs.' I mean, I thought I was losing my mind, that maybe I was seeing things! So I went upstairs just to prove to myself that I had just seen a ghost or something, and lo and behold, I open the door, and you're gone! I mean gone—like a little Houdini!"

I clapped my hands and laughed. "I love that story!"

"Well, you weren't laughing then. Not when your father came home anyhow."

"No. Unfortunately, Dad wasn't too impressed with my great escape."

Mom laid her head back against the headboard and closed her eyes. She breathed heavily.

I hesitated to add to what had been said, just in case she felt moved to say something further and tire herself out even more.

I found myself staring at the stars on her blanket.

Beyond the blue…So far away…I wonder….

Mom snapped me out of my musing. "I've been praying for you," she said.

"And I've been praying for you, Mother. And I've been thinking about the prayer of faith that James talks about. I really believe God is gonna heal you."

With her eyes still closed, she reached out for my hand. She squeezed it in her cold grip. "You're right, Son...And each day gets me closer."

I sat there silently for a few more minutes. Then I decided to let her get some rest. I was about to get up.

"You have to guard your heart, David."

"From what?"

"Oh…from envy and pride...covetousness...from bitterness and hatred…"

I cleared my throat.

"…These things lurk inside every one of us," she continued. "That's why we all have to guard our heart. It's a constant undertaking, you know."

"Yes, ma'am…I'm gonna let you get some rest now, alright?" I tucked her feet in. "I'll talk to you later."

"Thank you, David."

*   *   *

A few days later, Andrew came rushing down the stairs and into the kitchen. "You better come now!"

Evelyn and I followed him upstairs into the bedroom.

The three of us gathered at Mom's bedside. Her breathing seemed unusual, but I didn't think much of it. I just sat there in the chair, holding her hand, resting my forehead upon the mattress, praying.

Every now and again, I'd look up. Andrew and Evelyn were still standing, gazing down upon the bed. Tears ran down their faces as they tried to stifle their sniffling.

I placed my forehead back down on the mattress and prayed some more. I remained in that position for about another twenty minutes.

Then out of nowhere, Andrew came out with it—

"That's it! Mom's gone!"

Evelyn wept and wailed.

I looked up. "What do you mean?"

"Mom's gone!" Andrew said, sobbing.

I stood up. "She's gone?"

"She's gone!" Evelyn cried.

I looked down at Mom's body. The lack of awareness—the happy expectancy—it all began to fade as reality, cruel and unfeeling as it is, took over. Despite the wave of dizziness that rolled over my brain, one thing became clear to me—Mom was not there.

The anguish. The fury. The confusion that roiled in my heart all at once.

You betrayed me!

I staggered out of the room. I leaned against the wall and stared down at the floor. I jostled my head, trying to snap myself out of a bad dream.

With the support of the wall, I clambered down the hallway into my bedroom. I slammed the door behind me and plopped down on the side of my bed. Gazing down. My tears splashing on the floor.

I looked up. My out-of-focus eyes. But I could make out the black book on top of the dresser.

I grabbed it. I opened it. I tried to clear my eyes.

I found the page. I gazed at the hazy lines until the verses came into focus.

Faith will save the sick—liar!

Another surge of anger. It toppled the breakwall of my soul.

Before I knew it, my hand had struck the pages. I was gripping the clump of them in a clenched fist. And that's when I hurled it against the wall.

Chapter 19

Dad came home. Evelyn burst into tears again, trying to break it to him. She couldn't get the words out, but Dad knew. He took his hat off and heaved a sigh. His face grimaced as he fought to stave off the tears. He went up to his room and closed the door. That's when he let out a sob that could be heard throughout the house. That's when Andrew and I lost it all over again.

He finally returned downstairs. He paused by the landing and tried to say something.

Evelyn came up to him and patted his back.

Dad struggled for a moment then buried his head in his hands. "I wasn't there for her! I wasn't there for Mom's homegoing!"

Yet even Andrew and Evelyn, who had understood the urgency of Mom's condition, assured him there was little reason that morning to have expected it. That it wasn't until later in the day Andrew noticed the dire change in Mom's breathing.

Dad nodded his head, looking down at the floor. Then it occurred to him: "I wish I could tell her. Without any reservation whatsoever!"

"Tell her what, Dad?" Evelyn cried.

"How much I loved her!"

"But you did, Dad."

"No, I didn't! I wanna tell her how I really feel about her. Not just that I love her—I told her that each and every day—but that I really, really love her—more than anything else in this world! That if I ever tried to look her in the eyes and tell her the truth—the way I always wanted to—I'd break down and cry like I'm doing now!" He stumbled forward and leaned on the back of the dining room chair, sobbing. "I wanna tell her that now—I would do it—I would do it right now!"

Evelyn came up and wrapped her arms around him. "You loved her very much, Dad. And we all knew that. And Mom knew that. We all wish we could say the things that are in our heart. Everybody understands that. But you loved her very much."

My brother stood nestled in the corner, his forehead resting upon his hand. I sat on the floor with my back against the wall, blubbering and whimpering.

The hour went by. The back and forth between the sobbing and sympathizing abated. We left the dining room to begin our preparations. Evelyn filled the little basin with water and washed Mom's body down while Andrew and I went out to the workshop to help Dad put together a wooden casket. When all was ready, we placed the body into the casket. Andrew sealed it up. Then we carried it down the stairs and set it up in the living room.

We were grateful for the number of those who attended the viewing the next day. Mr. Bradford and Dr. Thompson and Aunt Mary came by to share their condolences. The entire Sawyer family came by as well, including Silas. One would have thought Silas had been part of our lives all along; that's how sincere and heartfelt he was. He put his arm around me and told me how sorry he was for my loss.

Pastor and Mrs. Richardson offered their quiet support the entire time. Mrs. Harrison attended with Beth who was especially heartbroken for my sister. Mr. and Mrs. Tamas and their son,

Stephen, were also kind enough to stop by and show their love and support.

To my surprise, Mr. and Mrs. Swanson drove in as well, all the way from Carlton. Dad had gone into town in the morning and telephoned them about Mom's passing. They brought Jimmy, Jesse, Carrie, and Catherine as well. I'll never forget the impression Catherine made on me that day. I hadn't seen her in years; she had become quite the beautiful girl. Her hazel eyes were full of sunshine, a welcome contrast to the somber setting.

The next thing I knew, Daryl and his mom were part of the intermingling of the room. I had a pit in my stomach to cope with now, in addition to the hole in my heart. I had no desire to see Daryl and wanted nothing more than for him to go away. I was supposed to be the guardian of good news for Daryl, and all I had was bad news. Worse than that: a hollow faith. Not only did my mother not improve, she declined. She wasted away as I wasted my words in prayer because I was foolish enough to believe a fable.

I might as well've prayed to a rock! Like the one that killed that sparrow!

My thoughts were confused and digressive. I held on to the mantel of the fireplace for a second. I felt lightheaded. I stared down at the buckling of the wooden strip and the nail that threatened to snag someone's foot.

The bird was nothing but an omen for my mom! I should've known better!

I took a few deep breaths. I was angry as much as I was embarrassed, and I was embarrassed as much as I was angry. I kept to my part of the room—at the head of the casket.

A few minutes later, Daryl approached me on his own. He hugged me. "I don't know what to say, but I just want you to know I'm really sorry."

I wiped my eyes. "I know, Daryl. I know. Thanks. Thanks for coming by."

He put his hand on my shoulder. "Your Mom's not suffering anymore."

"That's right...she's not in pain...That's how I'm trying to look at it."

The time came for the graveside service. A handful of men carried the casket out through the front door and into the wagon. Andrew and I hitched up the horse, and we headed off for the little graveyard on Snake Hollow Road where both Mary and June were buried. Mary was the sister I had never met. Andrew was the only sibling old enough to remember her. She had died at two months old.

We arrived.

The men unloaded the casket from the wagon and conveyed it to the hole that had been dug.

Pastor Richardson commenced the committal service by thanking all who could attend—"on behalf of the family," he said.

What's left of us!

Pastor prayed. Then he delivered a brief message about hope, salvation, and the resurrection of Jesus Christ. "Just as sure as God gave Doris this body the first time," he said, "God is going to raise her up and give her another body." He closed in prayer, asking God to be with our family.

Who you gonna take next?

"Amen."

The casket was let down into the ground, the dirt was shoveled in, and that chapter of my life was as sealed as my mother's grave.

It was an ebb and flow of emotion the following weeks. As angry as I was with God, I realized it only confirmed my belief in him. As devastated as I was, a part of me still believed deep down that Mom was in a better place—in heaven. With God. But then the thought of God would generate a swarm of anger, and the anger would well up inside until it erupted at last.

If there's a God, then God is cruel!

Yet with another passing hour, the eruption would peter out, and the molten rock of my anger would start to cool off, bringing about milder meditations.

What if he really makes it up to us?

Then the sequence of emotions and musings would start all over again.

Forget rewards and returns! Where's—God—right—now?

The weeks dragged on this way. Time eventually turned our attention to Christmas. The holiday season was a hollow season. It lacked the joy and charm that usually permeated our home, which was a credit to Mom's influence. Andrew and I didn't even want to cut down a tree. It was Evelyn who talked us into it. We obliged her by putting one up, while Evelyn went ahead and decorated it with all the various ornaments and bows and candles. She put out our favorite knickknacks and strung garland throughout the living room, and even went so far as to bake some of Mom's cookies.

Sad to say, I did not fully appreciate my sister's incredible effort to make Christmas special that year. I was too cynical and exasperated. Now it never ceases to bring a tear to my eye!

Dad was just as determined to celebrate Christmas in honor of Mom's memory. He reminded us that, as hard as it was for us, Mom was in "perfect peace." "She is awaiting our reunion in heaven," he said, "where we will be celebrating Christmas together forever."

Dad called us into the living room on Christmas morning. He opened his Bible and read to us from the second chapter of the Gospel of Luke. He reminded us of what Christmas is truly about: "Jesus left the riches of heaven to come to this world and be born in a mangy feeding-trough. For one purpose," he said. "To ultimately die on a Roman cross so that our sins could be atoned for. So that we could have a relationship with God and a home in heaven."

As angry as I was with God, I had faith in the story of Christ. As contradictory as it seems, a part of me still believed that "God so loved the world that he gave his only begotten Son." And it frustrated me to no end. I could hear the words of Pastor Richardson echoing in my head: "If God loved you enough to send his Son to die for you—which is the most he could've done for you—then why wouldn't he do the least? If God gave you his only Son, then why wouldn't he give you the ring on his finger? If God gave you his finest gold, then why wouldn't he give you his silver? God still cares about you and has a plan for your life."

But how could you say you love me when you lied to me!

I trudged my way through those bitter months. Like shoveling a walkway through deep snowdrifts.

One dark day at a time.

Chapter 20

The bleakness of winter gave way to the bloom of Spring. I finally warmed up to the idea of breaking out of my isolation and being more outgoing again. I had been thinking about Silas lately and had been meaning to ask him what he thought about going fishing together sometime. He had stopped by the house a few times over the course of the winter, and I could tell he wanted to be friends. Sorry to say, I was not only burned-out over my friendship with Daryl, I was too absorbed by my own pain and pessimism to want to pursue another friendship. Yet I think the sense of a new beginning that can come with the scent of fresh air, the blossoming of trees, and the rustling of green leaves, inspired me to reach out now. That said, my thoughts never materialized. I made little effort to actually walk over to the Sawyers and ask him. I kept putting it off and putting it off.

I went fishing down at Heron Lake by myself one day. It so happened, as I was hiking back from the hollow, that I spotted Silas up on the crag, right around the parking area. He, too, was carrying a fishing pole and a bucket, and he was returning home. I called out to him and waved my hand. He paused for a moment and seemed to look right at me. But either he didn't see me at all, or he didn't recognize me from that distance, because he proceeded to hike the hillside back to the main road.

I took the shortcut through the woods and scrambled along the footpath, trying to catch up to him. At last, I came out on the lake road, completely out of breath. I lumbered around the bend, just before the straight shot to the top of the hill. That's when I spotted Silas in the near distance. I paused to catch my breath. Then I cupped my hands around my mouth. I was just about to call his name when a horse and carriage came to an abrupt stop.

It was Sheriff Lockhart. He pointed his finger at Silas and hollered at him.

I stepped to the side and found cover in the branches. Then I hustled up the hill so as not to be seen.

"…I wasn't up to no good, sir. I promise."

Sheriff Lockhart stepped down from his carriage and swaggered up to Silas. "It's been a while since I last seen a black scoundrel in these parts. What do ya think you're doing?'

"Like I said, sir, I was just doing some fishing down at the lake." Silas showed him the bucket. "I caught these fishes here, and I—"

"I didn't ask you where you were coming from. I gather you were down at the lake. What I wanna know is where—look me in the eyes when I'm talking to you, boy! Right here! Now I want to know where you think you're going?"

"I was about to tell you, sir—I'm on my way home."

"Home, huh?" The sheriff pulled his knife. "You've got no idea how close to home you are."

"It's a half mile up the road. I'm telling you the truth."

The sheriff snickered. "Home's a whole lot closer than that, boy. Trust me."

"I live right up the road with the Sawyers. You could take me there yourself. I promise the Sawyers would vouch for me."

"You're nothing but a colored conman—I can vouch for that!" He spit on the ground. "Now what if I told you I thought you was a rat wandering through my county looking to spread your disease?"

He brandished his knife. "Now I can't let that happen, can I? And ya know, it's always in my mind to thwart an infestation in these parts—I've done so for years."

I was prepared to jump out if I needed to, but I didn't want Augie to know how much I overheard. The only thing I knew to do in the moment was withdraw down the hill as quickly and as quietly as I could and then make as if I had now arrived.

I did just that. As soon as I reached the bend, I spun around and darted up the hill, shouting and waving my hands. "Silas!" The two of them turned their heads. "Wait for me!"

Sheriff Lockhart put his knife away and took a step back.

"I've been looking for you!" I said, reaching the roadside. "Good afternoon, Sheriff."

"Good afternoon, David. You know this young man?"

"Yes, sir. This is Silas—Whew! I gotta catch my breath—He works for the Sawyer family, sir—I spotted you down at the lake, just as you were heading back. I yelled for you, but man alive, you must be hard of hearing!"

"Oh, that was you?"

"Yeppers. Man, you're fast!"

Sheriff Lockhart folded his arms. "So he lives with the Sawyers, does he?"

"Yes, sir. He works for them."

"Well, I'm glad to hear that. Puts my mind at ease. I never seen him before and didn't know what he was up to. I just needed to make sure he wasn't some lying and cheating vagrant. We've had those, you know. I'm sure you've read about them before in the paper. And around here, we, um, shall I say, *encourage* 'em to pull up their stakes and move on. But I'm glad you showed up, and I appreciate the clarification—So you're a working boy, huh?"

"Yes, sir," Silas said.

"You give that family an honest day's labor?"

"I do. They're good to me, and I try to repay them as best I can. I owe it to them."

"Alright then. I'm much delighted to hear this. No problem at all here. No problem at all." He started back to his carriage. "You just tell Pete and Erma the sheriff says hello."

"I'll do that, sir," Silas said.

Sheriff Lockhart was about to step up into the carriage when he paused. He turned about and pointed his finger at Silas. "Now mind your business!" He held his gaze for a second and then gave me a nod. "David, tell your father I said hello and that I hope the family's doing well."

"I'll be sure to tell him."

"Alright then. Good day, gentlemen."

The sheriff got in and took up the reins. "Yah!"

As soon as the horse trotted a good distance away, I turned to Silas. "I know what happened. I know exactly what happened. I heard enough." Silas looked at me with the most forlorn look in his eyes. "I'm gonna tell you right now, you can never roam this road alone. Never ever again. Promise me, Silas. Promise me you'll never go anywhere alone again."

"I promise I won't. I promise. I didn't know there was anything dangerous about heading down to the lake. Neither did Pete and Erma. I've been down here before, and I told them where I was going, but I didn't know. And I don't think the Sawyers know either."

"I understand. But now we know there's something terrible about that man. Something awfully terrible. I've heard stories before, but I've never actually seen that side of Augie."

I wasn't about to let Silas walk home by himself. We headed back to the farm together. Silas did most of the talking along the way; I just listened. "You remind me of a fella I used to know at the orphanage," he said. "He used to drop off the cabbages and potatoes. You look so much alike. Except your ears are bigger." I just laughed. "And you both say 'Yeppers.'"

He proceeded to tell me about his caretakers and wardens over the years and how the Sawyer home was by far the best home he'd ever had. It occurred to me he never mentioned his mom or his dad one time. He had no remembrance of them. None whatsoever. A fact I had known sure enough, but the extent of which I never fully grasped until now. Here I had been mourning the loss of my mom, yet at least I had the memory of my mom. And I had a dad who loved me very much. Silas had spent his childhood in poorhouses and foster homes. At least I had my family.

We arrived at the end of the driveway. I said my goodbye. It felt our hearts had been knit together. I was burdened now for a young man I knew was assailed because of the color of his skin.

I went home and told my dad about the confrontation I had witnessed.

"I'm afraid there's not much we can do about it," Dad said mournfully. "I reckon there are enough officials and men of stature in this county that are in the Klan, and they'd protect him at all cost. Augie's held in such high esteem that any such accusation brought against him would never be taken seriously. It'd be thrown out. In a heartbeat. I'm afraid Silas is gonna have to keep to the farm and not venture out on his own again. I don't know what else to say, David. All we can do is bring it before the Lord."

Chapter 21

Andrew's progress had been frittering away ever since Mom's passing. The times he'd sit with us in the living room tailed off, whereas he kept mostly to the bedroom. He had a tough time falling asleep at night and would lie there for hours. I recall waking up on a few occasions and finding my brother pacing the floor, or on the side of the bed with his head in his hands. He didn't take part much in the discussions at the dinner table and more or less stared down at his plate. So you can imagine how surprised we were when Andrew joined us on the porch after dinner one evening.

"Yay!" Evelyn cried. "Andy's here!"

"What a pleasant surprise!" Dad said. "Have a seat, Son. We were just talking about ole Halsted."

Andrew sat upon the railing and leaned against the post, with a drink in his hand. "It's funny, his reaper's been just sitting there and sitting there…."

"Gee, it's gotta been what, four years now?" Dad said.

My brother took a sip of his drink. "Yep. That was the last year the Halsteds planted anything in that field."

"I reckon it'll be there till the Lord returns."

"It's a monument for the ages," Evelyn said. She motioned with her hands, as if it were a grand introduction.

Andrew chuckled. "It's a monument alright. I'll never forget it: Mr. Halsted was out harvesting corn and had gotten to about where that elm is there. I'm on my way back in the saddle when, all of a sudden, I hear him yell, 'What the cuss?' I tried not to laugh 'cause I figured it must've been serious. He gets down to have a look around and then he yells, 'Mother of pearl!' Which I had never even heard anyone say before. Well, he looks up and sees me and says, 'The knife holder broke off...again!' Then he kicks the thing and says, 'I'm done!' I didn't know what to say, so I said, 'Sorry to hear that, Mr. Halsted.' He gives it one more kick and says, 'I'm not sorry—I'm done!' I figured he was done for the evening when he walked away, but that reaper sat there for days. And then I find out Mr. Halsted's got a job working at Grisham. Ha! When he said he was done, he meant he was done for good! Ha ha!"

"I guess that reaper gave up the ghost," Dad said.

"I guess Halsted's reaper met the Grim Reaper, huh Andy?"

"It sure did." He took another sip of his drink. "I'll never forget the time June and I were playing hide-and-go-seek around the house. I went around and hid by the steps. Well, the porch was home base, so she made a run for it but stayed far enough away in case I was stonewalling. I forced her to the front of the house, but then she takes off into the cornfield faster than Rouge can lick her dish. We were just youngsters, and that corn was about yea high over our heads—Ha! Mom would've killed us if she knew we were playing in Halsted's field—But anyways, June made me chase her all the way to that little orchard, where the runoff cuts through during the heavy rains. Then she stops in her tracks and shushes me with her hand, snickering. I can hear the Halsted boys playing nearby, and when I finally catch up, lo and behold, Lonnie's off by himself. Ha! And let's just say his feet were covered—but that's about all that was covered! Ha ha!"

Andrew laughed so hard he started to choke.

"Easy there, Son," Dad said. "We wanna hear the rest of the story!"

My brother was hunched over, trying to catch his breath. "So now June and I are both in tears, trying to keep quiet while Lonnie's making mulch, and you wanna know what she does? She picks up a walnut and chucks it at him and pegs him in the back! Ha ha! The funniest part is that he sees this walnut go bouncing by and retrieves it and is looking up at the apple trees, wondering where in the world it came from!"

"That's pretty comical," Evelyn cried. "I'll give you that. But you shouldn't have been such a bad example to your little sister."

My brother took another sip. "Pshh! You kidding me? It was June's idea in the first place. You all think I was the mischievous one? Uh uh. June was the mischief-maker and the daredevil. Like the time we came across a rattler, coming down the pike at Bear Lake. It was just minding its own manners, as mellow as can be, slithering its way across the path. But no, June goes and grabs a stick and says, 'We gotta wake this serpent up.' And sure enough, about a minute later she's got that thing rattling away. And then she says to me, 'Don't you just love that sound? It's so expressive!' That's what that girl said to me!"

"Ha! June sure was a feisty little thing," Evelyn said. "'So expressive,' she says. My goodness!—Though I'd have to say you're a little expressive yourself. What you been drinking?"

"Oh, this?" Andrew raised his glass. "Just some clove tea. Helps with my headaches."

"Well, that's good to hear. I know it helps me when I have a sore throat."

"That, too."

A couple weeks later, I was woken up in the dead of night by the chime of clanging glass. I didn't stir. I opened my eyes. Not that I needed to. I could smell it.

172

He poured himself a drink. Downed it. Then went back to bed.

Dad took Evelyn and me aside one evening and informed us that Mr. Bradford was worried about Andrew. Andrew had gone into work that day more jittery and muddled than usual. He kept forgetting where he had placed his tools and was dripping sweat. He said Andrew stepped out of the shop for a little while. When he came back, he had it more together; however, Mr. Bradford smelled liquor and feared my brother was dependent on drinking.

I came home early from the lumber yard the one day and met him on the stairs.

"You didn't go into work today, Andrew?" I said.

He held his hand to his head. "Um, no. My headache's pretty bad today. I'm just not feeling well."

"I'm sorry to hear that."

"I'll be alright. Thanks, little brother."

He struggled down the steps, sort of lugging his feet.

About a minute later, I heard him leave the house. I returned downstairs and peeked out the back window. He lumbered through the yard and eventually disappeared into the woods.

I relayed the incident to my dad and my sister. Dad led us in a word of prayer, then he told us it was time to confront Andrew as a family.

The next morning, Dad, Evelyn, and I were sitting in the living room. We assumed Andrew had already gone into work that day, since he wasn't home. We were somewhat relieved.

Just then, a horse and buggy stopped in our yard. Then the sound of boots across the porch followed by a solid knock at the door.

"Good morning, Sheriff," Dad said. "What can I do for you?"

"Good morning, Mr. Hayes. I apologize in advance for infringing on your morning like this."

"Oh, you're not infringing at all. Would you like to come in?"

"No, that won't be necessary, Mr. Hayes. My schedule is busy today, so I need to get straight to the matter. I regret to inform you that Andrew's been arrested."

"Arrested?"

"Yes, sir. He's been booked and is currently in the cell."

"What for?"

"He was caught stealing a case of whiskey from the drug store."

"Andrew, stealing? Are you sure about that?"

"Mr. Hayes, I'm very sure about what I do. I wouldn't be here at your house this morning if it weren't the case. Now a man was spotted coming out the back of Edward's and slinking over the embankment down to the river. The witness notified my office, and Deputy Shane went out to have a look himself. Sure enough, he found the delinquent cozying beneath the willows."

"Now, now, Mr. Lockhart. I am well aware my son has his flaws, but he's had his share of struggles, too. Do not refer to my son as a delinquent."

"Or what, Mr. Hayes?"

Dad looked down and rubbed his forehead. "Are you sure it was Andrew?"

"Unless he's got a twin."

"Anyway, Andrew's not a delinquent."

"Now I'm sure there's a dictionary somewheres in this house, so you just go right ahead and look up the word at your own leisure and judge whether I've strayed from the English language. But I'm here to tell you my deputy found him there lounging around the riverbank with the case of whiskey by his side and one of the bottles in his hand. Drunk—as—a—fly!"

Dad lowered his head. "I'm just dumbfounded. Absolutely dumbfounded. We knew about his drinking, but to steal...."

"It's hard to accept these sorts of things, Mr. Hayes. It's like getting struck by a carriage coming around a blind corner—that's bad enough. But then to go through life with one's eyes closed—well, that only makes things worse. Clearly, Andrew's intemperate manner of living has been nurtured under your very roof."

"I'll concede Andrew's intemperance, Mr. Lockhart. But to suggest it's been *nurtured*, as you say, under my roof is simply—

"Well, it wasn't under my roof!"

"You know as well as I, Sheriff, that he came back from the War a different man. And since then, he's been—"

"You'd be wise not to excuse your son's vices! That, sir, will never help him. And the sooner we humble ourselves under the mighty hand of God and accept these things, the sooner he can exalt us in his good time."

"I'm not excusing anything here. What I mean is for you to understand that Andrew's a good man at heart and needs our help. In fact, he needs *your* help. This could be what he needed to help him turn things around, you see. But while he'll get what's coming to him—after all, he did break the law—"

"Yes, he did. That's why I'm here."

"—*perhaps* you could help our family out by extending a little mercy! Andrew's going to need Dr. Thompson's assistance drying out as well."

"And I will notify the doctor as soon as I get back into town. I'm also aware this is Andrew's first offense...that I know of anyhow. But I recommend you get your household in order, sir. Alright? I'll be in touch. Good day, Mr. Hayes."

"Bye."

Dad shut the door then plopped down in his chair, wringing his hands.

Chapter 22

My brother's name showed up in the *Avondale Times Herald* the next day. The newspaper reported the entire account: from the break-in to the arrest. He was released from jail and committed to the care of Dr. Thompson. The doctor had him stay at his home to be monitored. He implemented a plan of treatment that would reduce my brother's dependency over the next week or so.

"I would just drink a little to cope after Mom's death," Andrew cried. "I felt myself losing it again. I was going backwards. I couldn't unwind my stinkin' mind, and it was driving me crazy. It helped me go to sleep—I couldn't fall asleep. It helped me feel normal again—I just wanted to feel normal again! It was easy to be around people when I had a drink. I wanted to be around people. I wanted to talk to people. I felt like a normal person. I didn't wanna get drunk. I just wanted to be normal. Why can't I be normal? Why can't I be my old self again?"

The tears streamed down my brother's face.

"We understand," Evelyn said. "And now you're gonna get help. There are people in this town who care about you."

Andrew clenched his hair in his fists. "I wanna feel normal again! Is that too much to ask?"

"We understand," Dad said. "Don't get yourself all worked up now. The family knows you've been through an enormous fight.

You've been at war since you came back from the War. We know. You're a great warrior, Andrew, and you're gonna get through this."

"I had the shakes so bad," Andrew said. "They were so bad, and I was so nauseous. I couldn't take it. I didn't know what else to do. I had nothing left to drink. I ran out, and I was too embarrassed to tell anybody."

As you may recall, Prohibition didn't ban the drinking of alcohol, but it did forbid the sale and manufacturing of it. People had to get the "medicinal whiskey" prescribed to them by a doctor.

"And now Dr. Thompson's gonna help you," Evelyn said. "And Mr. Bradford cares about you, too. He says he's gonna take you back as soon as you clean up."

Mr. Bradford was very gracious and wouldn't dismiss my brother. He knew firsthand how hard of a worker he was, and he witnessed the improvement he had made.

Andrew wiped his eyes. "I can't take it anymore!"

It was strange not having my brother around the house, but he returned soon enough. He said Pastor visited with him and prayed with him each day. On one occasion, Pastor told him about a veterans home in Fairfax County managed by a man who had a heart for those who served in battle. He encouraged Andrew to consider the offer. That maybe a change of scenery would be of some help, even if it was only a temporary arrangement.

We greatly encouraged the idea.

Andrew just shrugged it off. "Rather than rot somewhere else," he said, "it would be better just to rot right here." My brother seemed downright morose now. A deadness permeated his eyes.

Not a week later, I was woken up out of a sound sleep. I lay there in a clouded state of consciousness, trying to process what had just happened.

I was nudged again. And this time I knew I was awake.

I looked over. Rouge was by the side of my bed staring at me.

"Rouge," I murmured, pushing her away. "Lay down, girl!"

She nudged my arm yet again.

I sat up and pointed my finger. "Lay—down—now!"

She refused. Then she whimpered like she needed to be let out.

I plopped my head back down on my pillow. "You've got to be kidding me! You stupid dog!"

Just then, I heard a dull thud from downstairs.

I sat up again, all ears.

It sounded like the closing of the back door.

I immediately got up and checked Andrew's bed.

It was empty.

What's he up to now?

I jumped out of bed and threw on some clothes then took Rouge with me downstairs to the kitchen. I looked out the backdoor window. A silhouette wandered toward the woods.

After all you went through, and you're out there making moonshine again!

I slipped on my shoes and hurried out the door. "C'mon, girl! Go get 'em!"

Rouge put her nose to the ground and took off through the yard. I trailed behind, doing my best to keep up. Then she hurried into the woods.

"Wait up, girl!"

I followed her as fast as I could manage in the dark, putting my hands out in front to protect my face from the lashing of branches.

He ain't getting away with this one!

Before long, Rouge began to bark. I knew she caught up to him.

"Andrew!" I hollered.

I paused to listen.

Nothing.

"Andrew! I know you're in here, and I know what you're up to! Now answer me!"

Still no reply.

I whistled for the dog.

She barked again.

I darted in that direction until I was no longer sure of myself. "Where are you, girl?"

I could hear her whimpering and shuffling around excitedly.

I was so angry with my brother, I thought invoking God would drive my point. "God woke me up, Andrew! God sent me after you! I know what you're up to, so knock it off!"

Just then, I spotted Rouge beside a tree, wagging her tail and looking up.

I rushed over. Sure enough, on the other side of the tree stood my brother.

"You need to hear me out," Andrew muttered. "And you have to promise me you won't say anything."

"I can't promise that."

"You must, David! You must!" He began to sob. "I can't do this anymore...I'm an embarrassment to the entire family...There's nothing left for me here!"

No sooner did those words come out of his mouth than I caught a glimpse of the shotgun in his hand. Dizziness struck my brain, like someone had just punched me in the face without any warning whatsoever. I held onto the tree beside me, trying to find my footing. Trying to find the words to say.

"You're not an embarrassment, Andrew."

"I know what I am! And there's nothing you can say to change my mind! You know I'm a mess. I'm nothing but a mess. There's nothing left for me here. Absolutely nothing!"

He slumped to the ground with his back against the tree. He covered his face and continued to weep.

I reached down and took the gun from his hand.

"Why did I have to be the one?" he kept muttering.

"What do you mean, Andrew?"

179

"Why did I have to be the one? Why didn't I break the law *before* the draft? Why did I wait until now? I should've robbed the whole darn drug store a long time ago!"

"I don't know what you mean, but I'm trying…."

"Why couldn't I be like Henry Campbell? Why did *he* get to get out of the War? Why was *he* rewarded for breaking the law and I get to be punished just because I didn't? It's not fair! Why did my mind have to be filched just because I wasn't a convict? How come Campbell got to move on with his life and get married and have a blessed life? There's no woman who'd want me, David!"

The tears flowed down my face. I struggled to smother my own sobbing as I watched my brother flop to the ground and curl up on his side.

"Why did Butler have to fall on it?" he bawled. "Why couldn't I been taken out of this hellhole? How come I couldn't come home with a flag draped over my casket like Turner? Oh, all of Avondale would love me then! Avondale would honor me now, wouldn't they? But no! I gotta be the filth and hogwash of this miserable town!"

I could say nothing. I stood over him, listening.

"We went days, David. Days. So many stinkin' days with no sleep and hardly anything to eat at all, dog-tired and wearied, scarfing up what hardtack we had with no hot water, no cup of George. Chewing coffee like it was tobacco, till brains cracked like porcelain. Like Miller when we watched him lose his flippen mind till he didn't even know who the heck we were! Like I was some stranger. A complete stranger to him!—That's right, Miller, you just stay right here and sing us that good ole tune—No, Miller, you can't go out there!—His shell was still there moving around in that hellhole, but he was gone. There was nothing left in his eyes, David. Miller was gone. Even before he climbed out and left us for good!"

As my brother lay there bawling on the ground, the realization overwhelmed me: God had truly sent me to my brother that night, but for a different reason than the one I had held.

As frustrated as I was with God, I knew in my heart to seek his forgiveness. Somehow, I thought him good enough to grant me that forgiveness, even though he apparently wasn't good enough to save my mother. Yet at least he saved my brother. For now, at least. And everything I had been upset about concerning Mom's death, Andrew had been enduring it all as well. Except more. My problems seemed small now in comparison to my brother's. The hardness of my heart melted away. A stillness rolled over me I hadn't felt in a long time. In fact, it was that very night I even forgave Dominic.

At last, Andrew struggled to his feet, wiping his eyes. "You gotta promise me, David. Promise me you'll take this to the grave."

"On one condition," I said. "Promise me you'll take Pastor's advice about that veterans home. It sounds like a good idea, Andrew. You've got a story to tell, and you'll get to help others."

"I can't do that."

"Why not?"

"I don't know. I just can't. I have no desire to go."

"Then promise me you'll at least pray about it."

"Fine. I'll pray about it."

"You promise?"

"I promise."

Chapter 23

As soon as my eyes adjusted to the light, I rolled over. My brother was still asleep. The ordinary feeling of reality now contradicted the glorious impression I had felt when I went to bed. I lay there thinking about what had transpired that night. It couldn't have been an accident. The joy and peace that swept over my heart, it must've come from above. Nothing on earth could've made me feel that way. Most of all, the riddle of life had been solved with ease: There's a God. He loves us. He's in control. We need to trust him. Yet now it was all a strange dream. The riddle was problematic again. Not that I was bitter with God anymore—I was clear of that now—but I remained heartbroken and confused.

Why didn't you step in for my mom like you did for my brother? Why didn't you answer my prayer? Where've you been for Andrew all this time?

I marveled at how steady my father seemed through life. He always managed to keep his head above water while treading through life's trials and tribulations. He always made it back to shore with his faith still intact. Yet he had lost a daughter when she was but newly born. He had lost another daughter when she was nineteen years old. He had essentially lost his oldest when he went off to war and came back a different person. And now he had lost the wife of his youth.

Emboldened by the other occasions my father had helped me when I opened up to him, I resolved to visit the workshop that day.

I got straight to the point. "Dad, do you ever doubt God's existence?"

"Not really," Dad said, sanding the woodwork. "Not much anyhow. I mean the idea has fluttered around in my brain now and again, but it doesn't stay there long. Kinda flies away on its own."

"What do you mean?" I asked.

Dad pointed to the dresser he was working on. "What I mean is the world is too complex and elaborate for me to believe it just happened by chance."

"Well, Daryl admits it's not by chance, but he says it's because of Natural Selection."

Dad chuckled. "Yes, I've read about this selection business— like it's got a mind of its own or something. But what I'd like to know is where it came from? What started the process of tiny changes? Not to mention this so-called selection only deals with living things, so where did all the non-living things come from?"

"Hmm. I never thought of that."

"If it's not by chance, as Daryl admits, then what are the chances it's not by chance?" He paused for a moment. "I guess what I'm trying to say is, if there's no God, then this is all nothing but the byproduct of chance, no matter how you cut it, and I just can't bring myself to believe that sort of thing."

"No, I hear ya. But Daryl says if there's a God, then something must've created God?"

I'll never forget the puzzled look on Dad's face. "If something created God, then he was never God to begin with."

"I know, but Daryl says that's a lazy explanation."

"Well, I reckon I know what he's getting at. But Daryl can believe the universe always was, and I can believe God always was. From where I stand, he's got his faith as much as I got mine."

"He says science will probably discover the answers someday and that's why he'll never be religious like me."

"Well, he may not go to church anymore and pray or whatever, but Daryl's exercising his faith just a tad, don't ya think?"

"I guess you're right."

"And what's the basis of religion?"

"You mean faith?"

"Exactly." He placed his hand on my shoulder. "So, here's the dirty little secret: All of us are religious. Even those who say they ain't. 'Cause we all believe in something. We're all devoted to something—even if it's to ourselves."

"It's funny you say that," I said. "Whenever he talks about Natural Selection, it sounds like he's talking about God. He talks about 'the power of Natural Selection,' 'the majesty of Natural Selection.' Like it's a person."

"There you go. He's just glorifying the creation rather than the Creator, that's all. But you never know," Dad said, cackling, "Daryl might have a change of mind when he's married someday."

"Daryl says he's never getting married."

"Whatever then. That's between him and God."

"But what does marriage have to do with it?"

Dad stroked his face. "Well, take for instance the complexity of the human body and all the organs...and I mean all of them mind you." He cleared his throat. "Then there's the machine work of the brain, this piece of gray matter that somehow regulates a gazillion different things we don't even think about, right?...Then try to imagine the evolution of a man, this constant cycle of struggle and death—I mean what a pain *that* must've been, all those poor unfinished folks! And don't forget this had to happen twice to produce a man *and* a woman...."

"Alright...I think I'm following you...."

Dad squinted. "What I'm trying to say is—how do I say this without being out of the way?" He paused again. "Son, let me just say that what takes place between a man and a woman—ehem—I reckon that should be enough to convert the most hard-boiled atheist. That's all I'm saying."

I tried not to blush.

"I think you get the picture," Dad said, adjusting the sander.

"I hear ya," I said. "But I know Daryl. He'd still say it's because of Natural Selection."

"Well, the whole thing's horsefeathers, as your mom would say."

"But what about all the pain and death in this world?"

Dad pointed at me. "Now *that's* the atheist's toughest point. And I have to admit, it can be a mighty difficult puzzle to put together. But the truth is, pain and death weren't the result of evolution—pain and death were the result of sin. Sin is what messed this whole thing up."

"I know, but God's the one who's in control...."

"Yes, but he's got his own purpose and plan now in all this mess. He wants our faith—we may not like to hear it. We may not think it's fair, but he wants our faith. He wants to take the bad things and make something good out of it. So it all boils down to whether God can be trusted or not, and that's something you have to answer for yourself. No one can do it for you."

"Well, I just sometimes wonder where God was when Andrew had to leave home and go off to war?"

"Well, let me ask you, David. Where was God when Jesus left his home in heaven to come to this sin-sick world? Where was God when Jesus suffered? You wanna know where God was? Right there on the throne."

"But how can God just sit there and not do anything about it? That's the part that gets me!"

"Well, how could God just sit there while his own Son was being nailed to a piece of timber? The truth is, he wasn't just *sitting there*— He was working out his plan for our salvation."

I stood there with my arms crossed and gave it some thought.

185

My father sat down on the unfinished dresser and looked at me with tears in his eyes. "Despite all the pain and death, I have hope that God's gonna restore things someday. As difficult as it is to lose a loved one or know that someone has literally got away with murder, imagine if there was no God. No chance of ever seeing Mom again—no chance of ever seeing June or Mary again—no final justice—no paybacks for all our losses down here. Now what I wanna know is, how does someone like Daryl cope with that? And does he ever hope he's wrong?"

"I don't know," I said.

"Well, ask him," Dad said.

I pondered these things in my heart as my father resumed his work.

After a few minutes or so, he sprang up and slapped the sander down on the dresser top. "Here's what I do know: I need a haircut, and it looks like you could use one to. Whatta ya say we drive down to Foster's to get our ears lowered and then grab something from Cooper's?"

I licked my lips. "Sounds good to me."

"Then let's do it!"

I'll never forget that drive for as long as I live. There was such a bright blue sky, and the sun smiled on our recent discussion. That old workshop proved to be the best classroom I had ever attended. No, it didn't solve all my problems, but it certainly gave me hope. As we arrived into town, we talked a little bit about Mom and how hard it was to believe half a year had already gone by since her passing. I looked over while Dad remained focused on the road. The tears welled up in his eyes.

We pulled up to Foster's and headed in.

"Good morning, Mr. Foster," Dad said. "Good morning, Mr. Evans."

Mr. Evans waved to us from the barber chair. "Hey there, gentlemen."

"I do believe it is post meridian," Mr. Foster said, pointing to the clock.

"Er good afternoon I should say," Dad said, shaking his head. "How the morning has flown!"

"You two grab a seat," Mr. Foster said. "I'm just finishing up on Tim and will be with you momentarily."

"Sounds good," Dad said. "So whatcha been up to these days, Tim?"

"Oh, you know, working the ole farm," Mr. Evans said. "It never ends."

"I'm sure," Dad said. "Probably all you can do just to break away and get a haircut."

"Let alone get *all* of them cut."

Dad chuckled. "I bet."

"The Lord did say that we must work while it is day," Mr. Foster said. "For the night cometh when no man can work."

Mr. Evans closed his eyes. "Yep. We're mighty busy these days. Trying to get the new barn up. The old one done us good, but it can't handle the load no more."

"Sounds like a good problem to have," Dad said.

"Praise the Lord," Mr. Evans said. "Looks like it's gonna be a fabulous season."

Mr. Foster touched up Mr. Evan's sides. "If you ask me, it would behoove us to recall the rich man whose farm brought forth plenty. What did the farmer do? Well, he decided he would pull down his barns and build greater."

Dad and Mr. Evans looked at each other and smirked.

"I reckon Tim's doing more than just tearing barns down and building bigger ones," Dad said. "He lives the life pretty good if you ask me."

187

"Well, thank you, Millard," Mr. Evans said. "I hope so, but I like what Paul said: 'To judge nothing before the time until the Lord come.' And then I reckon we'll all hope we had done more."

"Amen to that," Dad said.

"Anyways," Mr. Foster said, "you brought up the farm, and one can't help but think of wood, hay, and stubble when thinking about the farm. The apostle instructed us not to build our lives with such burnable material, you know. We should build on the foundation of Christ with things such as gold, silver, and precious stones, forasmuch as these would survive the fire. All the other would be burned up at the judgment." He snapped his fingers. "Just like that!—What do you think, Mr. Evans? You want a little more off the side here?"

"No, sir. I reckon it looks good."

"To be sure," Mr. Foster said. He removed the chair cloth and wiped off Mr. Evans neck. "A little powder and that about wraps it up."

"Looks good, Mr. Foster. Here's your quarter, sir."

"Thank you, Tim. God bless you."

"Lawrence, Millard, take care now. You too, David."

"Have a good day, Mr. Evans."

Mr. Foster tossed the coin in his register drawer. "Alright, who's up next?"

"David can go ahead," Dad said.

I hopped into the barber chair, and Mr. Foster put the chair cloth around my neck.

"The usual, David?"

"Yes, sir."

"That's good. Because that's about all I can manage."

The room became quiet, only the sound of scissors cutting through hair.

188

Mr. Foster revived the conversation: "How are you gentlemen holding up these days?"

"We're doing well," Dad said. "Thank you."

"Sorry to see your son in the paper like that," Mr. Foster said. "What a shame. But if you ask me, it's not always a reflection on the parents."

Dad crossed his legs and picked up another magazine. "Well, it's certainly not a reflection on Doris, that much I can tell you. But Andrew has made things right. He's back to work and doing better."

"Well, I'm glad to hear that. What a shame though. What a shame."

Dad thumbed through a couple pages. "When you've walked in another man's shoes, then I think one is better suited to pass judgment."

Mr. Foster snuffled. "In my humble opinion, one doesn't have to go around breaking into drug stores to be *better suited* to pass judgment."

"Not what I said, Lawrence. What I meant was that Andrew has had his share of battles. Some he's won. Some he's lost. But perhaps a little mercy and consideration—and a little prayer—would be in order. That's all."

"And a little faith, Millard. Let's not forget that. What was it the Lord said?" Mr. Foster looked up at the ceiling as if the answer were there. "That's right, faith the size of a tiny mustard seed. It could move the mountain in his life. I mean removed." He snapped his fingers. "Just like that!"

"Well, we know the Lord can certainly move mountains. That's what we're praying for."

"Ehem. Knowing the Lord can move a mountain and believing he *will* are two different matters now. Right, David?"

I didn't respond, but my heart was beating faster.

Dad rolled his eyes. "That doesn't mean every mountain is meant to be moved, Lawrence. You can't just go ordering God around. Some mountains are part of his plan. Some mountains are meant to be climbed—"

"Well, you're entitled to your opinion. I'll have to side with Christ on this one."

Dad shut the magazine. "Excuse me, but I'm not siding *against* Christ. The main lesson of the scripture is *not* that we go about moving every mountain that stands in our way. The most important thing is to become more like Christ. Did God move Calvary out of the way?"

"A clever evasion, Millard."

"I'm not evading anything. If a mountain stands directly in the way of God's divine plan for our lives, then yes, God is obligated to move it and *will* move it."

Mr. Foster's mustache twitched. "Methinks you have need that one teach you again, Mr. Hayes. It's easy to excuse one's lack of faith."

Dad glared. "Are you suggesting that Doris died as the result of my lack of faith? Is that why God didn't *move* the mountain?"

"You brought it up. Not me—Is that enough off the top, David?"

Dad rose to his feet before I could answer. "Is that what you're saying then? Because that would be a pretty bold insinuation, Lawrence."

"I'm not insinuating anything, Mr. Hayes. I'm merely relaying what the Bible says. If you have a problem with anything that was said, then your problem's with God. Not me."

My dad drew closer. "So God took my wife because I—or my own godly wife for that matter!—because *we* didn't have enough faith between the two of us to make up one little mustard seed?"

"If you ask me, Mr. Hayes, your attitude and tone is quite telling. You just said so yourself that the main thing is to become like Christ. In my humble opinion, your manner is far from it."

"Deny it, then. Tell me right now I've misunderstood you. Tell me!"

"I refer you to the old black book. That is all—David, you are all done, young man. Perhaps you could have a talk with your father."

That was it. Dad grabbed the barber chair and whirled it around as hard as he could. "Let's go, Son!" he hollered. "Let's get out of here before I—" My father couldn't even finish his sentence before brushing all the bottles off the counter with one swipe of his hand. "Before I lose it!" He picked up the container of scissors and brushes and hurled it across the room then got right in Mr. Foster's face.

Mr. Foster stood there rigidly throughout the entire clash, only his mustache twitching. "I believe you've said enough, Mr. Hayes. I'll be sure to notify the sheriff. Now if you'll be so kind as to leave."

Dad inhaled and exhaled heavily.

He surveyed the mess all around him.

Then he turned to me. "Sorry you had to see that, Son...I'm really sorry...I shouldn't have lost my temper like that...I, uh...I'll be reimbursing you for all of this Lawrence...I'll be by tomorrow...Now if you'll excuse me, I should be going."

"I'll be right out, Dad," I said.

I rushed around the room and picked up as many items off the floor as I could and put them back into the container. Mr. Foster was already hunched over, salvaging some of the products by the counter. I didn't know what to do with all the shards of glass and the busted creams and lotions that were smeared across the floor.

"Do you have a broom and a dustpan, Mr. Foster? I'll sweep this all up and then I'll mop it for you."

"Never mind, David. I've got this. Your father's waiting for you."

"Yes, Mr. Foster." I went to the door and hesitated. "Please forgive Dad, Mr. Foster. I've never seen him get like that before…He just really misses Mom…I think it's really getting to him."

Mr. Foster looked up and gave me a nod.

I returned to the car.

Dad sat behind the wheel, staring straight ahead. "I should've just dropped the subject a lot sooner…Lawrence has his way, and he's got his views, but I shouldn't have done that…It's just the way Mom got pulled into the conversation. I couldn't bear to hear such drivel—I mean the very suggestion!"

"I know, Dad…Honestly, I wanted to tell him to put a sock in it!"

Dad turned to me and smiled. "Well, I'm glad no one else had to see that…I reckon I won't be getting a haircut today. Probably best we head back home now."

Chapter 24

My friendship with Silas improved through the summer. We worked on the farm together, and we fished at the lake together. It was the sort of friendship Daryl and I once had. Except Silas was more outgoing, more uplifting, and he involved himself more in the exchange of ideas. This is not a harsh criticism of Daryl. Everybody possesses a unique nature, and I know Daryl would've given me all twenty-nine volumes of his beloved Encyclopedia Britannica had I needed it. Yet try as I might—and I believe he tried as much—things just weren't the same anymore.

It was on the weekends that I offered a hand at the farm and got to work alongside Silas. I could hardly keep up with the fella. Thankfully, he had only an objective to accomplish and nothing to prove. He was not a hefty man to say the least, but he was "as sturdy as Bunyan and as strong as Hercules," to borrow Nathan's bookish compliment.

Once our farm duties were finished, we'd go down to Heron Lake together. The Sawyer boys would accompany us as well from time to time. Irvin and Wayne usually did some fishing while Allen loomed over our shoulder, inserting a comment here and there. Nathan didn't fish at all. He'd prop himself up against a boulder and pull out *The Adventures of Tom Sawyer*, which he had read half a dozen times already. Without fail, he'd tell us Tom Sawyer was his distant relative and then he'd drift away to his storybook world.

The dreadful impression from the roadside incident with Sheriff Lockhart had dampened with time. Silas knew better than to walk the road alone, but the temptation into town was compelling. He wanted badly to break away from the short tether of his existence. He enjoyed the lake, but he wanted something more. Something different. Upon further consideration, we both agreed there wouldn't be any harm in venturing into town, so long as we stayed together.

As we approached the corner of Snake Hollow Road, I said to him, "We should go this way and have a look at the Slater house. It's the longer way around, but you'll be glad, I promise. You gotta see it, Silas."

He was clearly amused. "You're really captivated by that place. You've been talking about it all spring and summer long."

"Because it's creepy. There's something frightful about it. I mean what kinda house has bones coming up through the ground like they're rising from the dead?"

"Not the kind I feel like visiting," Silas said, chuckling.

"Oh, come on."

"You just said so yourself, that it's creepy and frightful."

"Well, it is. But it's fascinating. Tell me you wouldn't be fascinated with finding skeletons in a yard and blood in the house." I had confided in Silas about my little housebreaking undertaking.

"I never said it wasn't fascinating," Silas said. "It *is* fascinating."

"Well, you never act like it. You never seem to understand how big of a deal it is whenever I talk about it."

"I was just joshing you, that's all. I believe you, David. I just haven't seen it is all. And I'm sure I'd be just as excited about it if I did. But I haven't seen the town either, and it's killing me like you don't even know. And you said so yourself that it's the long way around. I'd rather stay the course. I promise I'll go with you sometime to see this haunted house. I promise. But for now, I'd really like to see where you go to school and whatnot."

"Fair enough." I shook his hand. "David Hayes, at your service."

He grinned, and with that, we continued down Healy Road together. I decided to save the main part of town for last and show him the schoolhouse first.

"This is it," I said. "This took the place of the one-room schoolhouse we all used to have to cram in. Class had grown since the War, and we were running out of room. Ahh, class is so much better now. It has grown even more since we moved in."

Silas seemed awestruck by the building. "It sure would be swell to be able to go here with you...though it would feel so odd at the same time. It's hard to imagine not working with the Sawyer boys. And I must say, I really like the farm."

"Nothing wrong with that. You and Irvin must get along fine." Further along the way and we arrived at the baseball field. "See that graveyard over there? You remember me telling you about Jack Kingsley? Well, he can crack the ball all the way over there and peg those tombstones. He's done it many times before."

Silas's eyes grew big with wonder. "Holy mackerel! That's what you were talking about. This Kingsley kid's gonna be the next Babe Ruth."

"You ain't kidding."

From there, we headed over to the old Mill Street Factory. "And this is where my life changed forever."

"Whatta ya mean?" Silas said.

"This is the abandoned building I told you about, where I struck that sparrow. See that ledge over there—about where those shrubs are growing, the ones with the berries? That's where the bird was. And I was standing right here when I threw that stone."

"That *is* mighty curious."

195

"To say the least! Have you ever known anybody that killed a sparrow with a rock? Or any bird for that matter, let alone a tiny one. I mean, come on. It's not like I struck a pheasant with a brick!"

Silas laughed. "You're still all hot and bothered about that, aren't you?"

"Well, now that I'm here again—in the very spot! I can't help but get worked up. I just wanted you to see it for yourself. Now can you blame me for thinking I'm cursed?"

"Pshh! You're not cursed. I mean don't get me wrong; what happened there is pretty unusual. I'll give you that. But to go saying you're cursed because of some happenstance, now that's a bit too far, don't ya think?"

"All I know is a lot of people think it's bad luck."

He turned around for a second, putting his hands to his head. "Seriously, David? It was an act of God. It was out of—"

"See? You just said so yourself! That's the point. It was an act of God. It was God telling me something. It was God doing something!"

"No! An act of God—you know, something that's out of our control—like getting struck by lightning. It's just an expression. For the love of heaven, you're really hot and bothered now! We need to get you out of here."

"Listen, you're right. I'm really sorry. I just wanted you to see what I've been talking about."

"And I see it. I just don't see how it makes you cursed, that's all."

"Fair enough. I'll show you around town and then we'll grab some grub. Sound good?"

He grinned. "Now we're talking!"

We made our way back to the main part of town and strolled by the storefronts and workshops along Main Street and Center Street. We looped around the Broad Street Lumber Co. where Dad worked and passed by the Grisham Textile Factory where Stephen's parents worked. Then we circled back to Cooper's and went inside.

Mr. Cooper came out of the back room, tying his apron. "And how may I help you, gentlemen?"

I turned to Silas. "Now it's on me, so whatever you want. Personally, I'm getting a bowl of soup and then some fried pork rinds and a soda for after. But you get whatever you want."

"That sounds good to me," Silas said. "I'll just get the same."

"You sure?"

"Positively."

"Alright, Mr. Cooper. That'll be two bowls of the soup of the day, a couple scoops of pork rinds, and two regular cokes."

"Fantastic, gentlemen." He took the ladle and began filling the bowls. "So who's the young man here, David?"

"Oh, I'm so sorry, Mr. Cooper. How rude of me. This is Silas. He's a friend of mine. Works for the Sawyers."

"I see. Well, nice to meet you, Silas."

"Thank you, sir. That sure smells delicious."

Mr. Cooper set the bowls on the counter before us. "And it tastes even better!" He filled the bag with the rinds then retrieved the bottles out of the refrigerator. "There you go, gentlemen."

I handed Mr. Cooper the money. "Alright, we'll be sure to return the bowls. We're just gonna go outside and get some fresh air."

"Fantastic. You gentlemen have a good afternoon." He gave Silas a wink. "You'll do well. The Sawyers are real good people."

Silas nodded. "Thank you."

We sat down on the bench just outside the store.

"Mmm," Silas said. "This is some good stuff."

"Ain't it though?" I said. "It doesn't matter what the soup of the day is here. This place never lets you down. And I love how much meat and potatoes they add. The kind of soup that sticks to your ribs."

"It's a rip-roaring recipe, no doubt about it. And the onions, too."

"I know," I said, taking another spoonful. "Perfectly delicious. How can anybody not like onions?"

"They'd have to be jingle-brained. Especially in a soup like this."

"Well, then Evelyn's jingle-brained 'cause she won't have any of it."

"You're kidding."

"Nope. She don't like cooked onions. Won't eat 'em raw either. Says they make her breath stink."

Silas chuckled. "What's so bad about your breath smelling like onions?"

"Your guess is as good as mine. But she'll say, 'You never know who you might run into.' I said, 'Who cares?'"

"What she say to that?" Silas asked.

"'That's the point,' she'll say. 'You never know who might care.' Then she finally admitted to me she read it in a Listerine advertisement once, that no matter how pleasant and attractive you are, someone may not be willing to put up with your halitosis."

"What in the name of Sam Hill is hali-whatever-you-said?"

"Halitosis. It means bad breath."

"Then why not just say bad breath?"

"Sounds more serious. Like it's a disease or something."

"Well, isn't bad breath different than having onion breath?"

"You would think," I said. "But she insists onion breath *is* bad breath. So I told her, 'Then use some Listerine for heaven's sake!'"

Silas swigged the rest of his bowl. "What'd she say then?"

"She said, 'I did. But it only works for a minute. Then you can still taste 'em.'"

Silas shook his head. "Evelyn sure is funny."

"Well, wait till you hear this. So I asked her, 'Who you worried about running into anyway? And what business would he have being that close to your breath, huh?' She said, 'I can't tell you.' And I said, 'Oh! So there *is* someone!' She tried to play it off, but that's when I told her, 'Hey, you never know, Stephen Thomas may like your onion breath!' Ha ha!"

"Who's Stephen Thomas?"

"He's a friend of the family; works with my dad. My sister won't admit it, but she's got a crush on him. Has for years. I mean you should've seen the look on her face!"

"That's too funny."

At last, I finished my soup.

"Here," Silas said. "I'll take these in." Silas went inside to return the bowls. As soon as he came back out, he stretched his arms and breathed a sigh of relief. "It sure feels good to get away and see the sights. I feel like a free man again."

"I don't blame you. I'm really glad you could come along and that this all worked out. You wanna head down to the river now? I've got the perfect spot. Daryl and I used to go swimming there and jump off the stone wall by the watermill. Who knows? After we dig into these rinds and take our drinks, maybe we'll do a little swimming. Whatta ya say?"

Silas's face lit up. "That would be swell. Let's do it!"

We headed for the secluded scene along the Seymour River. We walked over the ridge and started down the bank. As soon as we came around the old Crawford building, my heart sank. I grabbed Silas by the arm. "Here, this way."

It was too late.

Sam Lockhart looked back and spotted us. "Whoa! What do we have here?"

"Now hold it there a minute, Hayes!" Dominic hollered, standing to his feet.

The Lockhart boys dropped their poles and hurried over.

"Well, I'll be!" Harvey said. "Looks like Hayes is hobnobbing with the devil."

"C'mon, Silas," I said. "Let's go."

Dominic grabbed Silas by the shoulder as he was turning around. "Why the hurry? You just showed up." He snatched the bag of rinds out of Silas's hand. "Hey, fellas! Looks like they brought us something to munch on. All we need now is little something to wash this down."

"Leave Silas alone," I said. "He hasn't done anything to you."

"Silas, huh?—Boys, this dingus has a name. Harvey, I'd like you to meet, Silas. Silas, meet Harvey." Harvey and Sam snickered. "Now the two of you shake hands."

Harvey spit on the ground. "He's a devil. And I ain't shaking hands with no devil."

"I'm sure Dad would take him for a ride though," Sam said, snickering.

"Your problem's with me," I said. "Not him."

"Whoa!" Dominic said. "Now hold your horses, Davey-Boy. You see, the problem's with you and ole Devil Boy here."

I grabbed Silas by the arm. "Let's go."

We scurried to the top of the ridge as quickly as possible.

Dominic followed on our heels and then got out in front of us. Fortunately, we were in the open again. I felt confident Dominic wasn't going to engage in an all-out fight there against the two of us.

"Before I bid you good day," Dominic said, "I wanna show you something." He reached into his pocket and pulled it out. "Guess what's in my hand."

"I don't care what's in your hand," I said.

Dominic got right in my face. "You better care what's in my hand, if you know what's good for you." He glanced over at Silas. "And if you know what's good for him!"

He held out his hand.

It was a shoelace. All bundled up nicely with a link around it.

"You remember ole Arthur Stockard?" Dominic said.

A chill ran through my body.

"And do you remember what happened to good ole Arthur Stockard?"

I was dumbfounded.

"Of course, you do. But the real question is whether Silas here knows who Arthur Stockard is."

I tried forcing my way past him, but he immediately repositioned himself.

"Move!" I said.

"Hold on, Davey-Boy. Silas here might wanna know where this shoelace came from."

"Get out of my way!"

Dominic turned his attention to Silas. "I guess you could say it's a little keepsake. Came from one of Stockard's shoes."

"What's he talking about, David?" Silas asked.

Dominic leaned in. "You see, Stockard was a black devil. Just—like—you!"

"Don't push him like that!" I took hold of Silas and pulled him away.

He let us go this time, but as we walked away, he said, "Tell him, David. Tell him what happened to Stockard."

I picked up the pace.

"Tell him, David."

We were almost at the corner of Dixon's Inn.

"C'mon, David. Don't make me tell him!"

We were turning the corner when Dominic yelled—

"He was lynched, Silas! He was lynched!"

*   *   *

It was nearly time to turn in. Andrew and I were in our bedroom going about our nightly diversions, trying to improve our thoughts. He sat on his stool in front of the easel, working on a painting. I sat on the bed with my legs crossed and my back against the wall, holding my Bible. It was opened to the section of crumpled pages. I had smoothed them out as best I could, but the tatters and creases were a permanent reminder of that dark day when I mistreated it. My eyes settled on a set of verses in Paul's epistle to the Philippians. I was fixed on the fact they were set aside within parentheses.

(For many walk, of whom I have told you often, and now tell you even weeping, that they are the enemies of the cross of Christ. Whose end is destruction, whose God is their belly, and whose glory is in their shame, who mind earthly things.)

I had no sooner read those words than a bright yellow light flashed through the window and flickered about the walls. I leaned over and looked out. A cross blazed in our yard by the road, and a dozen or so Klansmen stood by, glowing in their white garb, masks, and pointed hats.

"What's going on?" Andrew asked, rushing to the window.

"It's the Ku Klux Klan!" I said.

I hurried into the hallway. "Dad, we got Klansmen in our yard!" I pounded on my sister's door. "Evelyn, you gotta get up!"

I looked back in my room. Andrew was standing on my bed with his rifle in hand, peeking out the window.

Dad stepped out with his shotgun. "I heard ya."

Evelyn's door flung open. "What's all the ruckus for?" she cried, cinching her robe.

"The Kluxers are in our yard," I said.

"What for?"

"I have my guesses, but they're obviously trying to send a message."

"Fine with me," Andrew said. "I'll send a message of my own."

"Now don't go firing shots," Dad said, heading down the stairs. "I don't think much more's gonna happen, but I'll be posted in the living room."

"I don't understand," Evelyn said.

"It's not that muddled," Andrew said. "As far as they're concerned, I'm nothing but a sloshed jailbird. I'm a threat to their pious way of life, the whited sepulchers that they are!"

"I don't think it's just that," I said. "I've been keeping company with Silas, and I'm pretty sure word has gotten around about it. If you ask me, I think the sheriff's in on it, too. I've seen firsthand how much the Lockharts hate Silas, and I'm telling you right now, they don't want him around."

Andrew took another peek out the window. "Wouldn't surprise me. Word has gone around for as long as I can remember about Augie."

"They'll probably head over to the Sawyers, too," Evelyn said.

"Most likely," I said.

"Well, they better be careful then," Andrew said.

"Nah, I wouldn't worry about them," I said. "The Sawyers can fend for themselves."

"I wasn't talking about the Sawyers," Andrew countered.

"Ha! The boys won't take too kindly to them," Evelyn said. "Huh, Andy?"

Andrew snickered. "Never mind the boys. They better be worried about the missus. She'd give 'em a headshot they'd be sure to forget!"

Chapter 25

Thankfully, the remainder of the year proved to be uneventful for us. A welcome breather. Though there was plenty that took place around the country that created quite a stir. In September, the Great Miami Hurricane wreaked havoc in Florida. Less than a week later, Gene Tunney defeated Jack Dempsey to become the heavyweight boxing champion of the world. In October, the St. Louis Cardinals defeated the New York Yankees in game seven to win the championship series, thus breaking my heart. In November, the National Broadcasting Company radio network was introduced. And I would be remiss if I failed to mention the establishing of Route 66.

Yet as far as that which concerned our family, there were no more cross burnings, no more serious threats, no more furious altercations or lost tempers. And you'd be pleased to know Silas continued to flourish under the safekeeping of the Sawyer home.

Over a year had passed since Mom went home to be with the Lord. The holiday season rolled around again. This time, I was looking forward to Christmas. I had started a new part-time job at Simms where I serviced automobiles and worked the gas pumps after school let out. Mr. Henson also made an opening for me at the lumber yard on the weekends. In those days, I was permitted to drive the big Ford flatbed for deliveries despite not having my license.

At any rate, I had saved up enough money to purchase some gifts for the family, and I was eager to spend it. I thumbed through the Sears and Roebuck catalogue in search of something special, but I determined a trip to McMurray's Department Store would be more meaningful. It was the most prominent store in the region, the closest thing to Macy's that we had. The only drawback was that it was all the way in Carlton, about fifteen miles away. Nonetheless, getting there was a minor setback since I had my own means of transport unbeknown to all. All except Daryl, that is. The train was our best kept secret!

Growing up, Daryl and I would cut through the Slater property and hop the train during the summer months. The tracks couldn't have been a couple hundred yards behind the house. It was the ideal arrangement. The trains heading northwest moved slow enough as they departed from Avondale, so one could climb aboard the cars with little difficulty. The location was out of the view of town, so we never got caught. The same was true in Carlton. A rye field lay just outside the open market, behind the Old Lantern, where we would jump off and then mosey into town.

The trip to McMurray's would accomplish two things at once: Not only was I guaranteed to find some first-rate gifts, but it would also provide Daryl and me a chance to repair our friendship. So with less than two weeks to go till Christmas, I visited Daryl one morning to share my proposal.

Daryl's mom answered the door and invited me in.

"Thanks, Mrs. Mitchell."

"You're welcome. How've you been doing, David?"

"Very well. Thank you."

"That's good to hear. How's the family?"

"Wonderful. Andrew's doing much better, too."

"I'm so glad to hear that. My heart really goes out to him. Good. And your Dad and sister?"

205

"Dad's just as busy as ever. You know Dad, he never stops. I think it helps distract him from Mom."

"Aw! Your poor dad."

"But Evelyn's doing great as well. She's got a job at the general store."

"Well, good for her. I'm glad to hear."

Lucy shuffled into the room. "Hello, David."

"Hey there, Lucy. Always good to see you."

"Same to you," Lucy said, smiling.

"Daryl's right upstairs," Mrs. Mitchell said. "Feel free to go up. He'll be glad to see you."

"Sounds good. I'll see what he's up to."

I went upstairs and gave a little knock at the door.

"Come in."

"Good afternoon, Daryl."

"Hey, what are you doing here? Have a seat."

"Listen," I said, closing the door behind me, "I've got a grand idea."

"What's that?"

"Whatta ya say we hop the train and do a little Christmas shopping in Carlton?"

He shrugged his shoulders. "I don't know."

"C'mon. It'll be fun. Like old times."

"I'm not really in the spirit."

"To hop the train, or to shop?"

He leaned back into his chair. "Probably both."

"Forget the shopping then. At least come along for the ride."

"I'm not sure I'm up to it."

"Please? It'll feel fun and festive. Christmas is practically a week away. Let's do something exciting while we're on break."

"I don't know, David. I'm not really into Christmas."

"You don't celebrate Christmas anymore?"

"Well, the Mitchell household celebrates it alright, but I just kinda go along with it. More for Lucy's sake."

"How can you not celebrate Christmas?"

"Don't get me wrong, I think there's a lot of good that comes about this time of year. It's just I don't buy into the—"

"I get it, all the fuss over money and presents," I said. "I understand, but you don't have to do any shopping. You could just come along. Then we could stop by Davenport's to grab something to eat. It'll be on me. Now how do you say 'no' to that?"

Daryl raised his one eyebrow. "The food does sound good."

"Then let's plan a trip to Carlton. Let's do it tomorrow. Times running out, and I really need to get to McMurray's."

Daryl leaned forward and gave a clap of his hands. "I'll tell you what; just go without me. We could visit Davenport's after the new year sometime."

"Why wait?"

"Listen, David. I don't want to get into it. I don't do well this time of year. I haven't for a couple years now."

"Why not?"

"I just told you I don't want to get into it. It stirs things up, alright?" He wadded up the piece of paper on his desk and pitched it at the wastebasket across the room. "I just don't buy into the whole Christmas story."

"What do you mean?"

"You know what I mean—the whole God thing. I haven't changed since the last time we talked."

"It never seemed to bother you before."

"Well, it did. I just didn't tell you."

"Fine. I just thought you'd wanna do something other than just pass each other in class. We hardly even talk anymore."

"And I do," Daryl said. "I just don't do well this time of year, that's all. I don't know what else to tell you. Like I said, the message about giving and being kind and all that, I think that's a good thing. This world could use a little more of that." He looked down and shook his head. "I just can't deal with the whole virgin birth thing. I can't deal with anymore fables."

I was caught off guard and felt defensive. "Well, I don't have any problem with the virgin birth. If Jesus was only a man, then the whole gospel message falls apart. And honestly, there's no point in even celebrating his birth, since the point of his birth was his sacrificial death. If he was just a man, then we're still in our sins and wasting our time."

"That's my point, David! How could Jesus be born of a virgin without a male chromosome? I mean, seriously! That's not even scientifically possible."

"If God could create the world out of nothing, then I don't think he'd have a problem supplying the smallest material."

"Oh, stop it!"

"No, I'm being serious, Daryl."

"I know you are—stop!"

"Well, science still hasn't shown us how this all came about, yet you still believe it all evolved somehow, don't you?"

"That's different."

"How is it different, Daryl? It's still faith."

"Pshh!"

"Fine then. Just don't make it like what you believe is all scientific."

"You're the one who believes in a resurrection! How's that scientific? Have they ever tested that hypothesis?"

"And you believe life rose out of the deadness of God-knows-what. Has that ever been tested?"

"You're not even being reasonable right now."

"Listen, I've said enough. I'm sorry. I just wanted to see if you wanted to hang out together. I guess it's not meant to be. I'll let you go." I was about to open the door when it dawned on me: "Let me just ask you one more question," I said, "and I'll leave you alone."

He looked up at me.

"Do you ever hope you're wrong?" I asked.

"About what?" Daryl said.

"About God not existing. Do you at least hope you're wrong?"

Daryl looked back down and said nothing.

"I don't know what happened to you, Daryl. But with all the hurt and unfairness in this world, do you ever hope there's a God who will at least make things right in the next life?"

He sat there with his face planted in his hands and his elbows on his knees. At length, he mumbled, "I don't know."

"Fair enough," I said. "I guess I'll see you in class when break is over."

Chapter 26

I went home saddened by what had transpired between me and Daryl, but I was still delighted about finding something pleasing for the family, so the next day I headed to Carlton by myself.

Whenever I went to Carlton—it's humorous looking back now—it was like going to the big city. Not that it was much bigger than Avondale, but it had some of the glitz and glamor that Avondale did not. For one, Avondale had a small theater and a run-down nickelodeon that was hardly frequented, yet Carlton boasted of a movie palace with an elegant marquee trimmed in lightbulbs, just off the side of the street. And the courthouse in Carlton, with its pillars and statues, was much more impressive than ours.

Then there was McMurray's Department Store with live models posing behind the storefront glass, flaunting their apparels and furs. As soon as you walked through the doors, you were greeted by a salesman stationed by the glass case filled with jewelry. The walls were thick with everything from trinkets and household appliances to suits and ties and hats. The lofty ceiling, along with the balcony that wrapped around the room, added to the splendor of the place. Garlands and wreaths and red bows bedecked the store, and it all felt so jolly. I couldn't wait to have a look around.

It was quite the task, but I settled on my purchases after all. I got a letter opener for my father, with a little magnifying glass on the end that charmed me. A pair of emerald earrings for my sister, emerald being her favorite color. A fountain pen for my brother, which came in a plush display case. And then something I couldn't help getting the moment I saw it: a pocket New Testament for Silas. I envisioned him pulling it out and reading it while we were down by the lake.

Having paid for the items, I took my bag and headed for the door. At that moment, the embodiment of beauty entered the store.

It was Catherine Swanson. It had been a year since I last saw her at my mother's wake. I thought she was a beautiful girl then, but she had blossomed into a lovely young lady. Waves of medium blond hair adorned a forehead that looked about as delicious as a honey-sweet apple. She wore a long wool overcoat of velvety blue that had a matching belt and a large collar that wrapped snugly around her neck. Her eyes were full of life, and she had a smile that could've melted a frost.

"Catherine!"

"David!"

"It's so good to see you!"

"Yes, so good to see you, too. I would've never expected in a million years to see David Hayes here. What a pleasant surprise!"

"I was just doing a little Christmas shopping for the family. There's no place better than McMurray's. Unfortunately, there's nothing like it back home."

"I love coming here. It's such a marvelous store. Ahh! Just look at all the ribbons and wreathes. Aren't they wonderful? I just love Christmas!"

"They sure are nice. Almost as nice as that ribbon in your hair."

She tilted her head and patted the bow gently. "Aw! Thank you."

"You're welcome."

I was surprised at how comfortable I felt with Catherine. To be honest, she was as natural and sincere as can be and had a way of making you feel at ease.

"So where's the family?" Catherine wondered. "Are they here?"

Now I was nervous, which was no fault of her own. "Um, no. No, they're not here. I wanted this to be a complete surprise."

"I bet Evelyn's having a marvelous time up and down this street, looking over the windows and the displays. Is she nearby? I'd love to see her."

"Um, Evelyn's not here. She's home."

"Oh! Then I guess I won't be saying hello. How about your father?"

"Well, he's home, too."

"Oh, my! You're here all by yourself you mean—*that* kind of a surprise!"

"Yeppers. Like I said, a complete surprise."

"How was the drive? That's a bit of a long way."

"Well...how do I put this? Um, I didn't actually drive."

"Don't tell me you walked?"

"Alright, I won't."

"So you walked to Carlton? You can't be serious."

"No, I didn't walk."

Catherine scowled, which made her look even more adorable. "Well, I know you didn't fly, so what am I missing here?"

I sighed. "It's sort of a long story."

"So then you *did* walk."

"No, no, no. Not *that* long of a story."

"Alright then...."

"I just can't really get into it."

"Top secret, huh?" She flashed her eyes. "Are you a detective or something?—not that you could tell me."

I scratched my head. "Life can be interesting to say the least. Hey, what about your family? Are they here?"

"My parents are outside, just a few shops down. They've been chitchatting with about everybody they bump into. Carrie's with them as well. Jimmie and Jesse are over at Snyder's. By the look of things, I wasn't gonna make it to McMurray's by Christmas, so I told my folks I'd just go ahead and meet them all here—Oh! Surprise, surprise, here they are now!"

Mr. and Mrs. Swanson walked in, along with Catherine's older sister, Carrie.

"Well, look who's here!" Mrs. Swanson said. "It's David!"

"Good afternoon, Mr. and Mrs. Swanson. Hi, Carrie."

"Hi, David," Carrie said. "What in the world are you doing all the way in Carlton?"

"Oh, just buying a few gifts for the family," I said.

"What a coincidence," Mr. Swanson said. "Your father here?"

"No sir," I said. "I wanted this to be a, a surprise."

"You mean you drove to Carlton by yourself?" Carrie said.

I hesitated then gave a slight nod. "I did come by myself."

"My goodness!" Mrs. Swanson said. " I can't believe you youngsters. You're all so grown up now. I can't even bring myself to drive one of those things, and you drove here all alone? What if you break down on the way home? Oh, I can't even think about it!"

Mr. Swanson gripped my shoulder. "Your father trusts you with the car, huh?"

"He usually does," I said. "I've driven it into town a few times."

Catherine didn't say a word. She just smiled as she watched the conversation close in on me.

"Listen," I said, wiping my forehead. "I have a confession to make."

Carrie clapped her hands. "I knew he looked guilty!"

Mr. Swanson smirked. "You didn't drive here, did ya?"

"Um, no, sir," I said. "And seeing I didn't walk here either, I guess you could say I took the train."

"What do you mean you *guess* you could say?" Mrs. Swanson asked.

I felt like I was on trial in front of the entire department store.

"Good heavens!" Carrie said. "He hopped the train."

I didn't disagree, and that immediately prevailed upon Mrs. Swanson to put her hands around her throat. "David! You did, didn't you? You hopped the train from Avondale!"

Mr. Swanson burst out laughing, which was a tremendous relief. For some reason, I had pictured him being severe with me. Catherine held her hands over her mouth and snickered.

"Dan!" Mrs. Swanson cried. "It's not a funny matter. The boy's gonna end up getting killed doing that, and you're encouraging him."

"Dear," Mr. Swanson said. "I'm not encouraging the boy to get killed...."

"But you're encouraging him to be dangerous, and that's close enough. Now tell him not to do it again."

"Ha! I can't tell him that."

"Why not?"

"How's he gonna get home?"

If you could've seen the look on Mrs. Swanson's face when it occurred to her. "David!" she cried. "You're gonna do it again!"

"I'm sorry, Mrs. Swanson, but I've got a two-way ticket back to Avondale."

Carrie and Catherine burst into laughter.

"Wait till I have a talk with your father," Mrs. Swanson said, shaking her finger at me.

"Now, please, Mrs. Swanson. Please don't do that. This was supposed to be a secret mission. You see, I was just trying to buy something special for the family for Christmas. You can't ruin the surprise. I promise I won't do it again."

Catherine spoke up for me. "Mother, you can't tell on David. It'll spoil Christmas for him."

"Then I'll wait till after Christmas to do it."

"Aw! You can't do that to him. He said this will be the last— Didn't you, David?"

I put my hand over my heart. "I promise I'll never do it again."

"See, Mother?"

Mr. Swanson chuckled and shook my hand. "We'll let you go then, David. Just be safe."

"Thank you, sir," I said. "Yes, I should be going if I'm to get back home today. Getting stuck in Carlton wouldn't be good. That'd be sure to ruin the surprise."

Carrie laughed. "I have a hunch your folks would still be surprised."

"True."

Mrs. Swanson buried her head in her hands. "Ah! The very thought of it! Now I wish you drove the car."

"You're a mischievous young man," Carrie said. "I better not hear about you in the rumble."

"I'll be fine," I said. "You all take care. It was so good to see you." I made sure to look at Catherine.

"Be safe, David," Catherine said.

"Don't worry. I will."

"And be sure to keep your word," Mr. Swanson chimed in. "No more train hopping now."

"No more, sir. This is the last—Tell Jimmie and Jesse I said hello—Merry Christmas!"

Chapter 27

The entire town was abuzz with the news. No, it didn't concern me and any train-hopping. It was about Sheriff Lockhart's "daring raid." The word around town was that "Augie came to know" of the Schnilbacker brothers' making "panther piss" down in Chicken Coop Hollow. It wasn't the mere fact that "Augie took an axe to every still on the land," but that he shot and killed Roy Schnilbacker "dead on the spot" when he came out firing at the sheriff and his deputy. Sheriff Lockhart was heralded as the hero of the county. The front page of the *Avondale Times Herald* attested to his "investigative prowess," his "steadfast fight against wickedness," and the fact that he entered "a veritable lion's den of iniquity."

Christmas Eve arrived a mere two days after the sensation swept the town. It was a yearly custom in our home to attend the Christmas Eve service with Aunt Mary at the Union Street Church. We tried persuading Andrew to come along, but he felt uneasy with having "the whole world crammed in one place." "There's no sense," he said, "in being packed in a pew with one's heart in one's mouth." Thus Dad, Evelyn, and I drove into town that evening, while Andrew remained at home.

It seemed everybody in town was attending the Christmas Eve service that year. We had to park down the street then walk from there. As we drew near, a round of applause broke out.

"I can't go anywhere these days without all this fuss," Dad said. "I'm just too famous."

Evelyn and I laughed. We always appreciated Dad's humor. We paused at the church steps and looked across the street where all the commotion was.

It was Sheriff Lockhart. He was dressed in his suit and tie, long overcoat, and top hat. He stood arm in arm with Mrs. Lockhart who was as stern and proud as ever in her fancy white dress and showy hat. A crowd of admirers flocked around them as they made their way across the street. Trailing behind was Dominic, Harvey, and Sam—each one in their Sunday best, basking in the fanfare of their father.

I had a pit in my stomach that threatened to spoil the entire evening, but I determined I was going to remain focused on the purpose of the service. The three of us scaled the steps and walked through the doors.

As soon as we stepped foot into the entrance hall, Aunt Mary rushed over and showered us with hugs and kisses. Beth ran up as well, eager to see Evelyn. Bill and Sarah Harrison stood by, along with Vivian, Ada, Lester, and Lewis. I marveled at how laidback Lester conducted himself around me, knowing he had growled at me and chased me off that porch a couple years ago. It was as though it never happened.

Lawrence and Emma Foster brushed shoulders with us. Dad turned aside and said hello. Mrs. Foster presented a genial smile, while Mr. Foster gave a twitch of his mustache that seemed to acknowledge our presence. Trailing behind were their older children, Wanda and Jacob, who were in town for the holidays.

I spotted Jack Kingsley in the swell of the crowd, on the other side of the room. Our eyes met, and we waved to each other. Mr. Wagner patted me on the back as he proceeded toward the sanctuary. Then Mr. and Mrs. Mitchell walked in. Daryl held the door and assisted Lucy into the hall. As soon as he noticed me, he came over. He had a little wrapped box in his hand.

"Here," Daryl said. "I got this for you."

"For me?" I said. "You didn't have to get me anything for Christmas."

"I know. It's not just for Christmas, but I wanted you to have it."

"I feel bad though. I didn't get you anything this year."

"Don't worry about it. It's just a little something."

"Well, thank you."

"Go ahead. Open it up."

"Right here?"

"Sure."

"Alright then." I tore the wrapping off and opened the box. A pair of cuff links nestled in the packaging. "Wow, Daryl. These are swanky."

"I'm glad you like them...And I'm really sorry about last week."

"About what?"

"You know...I was in somewhat of a foul mood."

"Oh, don't worry about that."

"No, I'm really sorry. I was unpleasant. I know we don't see eye to eye, but you've been a good friend over the years."

"Well, I'll never forget the friendship we had, Daryl. Never. It's time we can never take back, and I wouldn't ever wanna take it back. And I really appreciate this gift. I love these. I'll be sure to—"

"Davey!"

I turned.

It was Jewel Pearce. She was with Glen and Rosa.

I looked back at Daryl and groaned. "Here we go again."

He smirked. "I'll let you go."

"Listen, I'll be sure to wear these. Thanks a million, Daryl."

"You're welcome."

Jewel came up to me. "Hi, Davey."

"Hi, Jewel."

She leaned into her shoulder, batting her eyes. "Fancy meeting you here."

"Yes. It's a fabulous Christmas Eve, isn't it?"

"Of course. This time of year is oh, so magical!"

I nodded.

"Believe you me," she said, playing with her hair, "I can't wait till tomorrow morning. Daddy says he's got something special for the prettiest girl in the world."

"Well, I hope you have a good Christmas," I said. "If you'll please excuse me, we really need to find a seat."

I directed my attention back to my family.

"…and just as sure as it is the eve of Yuletide," Aunt Mary cried, "I am positively sure this year's quilt making contest was fiddled. I—mean—fiddled! And I'm telling you right now, Edith Parks should've taken the cake, and it's a crying shame what those judges did to her!"

"Sorry to hear that," Dad said, moving away. "Hopefully they'll get some better judges next time 'round. But in the meantime, we probably should get going, or we ain't gonna have a place to sit."

We followed Dad into the sanctuary.

I spotted an open section of the pew on the left, near the back. I promptly claimed it for fear it would soon be taken. The room was filling fast. We sat down and waited for the service to commence.

Soon, the clock struck seven, and Reverend Sutherland approached the pulpit.

Just then, Dr. Milton Thompson roamed the aisle looking for an open seat. Sheriff Lockhart had his family scoot down along the pew and then motioned for Dr. Thompson to sit down. The doctor seemed not to notice and turned around to survey the room again.

"Good evening, ladies and gentlemen," Reverend Sutherland began. "I want to thank you for attending our Christmas Eve service..."

Dr. Thompson quickly plopped down next to the sheriff, clearly flustered.

"...It is my prayer," Reverend Sutherland continued, "that your hearts will be touched by the sacred music and the time-honored hymns familiar to us this time of year. May God's hand be upon tonight's sermon, and may the Holy Spirit bless his people. Let us shake off all distractions and the multiplied cares of this world, as we set aside this time to ponder the significance of the birth of our Lord and Savior. May the Spirit of the Lord fill our hearts tonight with his joy and peace and truth.

"But before I open with prayer, I feel it is only appropriate that we first take a moment to honor a special individual in our midst. I had noticed him and his dear family as I took to the pulpit just now. According to the epistle of Paul to the Romans, this gentleman is not merely an officer of our county, but indeed a minister of God, if you will. Ladies and gentlemen, in light of the recent bust that took place just a few days ago, we are reminded of how this man of God is truly a revenger to execute wrath upon him that doeth evil, and it is only right and proper that we give honor to whom honor is due. So without further ado, I would like us to give a warm and hearty welcome to the man whom we owe a debt of gratitude; a man to whom we owe our safekeeping and protection; a man who has been a faithful steward all these many years—ladies and gentlemen, the one and only, Sheriff Augustus Lockhart!"

The entire room rose to their feet and applauded.

Evelyn and I sat there, looking over at Dad. Dad sighed then started slowly to his feet, signaling for us to oblige the minister. So we stood up as well.

Sheriff Lockhart remained seated in his pew, sitting up straight and tall, donning a proud look I suppose was designed to convey humility and his utmost gratitude.

Strangely enough, Dr. Thompson remained seated despite the standing ovation.

"Look, Evelyn," I said. "Dr. Thompson won't stand up."

"I know," Evelyn said. "He doesn't look very happy either—look! He just glanced at Augie and shook his head—Davey, he's mad! He's not even clapping!"

There was no doubt about it: Dr. Thompson was refusing to join in.

"Thank you for your service, Mr. Lockhart," Reverend Sutherland said. "Thank you very much. We are beholden to your years of service, sir."

With that, the applause regained strength and grew even louder than before. The sanctuary and high ceiling reverberated with all the handclapping and cheers. Sheriff Lockhart stood to his feet. He turned to each part of the room, nodding his head and mouthing his thanks.

That's when Dr. Thompson got up from the pew and walked out of the service.

Chapter 28

Andrew woke us up Christmas morning to announce that breakfast was ready. We didn't need much coaxing. The smell of coffee lured us out of bed. We made our way downstairs and took a seat at the table, whereupon Andrew served us pancakes, an omelet, and sausages—what Mom used to make each year. He poured us our coffee and sat down as well.

I stirred in the cream and sugar. "It smells so good."

Evelyn took a sip. "Mmm. And it tastes as good as it smells. This is delicious, Andy."

"Sorry I didn't get you all anything this year," Andrew said. "But I hope this makes up for it."

"It sure does," I said. "I'll take this Christmas present every year!"

"I'll take it every day!" Evelyn said, chuckling.

"You didn't need to get us anything anyway," Dad said. "But thank you, Son. This means a lot."

"You're welcome."

Dad looked us over with his warm and welcoming smile. "Shall we pray?" He bowed his head. "Lord, we are always mindful of your great love and sacrifice for us, no matter what time of the year it is, but this is the day that has been set aside to celebrate your birth. Thank you for loving us enough to leave the riches of heaven to come down to this earth. You are a wonderful Savior. We are grateful to be able to sit down as a family with this delicious meal Andrew made for us, and to be able to spend this Christmas together. Now thank you again for your many blessings and for our home in heaven that you've prepared for us. In Jesus's name, Amen."

"Amen."

I drizzled syrup over my pancakes. "I can't wait to give my Christmas gifts to you all."

"Ooh!" Evelyn said. "I can't wait either. I just love getting gifts."

"Well, you're gonna love getting this one. Wait till you see it." I took a bite. "Mmm. Your gift is almost as good as this breakfast."

"That good, huh? I'm so excited. You should just go and get it now."

"Nope," I said, taking another bite. "You gotta be patient. In fact, I'm thinking about waiting till midnight to give you your gift."

Evelyn scowled. "That would be mean, Davey. Now why would you wanna do a thing like that? And like you should talk. You're the one who would go sneaking into Mom and Dad's room to have a peek at the presents."

"Please! I did that one time. One—time!"

Andrew chuckled. "I remember that."

"Now what's this all about?" Dad said, brushing off his necktie.

"We never told you that story?" Evelyn said. "Well, Davey thought he was getting a hunting knife for Christmas one year—"

"Because Mom made me think I was," I said. "Mom asked me what I wanted for Christmas, so I showed her the knife out of the catalogue. She even looked it over and nodded her head and said, 'I'll have to think about it, but I'll keep it in mind.' So what was I supposed to think?"

Evelyn touched Dad's arm. "So Davey goes and sneaks into your bedroom a week or so before Christmas—after Mom tells us not to. She specifically said not to step one foot in her room without her permission, or without you or Mom being there. Yet Davey, being the obedient child that he was, goes into the room anyway when Mom was outside. He sneaks into the closet where Mom hid the gifts and sees the box with the hunting knife he asked for. Ha! So he's as happy as a dog with two tails…" Evelyn burst out laughing.

"Man alive!" I said. "It's not *that* funny."

"Yes, it is! Ha ha!—So Davey wakes up Christmas morning and goes down into the living room and sees a box about the same size as the one with the hunting knife, all wrapped up under the tree—"

She couldn't even finish the story, she was laughing so hard.

"Wow!" Dad cried. "This must be real good. So what happened?"

I rolled my eyes. "So I looked down at the box—it's got Andrew's name written on it."

Evelyn clapped her hands. "Ha ha! Mom completely forgot and ended up buying the knife for Andy instead!"

Dad howled. "Ha ha! So then what did you end up getting?"

"Lincoln Logs!" Evelyn chimed in. "Davey got Lincoln Logs!"

Andrew smiled. "I still got that knife."

"Pshh! I still got those logs somewhere, too," I said, shaking my head. "I was crushed. I mean I can't tell you how crushed I was. It was so hard for me to pretend I was happy with what I got."

"Well, you must've done a good job then," Dad said. "I never knew any better."

"That'll teach you to go sneaking a peek at your gift," Evelyn said.

I smiled. "I never did it again."

"That is so comical," Dad said. He put his hand on my shoulder. "Well, I hate to disappoint you again, Son, but I didn't get you a hunting knife this year either."

We all laughed.

Despite finishing up our meal, we remained at the table and carried on with our wonderful time.

At last, we withdrew to the living room and gathered around the decorated tree. Dad grabbed his Bible off the end table and thumbed through the pages. In keeping with his tradition, he then read to us the portion of the gospel books that pertain to the Christmas story.

After that, Dad grabbed a few gifts from under the tree and passed them out. Andrew got a new set of brushes for his painting projects, Evelyn got a new shawl, and I got a new book. Then Evelyn wanted to be next to hand out her gifts and insisted we open them at the same time. Abiding by her rules, each of us ended up with a nice necktie for which we were grateful. Lastly, I handed out my gifts. Dad seemed pleased with his new letter opener. Evelyn went on and on about her new earrings, thanking me for not making her wait till midnight. And Andrew seemed to appreciate his new fountain pen.

"That's not all," Dad said. "I've got one more thing to give to each of you."

"Where?" Evelyn asked. "There aren't any more gifts under the tree."

"You got us more?" I said.

"No," Dad replied. "This is from someone else."

He got up and walked over to the fireplace. He picked up a few envelopes from off the mantel. "These are from your mother. Before mom went home...sorry..." Dad took out his handkerchief and wiped his eyes. "...Before Mom went home, she had written each of you a letter...She must've known she wasn't' gonna make it till Christmas...She placed these inside a book and told me to make sure you all got these on Christmas day last year. I feel terrible, but not only did I forget about them, Mom's book got moved somehow from the end table. I found these in the drawer just a few weeks ago. I almost gave them to you then, but I figured we were this close to

Christmas again that I might as well wait till today. I thought it would be sort of special. So anyways, here's yours, Andrew...Here's yours, Evelyn...And here's yours, David."

"Thank you, Dad."

We all did our best not to cry, but the dam was already broken. None of us wanted to limit the delightful time we were having with one another, but as soon as we could, each of us took our letter and went our separate ways for a while. I took mine upstairs and went into the bedroom and closed the door. The tears streamed down my face before I had even opened the envelop. I took the letter out and unfolded it. Through blurry eyes, I read:

Dear David,

I know your heart is broken. You believed with all your heart I was going to make it. And it's good you prayed because now God can never say you didn't ask. Because you did!

I didn't have the heart to break it to you, but I knew deep down the Lord was calling me home this time. You see, you were right. God was going to heal me once and for all.

Son, if it were the Lord's will to heal each and every time we prayed for it, we would never grow old and die. Realize that the prayer of faith did indeed save the sick. By the time you read this, I'll be home with the Lord. And someday he will raise me up just like he promised. You see, I was not only sick, I was saved! Saved by the blood of Christ!

Remember, there were times when even the apostle Paul was not at liberty to heal someone, even though he had the gift of healing. Even Paul himself was denied healing despite pleading with the Lord on several occasions. Sometimes God uses our troubles to keep us humbly dependent upon him, so that the power of Christ may rest on us. I can tell you this—his power rests on me right now.

Keep trusting the Lord and serving him. Our time on earth is but a vapor. Here one minute and gone the next. I look forward to getting together with you again!

Love,

Mom

Chapter 29

The Tamas family came over the house for New Year's Eve. It was a tradition that had been preserved for many years, apart from the year before when it was suspended on account of Mom's passing. We didn't mingle much throughout the year, but we had the sort of friendship which let you pick up where you had left off. There simply existed a free and natural understanding on both sides.

We were all seated in the living room with our drinks in hand, making the most of each other's company while soaking up the warmth of the fireside. The oil lamps were lit as well, their ruby quilted shades improving the mood of the room. They were pleasing to the eye and used to be Mom's favorite. Dad was sitting comfortably in his armchair beside the one. Evelyn was in the rocking chair beside the other. She swayed back and forth while twirling a lock of her hair, sneaking a peek at Stephen now and again. Stephen, Andrew, and I were seated at the game table in some folded-up chairs, with Rouge lying at Andrew's feet. Stephen's parents were on the sofa, holding hands.

I got up and tossed a couple logs into the fire. "I forget, how old were you, Stephen, when you came here with your parents?"

"Um, I vuz about eight years old," Stephen said. "Hard to believe I'm twenty-four now."

Andrew chuckled. "You're getting old."

Evelyn turned to Stephen. "I can't believe it either. I'm gonna be turning twenty this year."

"In other words, you're nineteen?" I said matter-of-factly.

"In other words, I'm gonna be twenty. Why do have to nitpick, Davey?"

"I have my reasons." I flashed my eyebrows and sneered. "Just like you have yours."

She rolled her eyes. "You need to respect your elders. Remember, I'm older than you."

"Pshh! By two years."

"I'm still your elder."

Andrew took a sip of his coffee. "Hard to believe I was twenty when I left for France."

"I know," Stephen said, patting my brother on the shoulder. "I feel so badly. I got to come to America and escape da hell of Europe, and you had to leave America and go fight in Europe."

Andrew shrugged. "That's just how life is. No fault of your own. Besides, you're a grateful person."

Stephen raised his glass. "I am. I'm in love with my country, and I'm grateful for you."

My brother raised his glass as well and chimed it against Stephen's.

"Ve have alvays felt very badly for Andrew," Mrs. Tamas said, putting her hand on her husband's knee. "Haven't ve, dear. Like ve are partly to blame."

"That is true, darling," Mr. Tamas said. "Little did ve know da war vood break out after ve left Austria-Hungary. And sadly, it vuz our homeland dat vuz vy Andrew had to go."

"Well, it wasn't exactly your fault that a single agitator shot and killed the Archduke," Andrew said.

"I know, I know," Mr. Tamas said. "But our country declared war on Serbia after dat."

229

"Well, it's nobody's fault," Evelyn said. "And we're all here together, and that's all that matters tonight. So what do you say we play a game or something?"

Dad sipped his coffee. "Go right ahead. That's what the game table is for."

"You gonna play with us, Dad?" Evelyn asked.

"Oh, no. I am happy as can be right here," he said, thumping the arm of his chair. "And I reckon Mr. and Mrs. Tamas are content on that couch as well. You know how it is with us; we usually just sit around and share stories about when we were young."

"You were young?" Evelyn said, with a straight face.

Dad raised his eyebrows. "Watch it there, young lady. I know it's hard to believe. But, yes, we were young once."

"Once upon a time," Mrs. Tamas said, chuckling. "And let me tell you, Mikklos could get down and do pushups vith vun hand."

"One hand?" Evelyn cried.

"Yes, vun." She stressed it with a single finger. "And many pushups. Not just three or four. I mean *many*. And he could run very, very fast. I mean fast like a marlin!"

Mr. Tamas nudged his wife. "I vuzn't swimming, darling. Marlin's don't run; day swim."

"You know vut I mean," she said, slapping him on the knee. "I just mean you were very fast…like a brown hare then." She gave a firm nod of her head and turned to me. "He vuz fast. Like from here to town in a few minutes."

"That's pretty good!" I said.

"Not anymore," Mr. Tamas said, adjusting his tie. "I can hardly run to da outhouse now. I have to pray dat I make it in time. But Csilla could run, too. Don't let her kid you. She was a vonderful tennis player—back and forth, back and forth, swinging and hitting da ball. She vuz a good swimmer too—fast like a brown hare!"

We all burst out laughing.

Then the room quieted for a moment.

"I got just the idea!" Evelyn said, clapping her hands. "How about we play a game of Mahjong?"

I shrugged. "Whatever. Sounds good to me. What do you guys wanna do?"

"I don't really care," Andrew said. "We've got plenty of vittles and tasty puddings, so that's all that matters."

"And I vill do vutever your sister vaunts," Stephen said.

"Did you hear that, Evelyn?" I said. "Stephen says whatever *you* want."

"Oh, goodie!" She sprang up from the rocker. "Then I'll go and get it. I'll be right back." She hurried out of the room and up the stairs.

In next to no time at all, she fluttered back down. Yet it seemed she was taking much too long to return. I leaned back in my chair and peered into the dining room. My sister was in front of the mirror, turning side to side, tidying her dress, touching up her hair. I leaned forward before she could notice.

"Look what I got!" Evelyn said, returning to the room. She held out the boxed set in the palm of her hand—like a waitress about to serve us our food. She raised it up over her head and twirled around. Then she stumbled over my shoe and lost control of the box, scattering tiles and game pieces all over the place. "Oh, my!" she cried.

Stephen sprang to his feet. "My goodness! Are you alright?" He practically hurtled over Andrew's lap to get to her.

"I'm fine," Evelyn said, kneeling down. "I tripped over Davey's shoe."

"Here, I vill help get doze for you." Stephen knelt with her.

"Aw! Thank you, Stephen."

"Not a problem, not a problem. I'm just glad you didn't tumble to da ground vith da game. Dat vood not be good."

"Aw! You're such a gentleman."

Andrew and I looked at each other and smirked.

"Yep, it's a good thing you caught yourself on that rocker," I said. "That was quite the close call."

"I know," Evelyn said. "I could've sprained my ankle, and it would've been all your fault, Davey."

"My fault, huh? It seems I remember another time you dropped your things. I wonder if that was my fault, too?"

Andrew and I snickered.

"I don't know why you find this so funny. You can come help us, you know."

"Nah. You two are doing a fabulous job. It couldn't have worked out better. Though if you had just fallen to the floor, then Stephen could've picked you up, too."

She looked up for the first time and eyed me.

At last, the two of them got everything put back into the box.

"I appreciate your help, Stephen."

"You are so velcome, Evelyn."

As soon as they returned to the table, we set up the game.

Evelyn chatted Stephen's ear off the entire time we played. She cheered him on so much that one would've thought a victory for Stephen was a victory for her. He didn't say nearly as much, but he clearly adored my sister.

At long last, Stephen ended up the winner. Evelyn clapped her hands in celebration.

"Funny how you seem happy you lost," Andrew said, putting the game away.

Evelyn held her nose up. "I'm not happy I lost. I'm just glad our guest has won. That's all."

"Yep, Andrew...*That's* all," I added sarcastically.

"Stop it," Evelyn said. "Don't make me punch you. Stephen's our guest of honor."

232

"Ooh! We don't just have a guest," I said. "We've got ourselves a guest of *honor*."

Stephen grinned. "I must say dat I feel honored and happy to be a guest in dis house. I alvays have a vonderful time vid you all."

"And you always seem to win, too," I said. "There's something suspicious going on here." "There's something suspicious alright," Andrew said, looking over at Stephen and Evelyn.

"Would you like something else to eat, Stephen?" Evelyn asked. "I'm headed to the kitchen, so I can grab you something."

He rubbed his belly. "Dank you. You are such a sveetheart, but I am so full. I've eaten vay too much today and vill probably put on fifty pounds. Ha! People vill ask me, 'Vut happened to you? You're so fat now.' And I vill have to tell dem, 'It's de Hayeses fault. Day feed me too much!'"

My sister put her hands on her hips and smirked.

"Did you hear that, Evelyn?" I said. "He called you a *sweetheart*."

"Of course, she heard," Andrew said. "Look at her face."

Evelyn made off to the corner of the living room and got down on her knees.

"There's nowhere to hide. So there's no use trying."

"I'm not hiding, Andy. I'm trying to find something."

"Well, there ain't no ring over there!" I hollered.

Stephen and Andrew burst out laughing.

"Don't be silly," Evelyn said. "I'm not looking for a ring—not over here anyhow."

Andrew and I pounded the table with our fists. "Whoa! She said it!"

Our parents looked at us like we were a bunch of rabble-rousers. They were shaking their heads and chuckling to themselves.

"Hooey!" Evelyn said. "Now where did I last put it? Oh, goodie, I found it!" She sprang to her feet and placed the record on the phonograph. She cranked it a few times and lowered the needle. "This is my favorite song!"

The Charleston began to play, and Evelyn began to dance around. As she reached over for Stephen's hand, Dad raised his eyebrows. Upon second thought, she grabbed Andrew by the arm. "C'mon Andy! Let's dance together."

Andrew stood up and got into it a little. Enough to make us laugh. He quickly returned to his seat. "I can't dance anymore. And to think I used to be pretty good at it, too."

"Not me," Stephen said. "I vuz never good."

Evelyn tapped me. "Let's do the Charleston, Davey!"

"You're crazy," I said. "What's got into you?"

"I think we all know," Andrew said. "It's called an arrow from Cupid's bow."

"Phonus-balonus!" Evelyn said. " It's New Year's Eve. You gotta have a little fun once in a while."

Evelyn's spirit was contagious; I couldn't resist. The two of us danced around the room, stepping forward and backward, moving our heels in and out, swinging our arms side to side. Dad didn't care for the song and would have normally told us to "pipe down," but he seemed amused now. Mr. and Mrs. Tamas were clearly enjoying the performance, so I think it helped Dad to loosen up.

Andrew turned to Stephen. "David's quite the Oliver Twist!"

Stephen leaned back and folded his arms. "It's vonderful! Look at de two of dem go!"

Chapter 30

After the new year, Stephen approached Dad at work and asked him for permission to start "courting" Evelyn. Of course, Dad said yes. Stephen was just an honorable man all around, and he had watched my sister grow up and become a wonderful young woman.

I took heart from Stephen's boldness and followed his lead. I asked Dad what he thought about my getting Mr. Swanson's permission to start writing his daughter. Dad wondered what "triggered" me to want to write her. I couldn't bring myself to lie; I was sure he could read my thoughts. I told him about my daytrip to Carlton and the "divine appointment" I had at McMurray's. I made sure to toss in a promise to "never ever ride another freight car for the rest of my entire existence."

He squinted in his usual way, but he just stared at me. I had never seen my father dumbstruck before. A smirk finally stole across his face, and he turned around and walked away. "That's fine. Just make sure you get her father's permission."

"Yes, sir," I said.

Then he halted and turned back around and pointed his finger at me. "Don't let me find out you snuck past her father like you snuck on that train. In fact, I wanna see his return letter. You understand?"

"Yes, sir. I will."

"Alright then."

On the outside, I appeared calm and self-possessed; but on the inside, I was jumping for joy and screaming at the top of my lungs. I rushed upstairs and rummaged through my belongings for a pen and some paper. Yet I couldn't find my pen. I got down on my knees and looked under the bed. Perhaps it had fallen. I couldn't help but think of the woman in the Lord's parable who had lost a piece of silver. I imagined calling my friends and neighbors together, saying, "Rejoice with me! For I have found the pen which had been lost!"

I couldn't find it though.

I dug through Andrew's belongings and came upon the fountain pen I had given him for Christmas. He wasn't home to get permission, but I assured myself he would understand if I borrowed it.

I set the paper down on my dresser, as if it were my desk. I sat on the edge of the bed with the paper before me. In a flash, the joy I had felt gave way to discouragement. I tried to encourage myself in the Lord—as King David had done when he discovered the Amalekites had smitten Ziklag, burned it with fire, and had taken his wives. Yet try as I might, my effort failed, and discouragement turned to despair.

Why would Mr. Swanson let me write his daughter?

My mind took off as if it were being drawn by wild horses. I could see Mr. Swanson asking me, 'Now why do you want to write my daughter?' I tried to look him in the eyes and answer him as best I could in my mind. Then it occurred to me I had hopes of marrying her someday, which made me feel like a villain. Not only had I dug through my brother's belongings without getting his permission, but I was plotting to steal another man's daughter under the guise of *getting* his permission!

I plopped my head on the dresser top. I remained there for about five minutes. At long last, I picked up the pen and started writing *something*.

Dear Mr. Swanson,

I am writing you that I may humbly seek your permission to write your daughter, Catherine. She seems like a fine young lady.

Sincerely,

David

P.S. I was honest with my dad about the train ride.

I read it over about ten times. I folded up the paper and placed it in the envelope and sealed it. But as soon as I filled out the address, I felt I shouldn't have used the word "humbly" in my letter. It sounded too pretentious all of a sudden, and for that reason alone, I felt sure I was guaranteed a denial.

I decided if I was going to do this, I was going to do it right, so I got another sheet of paper out.

Just then, I heard Andrew coming up the stairs.

What's done is done! I must leave it to the mercy of God!

I put away Andrew's pen and took the letter downstairs and fetched a stamp.

The next day, I rode my bicycle into town. The whole way there, I pondered how my future hinged on such a little item in my hand.

What if I run into Dominic and he takes it from me? What if a hawk swoops down and plucks it out of my hand?

I arrived at the post office. I gave the envelope a long hard look and then mailed it.

What if it gets lost in the mail? What if Catherine's dad throws it away without even telling her?

I took a deep breath and resolved once more to leave it in God's hands.

The entire month of January frittered away. Not a word from Catherine's dad.

However, in the first week of February, a letter came in the mail, not only addressed to David Hayes, but with a return address from Mr. Dan Swanson. The thrill of excitement and the fear of rejection gripped me at once.

I opened it. I felt the blood rush to my head as I read the first couple sentences.

David,

You and Catherine are both very young and need to be patient. It would be wise not to rush this chapter of your life but focus on establishing your future. Nevertheless, Mrs. Swanson and I have prayed it over, and we have decided that you may write Catherine. But no more than once per month. I have informed Catherine already of your intention, and she seems to have an interest in you. She is looking forward to your correspondence.

Sincerely,

Mr. Swanson

The relief that flooded my soul can hardly be overstated. I began deliberating at once about the subject matter of my first letter.

Chapter 31

Springtime brought not only the refreshing changes to our natural surroundings, but also some changes to our personal lives. Andrew surprised us at breakfast one morning with the news that he was moving to Fairfax County. "Arrangements have already been made," he said. "I'll be staying at Mr. Livingston's home with some other servicemen. In fact, I'll be packing my bags and leaving this Saturday. I'm to take the train to Royalton, and someone will be meeting me there to take me the rest of the way to Pickerington. It's something I've been thinking about for a while…" He paused and turned to me. "…and praying about."

We were startled by the sudden announcement, yet we were just as pleased. It was certainly what we had wanted for Andrew for quite a while, and now he was truly keen on the opportunity. We did nothing but encourage him.

The week slipped away. Before long, we were at the station saying our goodbyes.

Andrew hugged Dad. "Love you, Pop. Thanks for never giving up on me."

"Nah, I'd never give up on you, Son," Dad said. "I've always felt badly for you is all. And I always wished I had the magic key to open the door for you. I knew you'd been to hell and back. I knew that. We all knew that. But I'm happy to see you make a fresh start, and I believe it's gonna be a help to you. I believe you're gonna be a help to others, as well. But regardless of what you do, I just want you in God's will. That's all. Whatever that looks like—I don't concern myself with that. Just be in God's will. 'Cause in the end, that's all that really matters in this life." Dad patted him on the shoulder. "I love you, Son."

"Thanks, Dad."

"Take care now."

Andrew hugged Evelyn. "I guess I won't be teasing you much from here on. But I'm sure gonna miss you."

"And I'm sure gonna miss your teasing, Andy." Evelyn wiped her eyes. "It's not gonna be the same around here. But I really hope this works out for you. And I hope you're happy."

"Thanks, sis."

Andrew turned to me and gave me a hug, as well. "Thanks for putting up with me, David. I mean it." He stood up straight and grabbed hold of me by the shoulders. "I owe it to you. Take care of yourself, little brother."

"Thanks, Andrew."

With that, he boarded the train and sat down by a window. Soon, the steam engine was howling, the wheels were squealing, and we were waving goodbye.

That was it. Andrew was no longer part of the daily interactions and all the comings and goings. It felt strange having the bedroom all to myself. Rouge sniffed his bed and whimpered, clearly unsettled by his apparent vanishing.

Then not even a couple weeks later, Beth informed Evelyn that she, too, was moving away. She was to live with a "well-to-do cousin" in New York City. Before we knew it, Beth was hugging her family and Evelyn goodbye at the station.

"Oh, I'm gonna miss you, Beth," Evelyn cried.

"Me, too," Beth said. "I'm looking forward to moving to the city, but I'm really sad about leaving this old town. I've never been more torn about a decision. It's awful."

"I know. But we'll always be friends, no matter the distance."

"That's right. And nothing will ever change that."

"And at least we can write each other."

"Oh, Evelyn, I can't wait to tell you all about the city."

"Me neither."

With tears streaming down, Evelyn and Beth hugged each other one more time.

Beth made her way to the steps. She was just about to board the train when she hesitated. She handed me a letter. "Would you be so kind as to give this to Daryl?"

"I'll do that for you."

"Promise me you'll give it to him?"

"I give you my word he'll have this letter in his hands today."

"Thank you, David."

She turned about and flashed her dimpled smile, waving goodbye to everybody. She climbed the steps, blew us all one last kiss, then disappeared into the railcar.

That was it. Evelyn's lifelong friend had moved away.

I remember the newspaper accounts in the latter half of April describing the Great Mississippi Flood and the devastation it had wreaked on the lives of some seven hundred thousand people. I remember how grateful I was to have a house to go to and a bed to sleep in, and not have all my possessions and keepsakes swept away downstream. Our part of the country was experiencing a spell of summerlike weather. Granted a couple days got uncomfortably hot, but I was conscious of the fact that those less fortunate would've gladly endured the petty nuisance. Not to mention we were treated to a handful of agreeable picture-perfect days as well. The kind you wished were all year round.

Dad, Evelyn, and I had returned home from attending church that Sunday morning. The day was heavenly, and Dad was determined to "not let a day like this be lost by staying cooped up inside."

Evelyn agreed. "Let's have dinner in the backyard."

"Well, whatta ya say we go for a drive this afternoon?" Dad suggested.

"And have a little picnic somewhere?"

"Even better."

"That sounds wonderful!"

"It sure is gorgeous outside," I said. "Doesn't get any better than this. A perfect day to have the windows rolled down."

Evelyn clapped her hands. "This is just the bee's knees! I'll get some sandwiches made."

"There's leftover cornbread, too," Dad said. "Go ahead and throw it in that basket there."

"And here's a few bottles of soda," I said. "One for each of us."

"Splendid." Dad headed upstairs. "I'm gonna change out of my Sunday best and then I'll be ready to go."

Evelyn and I put the basket together. Then we changed out of our clothes into something more suitable for the picnic. We scampered out of the house and climbed in the car. Dad finally came out, carrying his Bible with him. He got in and started it up, then we headed for town.

We were approaching the intersection of Healy and Ludwig when Dad spotted Mr. Foster walking toward his house. "Hey, whatta ya know? It's good ole Foster."

Dad pulled up alongside the curb and laid on the horn just to be funny. "Good afternoon, Mr. Foster."

"Good afternoon, Millard. I see the horn works."

"Just making sure you're paying attention."

"I'm paying attention alright. The question is are *you* paying attention? You do realize what day it is?"

"Of course, I do. Why, it's a perfect day for a picnic. We're headed up to Hideaway Hills. Gonna enjoy the view from Mount Pleasant."

Mr. Foster shook his head. "Evidently, you're not paying attention. Either that, or you just don't care. You do realize it's the Lord's Day?"

Dad chuckled. "Sunday usually is."

"So you have no qualms then with your carrying-on, wandering around like a bunch of Israelites in the wilderness?"

"I'm hardly carrying-on, Lawrence. And I'm not wandering either—I know exactly where I'm going."

My sister and I chuckled, which Mr. Foster overheard. "So all the more obstinate then. You all don't seem particularly concerned about playing on the Lord's Sabbath. The very day set aside for solemn meditation."

"I don't think God's offended by me driving on Sunday," Dad said. "I drive the same on Sunday as I do every other day of the week."

Mr. Foster pointed his finger at Dad. "Now you're sitting in the seat of the scornful, Mr. Hayes. You might want to take heed."

Dad made like he was examining the inside of the car. "Nope. Looks to me like I'm sitting in the seat of a Ford. In fact, if I'm guilty of anything, Lawrence, it's trying to be neighborly. So may the Lord be gracious enough to forgive me for that. Good day, sir."

Dad put it in gear and started driving away.

Mr. Foster scurried alongside the car and peered through the window. "The Lord has a way of humbling us!"

Dad responded by speeding up.

Mr. Foster gave up the pursuit, hollering, "Prepare to meet thy God!"

Evelyn and I looked out the back window. Mr. Foster was standing in the middle of the road, pointing his finger at us.

That dreadful feeling came over me right then and there—the feeling of being cursed. I hadn't felt it in a long time, but the old sensation was back.

"I don't know about him sometimes," Dad said, chuckling. "I guess I won't be stopping anymore to say hello to *him*. Not on Sunday anyhow."

"What's gotten into him?" Evelyn said. "He seems grumpier than ever lately."

"Oh, you know Lawrence," Dad said. "That's just his way. I probably shouldn't have been so sarcastic with him. He just gets on your nerves after a while. Though you're right; I've never seen him quite like that before." Dad cranked his neck to get a look at me. "I guess it makes up for the way I lost it with him that one day. Right, David?"

"Most people would have," I said, having a look out the window.

"I don't get it," Evelyn said. "Why's it such a sin to drive on Sunday?"

"Well, in his mind, Sunday is the New Testament Sabbath," Dad explained. "So there's a lot that him and Emma won't do on Sunday that they consider to be work. Though it's kinda funny; he won't mow the lawn or go out to eat, but he's got Emma working in the kitchen making his meal. Ha! But it's not just them. His church is sort of like that."

Evelyn rolled her eyes. "First of all, the Sabbath was on Saturday. Second of all, we're told to not judge people anymore based on a holy day or sabbath day, so I don't understand."

"I know," Dad said. "I can't figure them out either."

"What an odd church," Evelyn said.

"Well, there's good people at Lawrence's church," Dad said. "Don't get me wrong. It's not their fault Lawrence is so ornery and pushy. Besides, we've got a few funny folks in our church, too, don't forget. Mr. Dowdy thinks it's worldly to drive a car. Not just on Sunday either."

Evelyn plopped back in the seat. "I guess so."

"Miss Browman goes to his church," Dad continued. "So does Mrs. Spencer and Mr. and Mrs. Randall. They're the sweetest people you'd ever meet. And what about Mr. Morris? Do you realize how much food he's given over the years to the pantry in town? And then there's Lawrence's own wife. Emma has always been friendly toward us. She's friendly to everybody. And I reckon she sort of puts up with him the same way everybody else does."

"I guess you're right...." Evelyn was looking out the window and seemed distracted. "But one thing's for sure, those are some dark clouds."

I leaned over to have a peek. "Man alive! I think we're gonna get some rain."

"I reckon a little rain never hurt anyone," Dad said.

I took another look. The sky was murky, and the clouds were churning. "I'm not so sure it's gonna be a little rain. I think a storm's headed right this way."

"Ah! I hope it doesn't spoil our picnic," Evelyn said.

"Nah, it'll be alright," Dad said. "We're almost to Turley's bend and then we start climbing. If we have to, we'll sit it out."

Just then, a gust of air blew through the windows. Evelyn's hair threatened to lash me in the face, so I leaned back in my seat. Within a minute, the air got cooler. Raindrops started to hit here and there upon the windshield, and another strong gust came through, spraying us in the face.

"Whoa!" Dad said. "I guess we better roll up the windows."

The wind intensified. A salvo of large drops splattered on the windshield. The trees began to sway, and daylight was soon swallowed up in darkness.

Then, as if the bottoms of the clouds had fallen out, a torrent was unleashed. The sound of thrashing rain grew louder until the clink and clatter of hailstones joined the ruckus. My heart pounded in my chest as I peered out into the blurry landscape. Through the wet smear of the window, I could make out the hustle and bustle of tree limbs threatening to break away.

Prepare to meet thy God!

Dad gripped the steering wheel. "Who would've seen this coming?" He strained to see the road.

"This is crazy!" Evelyn cried. "It was sunshiny just a few minutes ago!"

The car wobbled.

"Dear Lord!" Evelyn cried.

I expected a tornado to touch down on us any moment.

"I can't die yet!" Evelyn shouted. "I gotta get married first!"

Prepare to meet thy God!

Dad pulled over. We gripped our seats as the car trembled in the turbulence. Lightning flashed. The thunder detonated like a bomb, then it rumbled like a beast.

Another minute went by. It began to settle down.

As quickly as the stormed rolled in, it rolled out. The rain stopped. The entire event seemed like a wild and furious dream.

"Wow!" Dad said. "That was something else!"

"Look at that mess!" I said.

Large trees had blown over. Busted limbs and smaller branches littered the countryside.

"Man alive!" Dad said. "I wouldn't be surprised if a twister came through."

"I was just waiting for the car to get sucked up into the air," I said.

"Whew! You're not kidding," Dad said. "Or at least rolled over. I thought my heart was gonna beat right out of my chest."

"I was scared to death," Evelyn said.

Dad looked back. "Well, look at you. You've been raised back to life. And now you'll be able to get married."

"It's not funny, Dad. I'm being serious."

"I know you are, honey. I'm just teasing." Dad started the car and let the windshield clear up. "We might as well keep going. We made it this far, right?"

I pointed. "Looks like the sun's peeking out over there."

Evelyn's face lit up. "Our little picnic's not spoiled after all!"

We continued down the road. Rays of sunlight beamed down through a break in the clouds. We made it around the bend and started up the slope.

We reached the hilltop view and pulled off to the side.

We got out of the car and stretched. I breathed in the fragrance of the after-rain. The cool air stuck around, but the sun was shining again. We walked up to the edge and surveyed the majestic scene before us. We were overlooking the entire Rosedale Valley with the glow of daylight behind us.

Then traces of a rainbow emerged where the clouds still lingered. The bow improved. The faded colors became clearer and clearer. At last, the colors shone brightly, and a vibrant arch stretched out over the entire region.

"Amazing!" Dad said. "Reminds me of a sermon Pastor preached many years ago. I'll never forget it. It was titled *The Bow of Promise*."

"Sounds interesting," Evelyn said.

"It sure is," he replied, opening the Bible in his hand. "The verses are in Isaiah." He thumbed through the pages. "Here they are; I've got them circled. God says, 'In a little wrath I hid my face from thee for a moment; but with everlasting kindness will I have mercy on thee, saith the Lord thy Redeemer. For this is as the waters of Noah unto me: for as I have sworn that the waters of Noah should no more go over the earth; so have I sworn that I would not be wroth with thee, nor rebuke thee. For the mountains shall depart, and the hills be removed; but my kindness shall not depart from thee, neither shall the covenant of my peace be removed, saith the Lord that hath mercy on thee.'

"You see, no matter what God's child has gone through," Dad explained, "God promises never to leave us. Even during the most severe trials where we feel forsaken. When it seems his wrath is bearing down on us and everything around us is falling apart, God still loves us. He hasn't abandoned us. His kindness and peace are still certain. And the rainbow is God's reminder of this. Not only is it his promise never to destroy the world again by a flood, but it's a sign of his covenant of peace with his people."

My father's words dispelled the spirit of fear that had come over me. I basked in those words as much as the sunshine. The peace of God rolled over my soul once again. My eyes welled up, and I turned away and leaned against a tree so that neither of them could see.

"I remember what Pastor said," Dad continued. "The rain stands for the sorrow and hard times in our lives. The sun stands for Christ who is always there—even when the storm clouds hide his face from us. And without the sun *and* the rain, there'd be no rainbow. God uses both the sunny days and the rainy days in our life to work out something beautiful."

"That's wonderful!" Evelyn said. "It gives me goosebumps."

"It's a good message," I said. I pretended to scratch the corner of my eye.

"It sure is," Evelyn said. "Dad preaches better than Billy Sunday."

"Well, don't go singing my praises now," Dad said. "It's Pastor Richardson's message. Not mine."

Evelyn and I laughed.

"What's interesting," Evelyn said, "is out of all the signs that God could've given us, he gave us something that is round about his throne in heaven. The apostle John saw it and wrote about it. The bow reminds us of the glory of God and the beauty of holiness. And what's more, God's throne of judgment becomes a throne of grace once we accept his offer of salvation. Because of the Lord Jesus Christ, we don't have to fear the clouds of judgment anymore."

"Couldn't have said it any better, honey," Dad said.

"Hold on, there's more," she said. "It all makes sense: God not only chose a rainbow as his sign, but he put it—I mean he could've put a sign anywhere, right?—but he painted it on a cloud, so that we'd be reminded of his mercy."

My sister had no idea she was ministering to my heart. It was like God himself was speaking to me. I stood there facing the valley, still leaning against the tree, still pretending to scratch the corner of my eye. And while I continued to delight in the panorama, I called to mind a time in my life when I looked for a sign from God. It dawned on me that it was right there before my eyes.

Chapter 32

I borrowed the car and stopped by the Sawyer's after work one Saturday. As soon as I walked through the door, Nathan cupped his hands around his mouth and announced, "Hayes is here! Let the celebration begin!"

Ann marched through the room, crying, "Hooray for David and Silas! Hooray for David and Silas!"

Wayne came running down the stairs. "Why's Ann cheering for David and Goliath?"

"I said *Silas*," Ann protested. "Pin your ears back."

Allen turned to Wayne and nodded. "Yep."

Mr. Sawyer entered the room with a grin on his face and his guitar strapped around his shoulder. "It's merrymaking time!" Irvin pulled his harmonica out of his pocket and tested it out, sliding up and down the musical scale a few times. He gave his dad the nod, and the two of them began to play a catchy tune. We all joined in, clapping our hands and dancing around the room, while Silas sat there at the table with an expression of surprise and wonder on his face.

Mr. Sawyer finished the tune, giving it one last strum. "Ha ha! He's looking at us like we've got bats in our belfry! Give this man a round of applause!"

We all clapped and cheered. "Happy Birthday, Silas!"

Silas grinned. "Thank you. You folks sure are stark crazy. But that's what I love about you!"

"At least I know I'm crazy," Mr. Sawyer said. "Mrs. Sawyer here, she's crazy and doesn't even know it. Ha ha!"

Mrs. Sawyer nudged him. "I'm not crazy."

"See? She doesn't have a clue."

We all laughed.

"Listen to yourself, Pete. You're the one who's crazy, and everyone here knows it, too."

"And I know it, too. I just fessed up. But you done made me crazy."

"Now you're fibbing."

Mr. Sawyer raised his right hand. "I'm telling the whole truth, and nothing but the truth, so help me God—just as much the first time I told you I loved you. You made me crazy—crazy about you!" He gave her a big hug and lifted her right up.

"Put me down, Pete!"

"Now it's not polite to go putting people down," he said, circling around.

"Peter Sawyer! You know what I mean! You're gonna hurt your back."

He set her down and hunched over the chair, as if he were in a lot of pain.

"See?" Mrs. Sawyer cried. "You hurt your back."

He straightened right up. "Nah! I'm as spry as a kitten."

"No, you're as sly as a fox—*that's* what you are." She slapped him on the arm. "I don't know about you sometimes."

He took her back into his arms and kissed her. "Oh, I was just having a little fun with you, dearest. It's Silas's birthday."

"Daddy's just saying that," Ann said. "It's an excuse to act up."

"You tell him, Ann," Mrs. Sawyer said.

Mr. Sawyer patted Silas on the back. "I'm not just saying that. It really is Silas's birthday."

Ann rolled her eyes and huffed. "We already know that."

"And you wanna know how it's his birthday, David?" Mr. Sawyer asked.

"How's that?" I said.

"Because I picked it," Ann chimed in. She pointed to herself very proudly.

Wayne laughed at her. "Sure. You picked it out of a *hat*."

"So?" Ann said. "I still picked it, didn't I?"

Mr. Sawyer spoke up: "So we Sawyers reckon that a man ought to have a birthday. And it has therefore been decreed that this seventh day of May is the official day to celebrate Silas's birthday."

We all cheered.

"And I got to pick the number," Ann said, self-assuredly. She made sure to catch Wayne's eye.

"Did you hear that everybody?" Wayne hollered. "Ann got to pick her nose."

"I said I picked the *number!*" She rushed over and smacked him on the rear. "Take it back, you meany!"

Mr. Sawyer gave a hearty laugh. "Now don't go hitting people on the caboose, Ann. There's no reason to get yourself in a real tizzy. You see, I get to pick my nose *and* my guitar. So I'm blessed twice over." He began strumming the opening chord. "And we're all blessed to have Silas here with us on his birthday, so let's all sing the birthday song."

"Hooray!" Ann cried, bouncing around. "Happy birthday for Silas!"

"Ready? Here we go…."

Mr. Sawyer played, and we all sang. Except for Wayne; he just yelled. Mr. Sawyer then melded into a little ditty upon which we all clapped our hands and danced around the room like before.

The frolicking finally ran its course, and we joined Silas at the table. Mrs. Sawyer served beef steaks and chowder for dinner, and Nathan poured us all some sweet tea. Mr. Sawyer then led us in a word of prayer, thanking God for the food and for sending Silas their way. As soon as he closed, everybody jumped right in, gobbling up the food and gabbing about this, that, and the other.

Pete and Erma shared some memories of their children's first birthdays, which led into some embarrassing tales. When all the bantering settled down, Wayne proceeded to hop from subject to subject: how Colonial Air Transport had carried six passengers on a flight from Boston to Hadley Field, how New Orleans had over fourteen inches of rainfall in a single day, and how Chevrolet was becoming the frontrunner for General Motors.

Nathan then entertained us with a couple stories he had read: one about a factory, and another that involved a farm. Which led Irvin to chime in about his dream of running "a king-size farmstead" someday "with gasoline-powered tractors, electricity, and that new John Deere combine harvester." Meanwhile, Allen was busily nodding his head while he ate, adding "Yep" every now and then.

Ann, being the first to finish her food, got up from her seat and stood around the table. She commented on "the sweet songbirds" and "the flowers of Spring." Then leave it to Ann to veer off the flourishing path with a remark about the Saint Valentine's Day Massacre that had taken place that past February. Which prompted Mrs. Sawyer to object to "such a distasteful discussion at mealtime."

The meal was delicious, and it was followed up by some baked apple pies. When Silas finished with his dessert, he left the room momentarily and returned with his Bible—the one I had given him last Christmas. He had been reading Proverbs ever since, his favorite book of the Bible. He was excited to show me a set of verses he had read that morning. The verses were underlined: "Trust in the Lord with all thine heart; and lean not unto thine own understanding. In all thy ways acknowledge him, and he shall direct thy paths."

"Aren't those verses swell?" Silas said.

"They sure are," I said.

"My job is to acknowledge him as best I can," Silas explained. "And God's job is to direct my paths. You see, it's not my job to do the directing; God promises to do the directing. I just have to do my part in the acknowledging, and God will take care the rest."

"That's a good point, Silas. Very encouraging."

"I think so. And I'll tell you what: I love this Bible you gave me."

"Good. I'm happy for you. And you read it like you've been doing it for years."

"Thanks to Nathan. He was a swell teacher."

I took the last bite of my pie and leaned back in my chair with my hands folded behind my head. I chuckled to myself as I watched Ann toss a piece of corn at Irvin and then dodge behind her dad. Irvin looked at me, upon which I pointed at Ann.

"I know it was you, Ann," Irvin said. "So don't try hiding behind Dad."

"Howd'ya know it was me?" Ann wondered.

"I just know these kinds of things," Irvin said.

Ann saw me smiling. "*You* told him didn't you, David?"

"I promise I didn't say a word," I said. Which happened to be the truth.

She glared at me in her cute way. "I don't believe you. And Irvin's no prophet either, so you must've helped him."

"I didn't say a word, Ann."

Just then, Wayne tossed a piece of corn at Ann. It got stuck in her billows of hair without her even feeling it. We all burst out laughing.

"What's so funny?" Ann said.

"Are you saving food for later?" I asked.

254

"Whatta ya mean?"

"Here, turn around. You've got something in your hair. Looks like a piece of corn. See?"

"*You* did that, didn't you, David?"

"Whoa! I did *not* do that. I swear."

"Sure, you didn't. Look at you! There's guilt written all over your face."

"I guess you don't read well," I said, sitting back down. "I don't know what to tell ya. It looks like you're no prophet either—"

"*Prophetess!*—I'm a girl."

Wayne rolled his eyes. "Sure! And you're *so* prophetic," he said sarcastically.

"I am *not* pathetic," Ann said. "Take it back!"

"That's not even what I said!" Wayne cried. "Stop being a birdbrain."

Silas laughed, then he turned to me. "Listen, I wanna do something special for my birthday, David. I need to get out and do something fun."

I did feel badly for Silas. He was practically confined to the farm. He never ventured into town again after the incident with Dominic.

"We can go down to the lake again," I said.

Silas shrugged. "I don't know."

The lake seemed like the only safe place we could ever go, but I could see he was eager to try something new for a change.

"I got it!" Silas said. "What about that haunted house? I promised you I would go."

"We can't risk going into town, Silas."

"You said it's outside of town."

"Sure, but we'd still have to drive down Snake Hollow—which I guess we could risk doing in the car...though I'm not sure it would be a good idea to bring the car there. Someone would be bound to see us…I don't know. It would just be my luck to run into the Lockhart boys again."

We gave it more thought.

"*Unless*!" I cried.

"Unless what?"

"Unless we drive back to my house. Then from my house we could follow the creek. Cherry Creek twists and turns all the way to the west side of the Slater property. It's the long way though."

"I don't care! Let's do it!"

"Are you sure?"

"Yes. It's my birthday! It'll be a day I'll never forget!"

"Suit yourself."

Silas and I thanked the Sawyers for "the lip-smacking grub" and told them we were going on "a little birthday run." That prompted Irvin to crack a joke about the two of us being the "sliest bootleggers in all the county."

We hopped in the car and drove back to my house.

We cut through the back yard and wandered through the woods until we arrived at the creek. From there, we followed the creek's lead as it guided us to our destination. We climbed out and tramped through the undergrowth until the Slater house was within a stone's throw.

I glanced over at Silas. He was scowling.

"What's the matter?" I asked.

"Oh, nothing," Silas said.

"You look like you're in deep thought."

"It's this house. It reminds me of somewhere...."

"Well, let's go this way." I headed toward the front yard. "I'll show you those bones I was—man alive! That tree must've just blown over in that storm! That was never like that!"

"That tree's humongous!" Silas cried. "Look at it. Ripped right up by its roots!"

"Thank heavens it didn't hit the house. Can you imagine if that thing fell the other way? That house would be split in two."

"Honest-to-goodness!"

"Oh! Right here, Silas! I almost passed it. There's one of the skeletons. Pretty strange, huh?"

"Those are human remains alright."

"I know. It's creepy. They say the woman who lived here killed the trespassers and buried them in this yard."

Silas chuckled. "I know the story. You've told me it a dozen times already."

"Well, you have to admit it's pretty weird...."

Silas didn't answer. He was studying the house again.

"That's the old Slater house," I said. "A pretty fascinating-looking place, huh?"

"David, I've been here before."

"What?"

"I'm telling you right now, I've been to this place before."

"There's no way. You just moved here not that long ago."

"Then I used to live here at one time. I don't know what else to say. Everything's the way I remember it. I mean *everything*—the porch being high off the ground like that, the steps off to the right. And that tower thing—how could I ever forget that, David? I'm telling you, God as my witness, I used to live here."

He was transfixed by the sight of that old house. As much as I wanted to think he was confusing houses, the look on his face told me otherwise.

"Please tell me you're mistaken," I said. "'Cause this whole Slater thing is crazy enough as it is. I can't take it anymore. Skeletons—blood—a necklace. Oh, and that stupid wedding dress. I mean, for heaven's sake! And now you're telling me you used to live here. I can't take it anymore. I wish I had never seen this place before."

Just then, Silas pointed to the fallen tree. "Hey, look at those roots!"

"Holy smokes!" I said. "Looks like another skeleton."

We both scurried over and inspected it.

Sure enough, a complete human skeleton was entangled in the roots and the clump of earth.

"See?" Silas said. "Those murder stories are rubbish. How could the woman bury someone under a tree? That body was there before this tree even sprouted."

I stared at the roots, scratching my forehead. "I just don't...I mean how can..." The certainty made its way into my grasp. I took a deep breath. "Little did we know...."

Silas laughed. "You mean little did *they* know! They built a house on an old burial ground. Imagine that!"

I sighed once more. "Someone did say that before...It just didn't sink in, I guess...But what about the bloody cloth and that stupid necklace?"

Silas shrugged. "I don't know."

"See?" I cried. "That's what I mean! You solve one part of the mystery and there's still another part unresolved. It's always something with this stupid place! It never stops!"

Silas got up and started toward the house. "Trust me, you're not the only one bewildered."

"There's a way in from the side window, you know."

"I'm not sure that'd be a good idea. If we got caught, I'd be in a whole lot more trouble than you."

"On second thought, we better not," I said. "Hey, someone's been here recently!"

"Those tire tracks? I just saw those. Pretty fresh, huh?"

"They are."

I was no longer comfortable about getting on the porch, but I followed Silas up the steps anyway. We walked up to the windows and peered in.

"Alright, I am *not* losing my mind!" I cried. "That couch was not there the last time Daryl and I were here. That couch was against the wall, over that way—and I don't even remember that chair. Holy smokes! The floor's been swept over here."

"It's because someone's been in the house."

"Really?"

As confident as I felt, it still surprised me to hear Silas say it.

"Come look," Silas said. "There's a pair of boots right by the door."

I went over and peeked inside. "Man alive!"

Silas kept his face pressed against the glass. "Funny how this place seemed like a mansion when I was little. But it's the same layout alright. Nothing's changed."

I crossed my arms. "Alright then, describe the upstairs to me."

Silas pressed his hand to his forehead. "So when you reach the top of the stairs—by the way, the very staircase that fans out at the bottom before you even go up. Just thought you'd like to know. Anyways, when you reach the top, um, there would be two doorways on the left...close together. Those would go to the two bedrooms or whatever, but to the right was a door in the center of the hallway. I remember it was a special door in my mind because there was this pretty woodwork or molding all around it; so, as a kid, you just knew it was a special kind of room. Inside was an enormous room overlooking this yard. I'll never forget it 'cause I would stare out those windows. I happened to see a Tin Lizzie drive by on this road once—which was rare in those days—but in my little childish mind, I expected to see it every time I looked out the windows...."

"Unbelievable!" I said, shaking my head.

Silas grinned. "Told you!"

"Unless you're some kind of soothsayer or something...."

"Oh, and I remember the lady well."

"Faye?"

Silas looked puzzled. "I remember the name Sheila...She was a nice lady though. She took care of me for a long time. At least that's how it seemed at the time. I'm trying to think how old I must've been...I couldn't have been more than three years old."

"You must have a really good memory."

"I do. It's like having an extra life. Ha! But I remember how much she took care of me. For whatever reason after that, I ended up living with another family down in Lyon. The rest is history. But I always wondered where this place was. No one claimed to know for some reason."

Just then, a car could be heard sputtering down the road.

"Over here," I said. "Duck down."

We waited for the car to go by.

Yet it didn't seem to go by. In fact, it seemed to be getting closer.

I peeked around the corner.

The car was pulling right into the yard.

"They're coming here! Let's go!"

Chapter 33

Evelyn's birthday fell on a weekday, but arrangements had been made to have a big celebration that Saturday. The party was top-secret. Evelyn had no earthly idea. And the man at the helm of the conspiracy was none other than Stephen Thomas. Though it would not be untrue to say he had gotten a little help from Dad. Evelyn and I sat at the dining room table while Dad finished up with his hours-long preparation of roast duck and baked potatoes—his famous recipe. He took the baking sheet out of the oven, untied the legs, and laid out the toasted brussels sprouts and pecans. As soon as he set the sheet on the table, there came a knock at the door.

Evelyn got up to answer it. "I knew I heard someone pull in the yard."

Dad turned to me and smiled.

"Surprise! Happy Birthday!"

"Stephen! I thought you forgot."

"Me, forget? Ha! I vood never forget my lady's birdday."

"Oh, my! Why, hello, Mr. and Mrs. Tamas. Come in. What a surprise!"

"Good evening, young lady," Mr. Tamas said.

Mrs. Tamas gave Evelyn a kiss on the cheek. "Happy birdday, sveetheart!"

"What's all this?"

"It's food for da party."

"Party? What's going on here?"

"You vill see, darling."

I helped bring the food in and set it on the dining room table. The Tamases had barely gotten their coats off and hung up when there were more knocks at the door.

"Happy Birthday!"

"Pastor and Mrs. Richardson! What a surprise!

"So good to see you, girl."

"Thank you. So good to see you, too—Is this your doing, Stephen?"

"I cannot say. Othervise, perhaps."

"You mischief-maker!—Here, I'll take that. Thank you."

"Looks like more just pulled into the yard."

Evelyn peeked outside. "It's the Sawyers! I can't believe this!"

"Happy Birthday!"

"Happy Bir—why am I saying Happy Birthday? I can't think straight right now."

Stephen burst out laughing.

"Howdy, Pete," Dad said. "Howdy, Erma. Let me take these. You folks come in."

"Ha! This place is filled already."

"Hey, Allen! Hey, Wayne!"

"Happy Birthday, Evelyn!"

"Thank you."

"Hey, everybody! Silas is here!"

"Ladies and gentlemen, the man of the hour!"

Silas strode through the door, his face lit up. He pretended to tip his hat, which he was not wearing.

"What's all the fuss about?" Nathan said, barging through the door.

"I heard there was a party!" Irvin shouted.

"Me, too!" Wayne said. "I wasn't invited though."

"You guys are too funny! C'mon in."

Irvin took Nathan's hat from his head and tossed it across the room. "Gimme some elbow room."

"You boys are crowding the doorway," Mr. Sawyer said. "The young lady's trying to get through."

"And you're too loud," Mrs. Sawyer said, rolling her eyes.

"Mattie!" Evelyn cried. "You, too?"

"And I brought Alice and Ruby," Mattie said. "They're on their way in."

"You can't be serious! And you all got here pretty much the same time. What is it, six o' clock?"

Stephen thumped his chest. "Ven I plan someding, I plan it da right vay and only da right vay."

Evelyn smacked him on the shoulder. "You mischief-maker! I can't believe you!"

"Happy Birthday, Evelyn!"

"Ruby! Alice! I didn't know my twentieth was that special, but thank you for coming."

"We wouldn't have missed this for the world."

"I'll get those off your hands," Dad said. "There we go."

"Here, let me get your coats," Evelyn said. "Oh, my! I don't think there's enough seats in this house for everybody."

"There's plenty," Dad said. "David's going to set up chairs in a moment. Everything's covered, honey. Just enjoy yourself."

The chattering and cackling echoed throughout the house. Before long, everybody was lined up, ready to fill their plates and pour their drinks. Supper was spread out upon the dining room table like a vast buffet. There were platters of finger foods like deviled eggs, cheeses, roasted nuts, and olives. In addition to Dad's roasted duck and baked potatoes, there were pastry pigs, meatballs, and

Caesar salad. For drinks, there was tea and lemonade; and for dessert, lemon cake and cookies.

Meanwhile I was setting up the old wooden folding chairs as fast as I could. It turned out we didn't even need them. The Sawyer boys plopped down on the floor, sitting in a circle with their plates of food. It was amusing to watch them chomp and chat at the same time.

Irvin straightened up and hollered, "Someone's at the door."

I got up and answered it. "Beth?"

I was mystified. I would've thought Louise Brooks or Colleen Moore was standing at my door. She had a short sleeveless dress with velvet layers and sequins, and she wore long satin gloves that went nearly to her elbows. Her hair was shorter than before and flaunted a beaded headband. She was an entirely different woman, yet it was Beth's face.

"Hi, David," Beth said.

I gave her a hug. "What a surprise, Beth." I had never smelled cigarette smoke on her before. "Come in. Make yourself at home."

"Thanks, David."

Dad waved from across the room. "Hello, Beth! Come join us!"

"Beth! Beth! Beth!" Evelyn cried, scampering from the kitchen. "You're back!"

Evelyn came rushing into the living room. You could tell she was taken aback. She handled it well, though, and bombarded Beth with the biggest hug. "Oh, my!" Evelyn cried. "Look at you!"

"Oh, this?" Beth said, pointing to her outfit. "Maggie spoils me with all these flapper dresses. She's got the money. Besides, I've got a decent job as a switchboard operator."

"That's wonderful, Beth!"

"The supervisor likes my voice. He says it's warm and calming."

"That's great," Evelyn said. "Well, it's so good to see you. Tell me you didn't travel all that distance just for my birthday."

"Well, it's bittersweet, really," Beth explained. "Aunt Mabel actually passed away...."

"Aw! I'm so sorry, Beth—"

"No, it's alright. We're sad, of course, but she was hurting so badly. I was at least in town, and I got word from Daryl—"

"You ran into Daryl?" Evelyn said.

"Well, I stopped by his house," Beth said. "I guess David had told him in passing."

Evelyn eyed her. "Are you and Daryl...."

Beth blushed. "No, not quite—well, maybe a little. We'll see."

"Beth, I'm happy for you! You've always had a crush on Daryl."

Beth shrugged. "We'll see what happens. We've been writing. He says I look good."

"You do. And you look thinner, too."

Beth leaned in. "The Luckies help with that." I could tell Evelyn didn't know what she meant. Beth put a couple fingers to her lips. "You know, the gaspers."

"Oh!" Evelyn said. "I did read that before in a magazine. They say it helps."

"So far. And it helps with the jangled nerves as well."

"I see. Well, come in. Please. Grab something to eat."

"Oh, no, thanks. I've eaten already, but I'll be happy to visit with you all."

Dad waved again. "Good to see you, Beth."

"Thank you, Mr. Hayes. Good to see all of you."

Beth mingled with the ladies, and I sat down next to my father where a group of men had already been in the middle of a conversation.

"...and then there's good ole Lindbergh," Pastor said. "Hard to believe what he did, huh?"

Charles Lindbergh had been the talk of the town that whole week. He had made his solo flight across the ocean just a few days earlier.

"You couldn't get me across that water," I chimed in. "I don't care if there was a crew of people who came with me. And then to fly an airplane all by yourself. Man alive! One little mistake and to the sharks you go!"

"You couldn't get me up there over the county," Mr. Sawyer said. "Let alone the Atlantic."

"Quite a feat," Dad said, taking a bite of his roast.

"What was it," Pastor said, "some fifty plus hours they said that he went without sleep? My goodness!"

"You're not kidding," Dad said. "And no sooner did the boy arrive and the Paris folk went absolutely wild. They practically ripped him from the plane."

"All in all, not bad for being raised on a farm," Nathan said. "Pretty crazy though."

Mr. Sawyer chuckled. "The farm'll do that to you!"

"His life will never be the same," Dad said. "He's got nowhere to hide from all those cameras. He might as well have tripled Babe Ruth's homeruns last year!"

"Imagine," I said, "if the Great Bambino cracked the ball out of the park and all the way to Paris. That's about what Lindbergh did. Ha!"

Suddenly, my ears picked up another conversation. I could've sworn I had just heard someone say something about Jewel and smallpox. I turned my head.

"...And that's why she hasn't been around," Mattie said.

Evelyn's mouth gaped open. "I can't believe it! What a terrible thing to happen to you."

"I know," Mattie said. "Especially all over your face like that. They said she had never gotten it before."

"I got 'em when I was little," Alice said. "I'm so glad that's done and over with."

"Gotten what?" I said. "I overheard you say something about Jewel being sick."

"She's got chickenpox," Evelyn explained.

"Oh! I thought you said smallpox."

"No, but Alice says it's really bad."

"That's what Betty Quinn and Mae Stone told me," Alice said. "And Mae's dad is good friends with Dr. Thompson."

"And Jewel's never got chickenpox before," Mattie added.

I cringed. "That can't be good."

"Not at all," Mattie said. "She had a dreadful fever. They thought they were gonna lose her."

"Oh, my!"

"Aw!" Evelyn said. "That poor thing."

I sat there mulling over the misfortune when Stephen rose to his feet. "If I may have your attention!" he hollered.

The room settled down, except for Nathan and Wayne who were still snickering and clowning around. Mrs. Sawyer reached over and took Nathan's hat from his head.

"Everybody keeps taking my hat!" Nathan said.

"I'll give it back if you can hold your tongue," Mrs. Sawyer said. "Mr. Thomas is trying to speak."

"Oops!" Nathan said. "Sorry, Stephen."

Stephen beamed. "Dat's alright. I first vaunt to dank all of you for coming out tonight. Of course, Evelyn had her twentieth birdday a few days ago. I vent to you all to plan dis special evening—and I couldn't have done it widout your help, Mr. Hayes. And, of course, you all know da reason ve are here. Ha! You did so vell to keep dis a secret. Give yourselves a hand!"

Everybody cheered and clapped.

"So I vaunt to say a few vords to you, Evelyn—here, you come sit right here in this chair—right beside me. Perfect! So I first vaunt to say dat you are a vonderful young voman—how about *lady*? Much better? She makes fun of my English, but I can't help it."

"I love your English!" Evelyn cried.

"Vell, dank you. You are a vonerful lady," Stephen continued. "You have a kind heart. A varm heart. And you are a beautiful voman—that I *can* say!"

The Sawyer boys hooted and hollered.

"But not just, uh, beautiful on de outside. You have a beautiful soul. You are my best friend in de whole vide vorld. And before all dese d-dear people..." Stephen nervously pulled it out of his pocket and got down on one knee. "...I vaunt to ask you someding. Evelyn, vill you marry me?"

"Is this for real?" Evelyn cried. "At my birthday party?" She just stared at the ring.

"Everybody here knows," Dad chimed in, "that this was never *just* a birthday party."

"You can say that again!" Silas shouted.

The look on her face when it dawned on her the entire occasion had been planned!

"Oh, my stars!" Evelyn cried, her hands to her face.

"So vill you marry me?" Stephen asked.

"Well, yes!" she cried, springing up from her seat. "By all means, yes!" She planted a kiss and held him tightly. "You mischief-maker! I can't believe you, Stephen!"

"Vell done, Istvan!" Mr. Tamas said. "Vell done!"

Mrs. Tamas came over and hugged them both.

Neither Stephen nor Evelyn could stop giggling. The two of them were suddenly engaged to be married. The whole plan had worked out perfectly. Evelyn gave Dad a big hug then made her way around, thanking everybody who came.

"Oh, Beth!" Evelyn cried, hugging her. "You were supposed to be my maid of honor! And now you've moved away."

"No worries," Beth said, fixing her gloves. "I'll be back for the wedding."

Chapter 34

Evelyn and I arranged for Stephen and Silas to join us down at Heron Lake for a picnic. The plan was for Silas and me to do the fishing while Stephen and Evelyn basked in their romance. To be fair, Stephen did agree to cook the freshly caught fish over a campfire. He was the master at cooking fillets that were golden brown on the outside yet tender and moist on the inside. So it was the ideal arrangement.

Evelyn and I left the house together and started toward the lake road. I carried the picnic basket, and she carried my fishing pole.

"Ahh! Not a cloud in the sky," Evelyn said. "Ponder that, Davey."

"It is gorgeous," I said. "Not too warm either, especially for a fire."

"Mmm. The thought of fish, especially the way Stephen makes it."

"He's no doubt the best. I could live off that fish for the rest of my life and never tire of it."

"It's the tastiest, and it's making me hungry."

"I hope you aren't too hungry. I don't think Silas and I will have much trouble catching anything, but you never know. It might be a while."

"No, I'm alright. I had a bowl of that raisin bran Dad bought the other day."

"Whatta ya think of it?"

"It's yummy. How about you?"

"I still prefer eggs and sausages fresh off the hot stove, but the new cereals aren't bad. I like the crunch."

"Oh, I love the crunch. And with fresh milk. Mmm."

I chuckled. "If Mom knew we were eating cold cereal, she'd be fit to be tied."

"Ha! Ponder that, Davey."

"Hey, here comes Silas—Howdy, Silas!" I yelled.

"He seems excited," Evelyn said.

"He has every reason to be. I told him all about Stephen's cooking. Ha! Look at him run."

"Stephen's really fond of Silas," Evelyn said. "He knows how close you two are. He said he wants him to be part of the wedding."

"Really?"

"Yep. We talked it over already. We thought that perhaps you could escort Aunt Mary down the aisle and Silas could escort Mattie. I don't think Mattie would mind at all. Andrew would be paired with Beth, then Wayne and Ann can go down together."

"That would be great—Hey, did you tell Stephen to meet us down at the lake?"

"I don't think so. Why?"

"Hmm. I thought maybe that was his car, but no one's in it.

"No, I'm pretty sure we were supposed to meet by the road...but maybe I misunderstood."

"Either way, he knows where to meet us," I said. "So anyway, that's wonderful about Silas. I can't wait to tell him."

"Yep! Stephen mentioned it all on his own."

"That was really nice of him—Hey, we were just talking about you, Silas."

"I hope it was good," Silas said, catching his breath.

"You're in the wedding!" Evelyn said.

"That's swell! I don't even know what to say!"

"You don't have to say anything," Evelyn said. "You just have to show up."

Silas beamed. "Well, thank you."

I laid my hand on his shoulder. "See? You're part of the family."

"Holy mackerel! That means I've got two families now! The Sawyer family *and* the Hayes family!" Then he leaned in and smirked. "Just do me a favor and don't go treating me like family, that's all. Ha ha!"

Evelyn smirked. "What do you mean?"

"I'm just joshing you," Silas said. "Wayne threatened me the other day saying he was gonna treat me like family by stuffing a soggy tomato in my pillow. Ha!"

"What for?"

"Well, he was sore 'cause he lost a game of euchre. Allen and I were down by three, and him and Irvin only needed one to win. Well, it's Irvin's turn to deal, and he turns over the nine of clubs. I about fell over—I had the right and left bower, the ace, and a couple good ones. So not only did I tell him to pick it up, but I told 'em I was going alone. Ha! I took all five tricks and stole the game right then and there. Allen and I are jumping for joy, and Wayne's so mad he says he's gonna stuff a soggy tomato in my pillow. And I said, 'You would do that to a lodger?' And he says, 'You ain't no lodger. You're family now." And I said, 'You'd do that to family?' And he says, 'No different than what I've done to my own brothers.' So I said, 'But I'm not family, and my skin can testify to that.' Well, Wayne calls Allen back into the room and says, 'Is Silas a lodger or a brother, Allen?' And, of course, Allen says, 'A brother.' And Wayne says, 'See? It's done and dusted. You're family whether you like it or not, and that means I get to—'"

All of a sudden, Silas turned his attention downhill.

"What's the matter?" I said. "See something?"

"Yes. Something just moved over there. I could've sworn it was a person, but then it sprang back behind those trees."

"It's probably Stephen," Evelyn said. "The little mischief-maker that he is, he's probably hiding on us."

Silas shrugged. "Meh. I'm probably just seeing things."

"It's probably a deer," I said. "I was coming up the trail just the other day, and the deer were all over the place. Right about where you pointed. There were like eight of them bedded down, and a ten-point buck standing nearby. You should've seen them take off when I came 'round that bend. Ha! I'll tell you what, we probably should be hunting instead of fishing. Does Stephen cook a good backstrap?"

"It wouldn't surprise me," Evelyn said. "But I'll have to ask him."

I licked my lips. "Ooh! A teensy bit of salt on that venison, and *mmm*!"

"Aw shucks!" Evelyn said, smacking herself on the forehead. "I forgot the salt and the butter."

"Are you serious?" I opened the basket. "Stephen needs them for the fish."

"They're not in there. I'm sure of it. I was gonna put them in the basket, but I set them down on the counter and then got distracted. I'll run and get them."

"No, I'll go back. It's not a big deal. You two just wait here. I'll be just a few minutes."

I returned to the house and found the salt and butter just as Evelyn had said. I tossed them into the basket and hurried back. To my surprise, Evelyn and Silas weren't there waiting by the side of the road. I arrived at the lake road and paused to listen. I heard voices nearby.

Ha! They must've found Stephen.

273

I hobbled down the slope as best as I could with a loaded basket in my hand. I was approaching the bend when I heard Silas say, "...but Evelyn's already taken."

"I told you to mind your stinkin' business! I'm not talking to you. I'm talking to her."

"What would Jewel think if she knew you were on the make, calling me Sheba like that?"

"It doesn't matter what Jewel thinks. I'm not with that floozy anymore."

"Why not? You were stuck on her, and she was stuck on you."

"Pshh! She loved me 'cause I was the sheriff's son."

I had fumbled the basket by accident and was trying to pick up the things as fast as I could.

"Well, it doesn't matter. Stephen and I are engaged to be married, and that's that."

"That's too bad. Such a beautiful thing gone to waste."

"Get your meathooks off me, Dominic!"

"You shouldn't touch Miss Hayes that way."

"Did you just swat my hand?"

"I don't mean no harm, but Miss Hayes is already taken."

I came into the open just as Dominic rammed his fist into Silas's chest, shoving him back.

"Leave him alone!" I yelled.

"Whoa!" Dominic said. "Fancy meeting the Cursed One *and* ole Devil Boy in the same place!"

"I wasn't looking for any trouble," Silas said, rubbing his chest. "It's just that you shouldn't treat Miss Hayes that way. She's a lady."

Dominic rushed Silas. "I told you to shut your mouth!"

Silas stepped back and seized his wrist with one of his hands. Dominic tried to shake it off, but Silas wouldn't let go. Dominic threw with his left hand, while Silas skirted out of the way.

Dominic rushed him again and tried clobbering him. Silas dodged the strike and took hold of his other hand as well. Dominic couldn't lift his arms, so he tried thrusting his weight forward. But Silas backpedaled, pulling him to the ground. I couldn't believe my eyes: Dominic was on his hands and knees before Silas.

"I don't want no fight," Silas said, stepping away again.

Dominic didn't say a word this time. He just looked up, glowering at him. His eyes burned with fire, and the vein in his forehead bulged.

At that moment, Sam and Harvey could be heard coming up the lake road, laughing and carrying on. Clearly frightened, Silas started up the hill.

Dominic hurried to his feet and pressed him again, bobbing and weaving.

"I don't wanna fight!" Silas cried.

Dominic threw two quick jabs and a cross. Silas evaded the flurry and seized his wrist again with both hands, absorbing a couple shots to the side of his head.

Then Dominic grit his teeth and threw a hook with all his might. Silas dodged the blow and instantaneously countered with his own, striking Dominic square in the face.

It was over. Dominic was already limp on his feet before his body plopped to the ground.

There he lay. Twisted limbs and all.

Knocked out cold.

Chapter 35

"We gotta go *now*!" I cried.

"What are we gonna do?" Evelyn said. "They'll kill him!"

"I know! I know!—Let's go, Silas! We gotta get you out of here!"

We scampered up the hill.

"They're gonna kill him!" Evelyn kept saying.

"We gotta get you back to your house," I said.

"But the Sawyer's weren't home!" Silas said. "What if they come for me and they're still not there?"

"The Sawyers got plenty of guns," I said.

"I can't do that," Silas said. "How's that gonna end for me?"

"Dash it all!"

"What about our house, Davey?" Evelyn said.

"I'd feel better if Dad were home," I said. "You know Augie's gonna be at our door."

"Oh, I can't bear the thought. If the Klan doesn't kill him first, Augie will see to it he's put away."

"I know. Just what they did to Samuel Rhodes!"

"But I wasn't looking for trouble!" Silas said.

"We know, Silas."

"I even tried to get away. I could hear more of 'em coming. I got scared, that's all. I never meant any harm!"

"You did nothing wrong, Silas. We just gotta get you somewhere safe."

We tried desperately to conjure up a plan. Thank God Stephen pulled up just as we reached the road!

"Stephen!" I cried, running up to the window. "I'll explain later—You two hop in—Take us to my house quick!"

Stephen turned around, put it into high gear, then went full throttle.

We arrived in hardly any time at all.

"Come with me, Silas!" I said. We hopped out of the car. "Take Evelyn back into town and get Dad. He's at the lumber yard. We can't have her here at the house alone."

Stephen nodded. "I'm going now."

"Then where are *you* going?" Evelyn asked.

"I'm gonna take him to the tracks. We'll hide out there and hop the first train leaving town. I can at least get him to the Swansons and figure it from there. Now go!"

"Be safe, Davey!"

I ran into the house and grabbed my rifle then stuffed a handful of rounds in my pocket. "Let's get outta here!"

Silas and I left the house and sprinted as fast as we could into the woods. We scampered down to the creek and chased the water's edge all the way to the Slater property. We arrived at the brushwood border.

"The tracks are behind those woods," I said, trying to catch my breath. "We'll hide out there until we get our break."

"My goodness, I'm so winded!" Silas said.

"I know, but we can't stay here. We've gotta get to those woods. Just a little bit more. You ready?"

"Look! That car's there!"

Sure enough, a car was parked in front of the house.

"My God!" I said. "Let's pray they don't squeal on us. C'mon, we gotta make a run for it!"

We sprang out of the woods and darted toward the clearing on the side of the house. We were just about to leave it all behind when someone came out of nowhere from behind the corner. Before I was even aware, I plowed right into them, knocking them to the ground.

"Dear heavens!" I handed Silas my gun and got down. "Are you alright, ma'am?"

"Whew!" she said, taking deep breaths. "That was a trip."

"I feel so terrible!"

The older woman sat up and leaned on her side. "I'm alright, I'm alright."

"Are you sure?"

"Yes. Just startled."

"I'd say so. You've got to be hurt."

"No, no—whew!—I'm more startled than hurt. You caught me just enough in the shoulder. I'm fine, though. I assure you."

I gripped my forehead. "I can't believe this!"

"I must say that's gotta be one of the biggest surprises I've ever had. Honestly, though, I'm fine. It looked worse than it really was."

"The pain must not've set in yet!"

She chuckled and started to her feet. "You're more worked up than I am."

"That just had to hurt."

"You boys were in a hurry, that's for sure."

"It's a long story. I promise we're not up to no good."

"I hope not—say, aren't you the boys that were on my porch a few weeks ago? Ha! You took off like white-tailed deer as soon as I drove in."

"Ma'am, I promise Silas and I were just being curious. That's all. Just curious."

She finished dusting herself off and looked up at me. "Did you say *Silas*?"

"Yes, ma'am. Silas here is a good man, and we're no troublemakers."

She turned to him. "Your name is Silas?"

Silas eyed her. "Yes, ma'am...."

"It can't be." She walked up to him and looked him over. She placed her hand on his temple. "My goodness, the scar!"

Silas stood there gazing at her. "Sheila?"

"Oh, my God!" she cried. "It's you! It's really you! I can't believe this is happening!"

"Holy mackerel! It's really you! I can't believe this either!"

"I remember when you got that scar. My goodness, I felt so guilty. You had climbed on the chair and, oh, you fell and hit your poor little head right on the corner of the chest!"

Silas reached over and hugged her. "That wasn't your fault. Not at all. You were good to me. You did so much for me, and I never forgot you."

"I've been praying for this day for years! Oh, my God! My prayer finally came true!"

"I've never forgotten you, Sheila."

"Listen!" I said. "This is truly amazing, and it's more than I can even handle right now. Trust me. But we can't sit here. Silas's life is in serious danger. It's a long story, but we've got to get him outta here before the Kluxers get hold of him!"

"So that's why all the rush?"

"Yes, ma'am. It's not good. Not good at all. They'll kill him! And if not, they'll put him behind bars for good!"

She clapped her hands. "Come with me!"

The woman ushered us inside the house and bolted the door shut. "By the way, my name is Faye—I'll explain later Silas."

"I'm David. David Hayes."

"Oh, my goodness! You're all grown up."

I smiled.

"Honestly, I don't think you have a thing to worry about," Faye said. "They're not gonna suspect you here in this house. This is my house—not what it used to be. But anyways, if they're hot on the trail and come knocking at this door, I'll just tell 'em I saw you two headed toward the tracks. That'll throw 'em off for sure. Not to mention, there's enough places in this old house to hide the both of you. Though I don't think I'll have to go and make like Rahab."

"But whatta we do from here?" Silas said.

"Don't worry about that, honey," Faye said. "First things first. You're about to find out a whole lot right now. In fact, I think *everybody* in this town's about to find out the truth once and for all! Here, let's head upstairs, and we'll watch the yard from my room."

It felt dreamlike being in the house Daryl and I had broken into. The place looked lived-in now and felt like a home rather than a haunted house.

We went upstairs into the master bedroom.

"Here's a chair for one of you," Faye said. "And then I've got this long seat over here. I'll be fine sitting on the bed—Here, you can set that rifle down here, David." Faye sat down and took a deep breath. "I can't believe this is actually happening."

"I remember this place so well," Silas said. "It doesn't seem like a big castle anymore, but it's the same place alright."

"Well, after Momma went home, Papa married again and moved away, leaving me the house. My sisters were already rooted in distant places and had no interest anyhow. It was much too big for a woman like myself, naturally, but I was at least cared for. My father was good to me and always saw to it that I was looked after—you know, being on my own and all. I was supposed to get married, but it didn't work out. But anyways, that's for another time.

"It came to pass that my father found himself alone again. My poor father, he lost another wife and became ill. I moved to Illinois to help him out. It was my turn to take care of him now, after all he did for me through the years—dear heavens! Where's the time even gone? But he eventually passed away, and I felt led to move back here." Faye smiled at Silas. "And now I know why! I still can't believe this! It's so good to see you again. You really remember me, huh?"

"Yes, ma'am," Silas said. "I remember you well. You were very kind to me."

"Well, you were a joy to have around. I was so sad to give you up, but I had to go away and help Papa. I always wondered what happened to you. So what brought you back?"

"Do you remember Pete and Erma Sawyer?"

"I sure do."

"Well, they got that farm in Belfast, and I moved in with them to help out with all the farm work. They've been good to me, too."

"That's wonderful. I remember Pete and Erma very well. That was so nice of them to take you in like that. Were you still down in Lyon?"

"Yes, ma'am."

Faye shook her head and sighed. "Well, there's a reason you know me as Sheila. You see, I took you in secretly. Only a few people knew. I'm not sure what difference it made, but at the time, I thought it best to have you call me by another name. I guess I was afraid— are you ready for this?"

Silas nodded.

"It's a remarkable story," Faye said. "Yet it's a true story, and there are witnesses. Believe you me. And they're still alive. Right in this very town—but I'm getting ahead of myself." Faye patted her chest, trying to catch her breath. "On one hand, I'm overjoyed to tell you your story..." Her eyes welled up. "...but on the other hand, it's a sad story, Silas. It involves your dear mother."

281

"You knew my momma?"

"I did. Her name was Clara. Clara Moore. She was a beautiful young lady. Sadly, she became the mark of a man's lust. Your lovely mother was a housemaid down in Richland. She was on her way home one evening when she was picked up by a man. A not-so-good man." Faye paused to wipe the tears from her eyes. "Well, he forced your momma—not just into his carriage. Though he did point a gun at her head. But I mean after he took her away, he forced himself on her and defiled that poor girl. Then he took her with him back to Avondale.

"But your momma was as tough as she was beautiful. She broke away from him and jumped off onto the side of road. The poor thing sprained her ankle, but she shuffled into the woods as fast as she could. She looked back and could see him coming after her."

Silas was in tears.

"I know, honey," Faye said. "As much as I dreamed of one day telling you your story, I knew it would be just as hard."

Silas cleared his throat. "No, I appreciate it, Sheila. I want to hear it. What happened next?"

"Well, God only knows where that monster had been planning on taking your momma, but they were just outside of town when she got away. She kept on through the woods until she reached the old convent on Abbey Lane. She pounded on one of the doors. Fortunately, Edna answered."

"Who's Edna?" Silas asked, wiping his eyes.

"Edna was a good friend of mine. One of the nuns there. Your mom told her everything that happened and warned her the man was following her through the woods and was wearing a sheriff's badge."

A chill ran through my body.

"All of a sudden, there was this drumming on the door. A couple of the nuns took Clara by the hand and hurried her off down the hallway to hide her. Edna said she calmly answered the door—leave it to Edna to be able to pull that off! I know I couldn't have done it. Anyways, she opened the door.

"It was Sheriff Lockhart. He asked her if a young black girl had come through in the last few minutes. Edna told him 'No' and then asked him what the matter was. He said he was returning home that night when he spotted a girl on the corner of Wilkins who matched the description of a certain 'lady-of-the-night' who had been 'all over hell and half of the county,' he said, and was also 'wanted on account of some burglaries.' He said he stopped to ask her some questions and that she took off down Lorigan Alley Way. He said he gave chase and followed her all the way to Gooseneck where she ran into the woods.

"Once more, Edna told him she hadn't seen any black person whatsoever. He elbowed her out of the way and stepped inside and looked around. Then he asked her if he was to inspect the buildings whether he would find the girl? Edna assured him there was no such girl. That's when he gave her the look of death, Edna said. He walked back outside and turned around one last time and told her to mind her business."

I buried my head in my hands.

"It wasn't much later," Faye continued, "it became clear that Clara was with child. So what were they to do now? Well, the women vowed they were gonna foster the young lady and help her with the child. They resolved to dedicate the child to God and to keep the whole thing hush-hush until God made it public, they said. Of course, they *had* to keep it secret—for the safety of the young mother and her child. Not to mention, the safety of the nuns as well. There was no way they could trust the law. And the Ku Klux Klan had already been burning down Catholic churches, so the women were just waiting for the convent to be next."

I looked up. "Where do you come in, Faye?"

"Well, Edna and I had been friends since our childhood. She confided in me at the time because they needed help with some of the provisions. Thankfully, I was able to help get it out to them. It was all the Lord, the way it worked out. Well, your momma was getting really close to having you, and I rode up to the convent one night..."

Faye sobbed again.

"Sorry, I'm trying, but I still see it like it happened yesterday...Ehem...As I was approaching, I hear gunshots fired…My heart sank. I just knew it. And then I see him riding away on the horse. All dressed in white, the mask and all…I raced as fast I could…And there she is, lying on the ground, your poor momma gunned down..."

Faye took out her handkerchief then motioned for us to give her a moment. After wiping her eyes, she got up and went over to the dresser. She opened the bottom drawer and took out the books and set them on the floor. She reached in and pulled out the bloody cloth. She came back and set the bundle on the bed, then she sat down again.

"So your momma's still breathing," Faye continued. "And I'm lying next to her, trying to get her to respond. 'Can you hear me, Clara? You gotta stay with me, alright?' She moans and says, 'I'm here.' Florence and Josephine run out into the yard, and I yell for them to go get Edna. Edna runs out asking if she's still alive. 'She just answered me,' I said. And that's when Edna says, 'We need to get to Milton now!'—Milton is Edna's cousin. You know him as Dr. Thompson, David.

"But thank God, Dr. Thompson lived on Aspen Way, just around the corner. I told Edna to stay with your momma, and I mounted Della and took off down the road at full speed. I pounded on Dr. Thompson's door. The door flung open, and I was so frantic telling him what was going on and how Clara was due any day now to have her baby. He rushed back into the house and grabbed a bunch of his things and some bottles and tossed them in his bag and hurried out the door.

"We raced back as fast we could. I never saw Dr. Thompson move so fast in my life. 'Is she talking, Edna?' he asks. 'Very little,' she says. Then Dr. Thompson gets down and looks Clara over. He leans over and whispers to me, 'She's not gonna make it much longer.' He tried asking her a couple questions. It was like Clara didn't even hear him...She just kept moaning and saying, 'My baby.'

"Dr. Thompson opens his bag and takes out a bottle and a towel. 'Clara, can you hear me?' he says. 'My baby,' she keeps saying. Dr. Thompson looked up at the both of us and says, 'I don't think there's much choice.' He leans in again and says, 'Clara, we're gonna save your baby, alright? Can you hear me?' Clara answers him and says, 'Save my baby!'

"So Dr. Thompson opens the bottle and pours it into the towel, then he twirls it and sets it over her mouth. And I hear him mutter, 'Dear God! Just a little longer!' He held the towel while Edna and I rubbed Clara's arms and legs and talked to her. It seemed like forever, but Clara finally fell asleep. Dr. Thompson immediately started the surgery, and there's at least this hope that the baby's gonna make it. But then Edna starts crying, 'She's gone! She's gone!' Dr. Thompson says, 'Are you sure?' And Edna says, 'There's no heartbeat!' My spirit sank, and I burst into tears. But then Dr. Thompson said those words—I'll never forget those precious words—'We're almost there!' he said. And not even a minute later, you made your entrance into the world, Silas."

Faye reached for the bundle. She opened it and dangled the necklace. "I saved this all these years for you. It was your momma's. Edna undid it from her neck and wrapped it in this old rag. The plan was to have you nursed here at the house all along, so she handed it to me. I hid it in that drawer all these years."

Silas wiped his eyes and got up. He held out his hand.

Faye let the necklace down into his palm then closed his hand in hers.

Silas heaved another sigh. "Thank you, Faye."

"You're welcome, honey."

"What about her body?" I asked.

"We carried her body to the cemetery right on the property and buried her as quickly as we could just in case someone came back. And sure enough, the sheriff's deputy—Deputy Patterson at the time—he came by the next day. Edna told him that a Klansman shot the girl several times before fleeing the scene and that the young girl had bled to death. They showed him where she died and then took him to the burial place. Deputy Paterson took his hat off, they said, and folded his hands and stared at the ground for a minute. He then offered his apology and bid them all a good day. Nothing was ever made public. Not even the slightest mention of the murder in the paper. But I know the truth of that night. Those women know the truth of that night. Dr. Thompson knows the truth of that night!"

Silas wiped his eyes. "I want *everybody* to know the truth of that night. I want to see him."

"See who?" I asked.

"The sheriff."

"Are you sure, Silas?'

"Yes, I'm sure. I want to look him in the face and tell him myself."

I turned to Faye. "Is that even a good idea?"

"If he wants to," Faye said. "Silas just might be the person for such a time as this. Where's the sheriff likely to be?"

"At the Sawyers or my place," I said. "But the Sawyers aren't even home right now, so my place would be next, no doubt."

"They might be back by now," Silas said. "They were only in town."

"Now how did you two get here?" Faye asked.

"We followed the creek from my house."

"Then why don't you both head back that same way? I don't think they know where you are; they would've showed up by now. You two did good work."

I grabbed the rifle from the bed. "Then we'll head back to my house. Dad's there by now I'm sure, and he's got the shotgun and the other rifle."

Faye stood up. "I'll drive to the Sawyer's. Are they still on Healy?"

"Yes. Right up the road from us."

"Great. I'll head there now, alright?"

"Sounds good."

"Then let's be going."

Chapter 36

Silas and I left the Slater house and hustled back, arriving at the edge of my backyard. We surveyed the area from behind the trees, then we took off through the yard and darted for the door.

We went inside. Dad and Evelyn came hurrying into the dining room.

"What's going on?" Dad cried. "Are you alright?"

"We're fine, but you're not gonna believe this." I was hurled over trying to catch my breath. "Is the front door locked?"

"Yes."

Evelyn ran back to double check.

"Alright. So I'm sure Evelyn told you about the fight. It was a prize fight, that's all I can say about that right now. A prize fight! But you're not gonna believe what I'm about to tell you."

"Wait, wait, wait!" Evelyn cried, hurrying back. "So what happened?"

"So Faye Slater's back in town," I said.

"You can't be serious!"

"I'm dead serious," I said. "She's moved back into that old house, and Silas and I ran into her when we were cutting through the property trying to get to the tracks. Are you ready for this?" I paused once more to catch my breath, then I blurted it out: "Faye took care of Silas when he was a baby!"

"What are you talking about?" Evelyn said.

"I know, I know. This is gonna sound absolutely crazy, but you gotta believe me. And you need to listen fast right now. I don't know how much time we have, so here's the story: Silas's mom was hiding out at Saint Mary's right here in town—before Silas was even born. And you'll never believe who she was hiding from."

"Well, who?"

"Augie!"

"Sheriff Lockhart?"

"The one and only!" I said. "Silas's mom was hiding from Augie 'cause he abused her. And I mean in a terrible, terrible way."

"Are you sure about this?" Dad asked.

"No two ways about it! His mom got away and ran for her life to Saint Mary's. The nuns hid her there the entire time she was expecting, but Augie had chased her through the woods and had a feeling she was there on the property. Somebody must've been snooping on her 'cause the Klan shot and killed her when she was out in the courtyard one night. But listen to this: Dr. Thompson was able to save the baby!"

"Goodness gracious!"

"Here's the thing," I said, "Augie never knew he fathered a child, and he's probably on his way now. And Silas wants to confront him, but he's gonna need some protection."

Just then, somebody pounded on the front door.

"Oh, my God!" Evelyn cried. "He's here already!"

Dad pumped the shotgun. I loaded the rifle. We went into the living room.

"Who's there?" Dad shouted.

"This is Pete here, Millard."

Dad opened the door. "Oh, good. It's you, Pete—hey, you folks c'mon in!"

The entire Sawyer family marched through the door, each one carrying a gun. Except for Ann, she had her pocketknife.

"We already know," Pete said. "Miss Slater here filled us in."

"Faye!" Dad cried. "I can't believe it! David told me everything. I don't know what to say. It's so good to have you back in town, though."

"So good to see you, Mr. Hayes! What a way to come back, huh?"

"You're not kidding." Dad shut the door and bolted it. "I just can't believe this is really happening. Maybe I need to pinch myself and see if I'm even awake—no, I'm awake alright. So I reckon I've never had a dream so peculiar as this. Anyways, I'm not sure how this is gonna go down, but Silas here feels led to confront the man— Is that right, Son?"

"Yes, sir," Silas said.

"Well, that's a mighty brave thing, if you ask me." Dad looked over the room. "So the man's bound to be here by evening. Probably sooner than later I imagine. Evelyn says the Lockhart boys drove the motorcar to the lake, so my guess is they made like the wind to track down their father. Now I suppose the best thing to do would be to see what sort of mood Augie's in when he gets here, before we go ahead and let him in. If he seems pretty sensible—and we'll be able to tell, looking out that window—but if he does, then I'll go ahead and open the door. That's where you folks come in. Now don't go pointing guns at him yet. He'll see them sure enough. And that's when I'll introduce Silas and give him the floor. Sound like a plan?"

"That'll work," Mr. Sawyer said.

"Good. Then we wait."

Dad managed the window while we conversed amongst ourselves and chatted with Faye. Everybody tried to catch up on the last fifteen years. Meanwhile, Evelyn bounced back and forth between rooms, serving sweet tea to everybody. She offered a glass to Silas as well, which he thanked her for, but kindly turned down. He said he didn't think he could hold anything down at the present time. Evelyn patted him on the shoulder before walking away. He just sat there in Dad's chair, staring down at his hands.

My heart was heavy for him. I couldn't begin to imagine what must've been running through his mind. How was it possible to process all that had bombarded him in such a short span? It was beyond belief. Here we were, all willing and waiting to take action on account of an abrupt lesson!

I sat down on the floor beside the phonograph and leaned against the wall. I took a sip of my glass.

Did Silas really pummel Dominic? Aren't we supposed to be in Carlton by now? Did Faye Slater just reappear into our lives like a ghost? Is this the same Silas I've been friends with all along?

"Here comes Dr. Thompson!" Dad said.

"Oh good!" Faye said. "I stopped by and told him what's going on. He said he wouldn't miss this for the world and that he'd be on his way."

I got up and opened the door. "C'mon in, Dr. Thompson."

"There's a doctor in the house!" Dad announced.

Everybody cheered.

Dr. Thompson waved in his own gentle manner. "Hello."

Silas got up from the chair and shook Dr. Thompson's hand. "Thank you, sir. Thank you for what you did that hectic night many years ago. I don't know what else to say. I don't know how I could ever repay you, but I want you to know how grateful I am for you. Thank you for caring."

With the sincerest expression on his face, Dr. Thompson said, "I was just doing my job, but thank you, young man."

"Right here, Dr. Thompson." Faye pointed to an open seat.

He nodded. "Thank you, Faye."

"Man alive! I guess the sheriff was right on your tail, Doctor," Dad said. "That's him alright!"

The room got quiet.

"And whatta ya know?" Dad said. "Looks like Carl Shane is coming along for the ride as well."

"Curtains are up, boys," Nathan said.

"We'll see if they head to your place first," Dad said. A few seconds later, the sputtering of the motor toned down. "Nope. I reckon all the vehicles in the yard tell the story well."

The motor died out.

"Are they coming?" Wayne asked.

"Not yet," Dad said. "They're sitting there chatting with each other."

Mrs. Sawyer chuckled. "Tell 'em it's impolite to keep people waiting."

"Alright, here they come," Dad said. "So remember the plan. No pointing guns...Not yet anyhow."

"Yes, sir."

Dad turned to Silas. "You still wanna do the talking, Son?"

"Yes, sir." Silas repositioned the chair to face the door.

"Alright. But we're here for you whenever you decide you've said enough."

Silas nodded his head and took a deep breath.

The thud of boots and the creaking of the porch heightened the tension. Then the solid rap at the door.

Dad left the window and gave us all a thoughtful nod.

"Sheriff, Deputy, good evening."

"Good evening, Mr. Hayes," Sheriff Lockhart said. "It's my understanding that the Sawyer boy—the adopted one, that is—well, he assaulted someone earlier today. That's what's been reported. I'm told he was with your son, David, at the time of the assault. Does the young man happen to be with him still?"

"Yes, sir. As a matter of fact, he is. Please, come in."

"Thank you, Mr. Hayes."

Sheriff Lockhart and Deputy Shane walked through the door, both in uniform and with a six shooter at their side.

"Good evening to you all," Sheriff Lockhart said, tipping his hat. "Sorry to interfere with your, um, little get-together. I had an unfortunate call to make, so if you'll please excuse me. I regret to inform you that this here young man assaulted someone today. That someone happens to be my son—which is neither here nor there—but that is the fact anyhow. And the rule of law says we can't have this sort of bad behavior going on in our society. So again, if you folks will excuse me while I carry out my obligation here." Sheriff Lockhart turned to Silas. "Now do you have anything to say for yourself?"

"Yes, sir," Silas said calmly. "I was attacked."

Sheriff Lockhart folded his arms and peered down at him. "You were attacked you say?"

"Yes, sir. Dominic made some wayward comments to Miss Hayes here and then laid hands on her. I spoke up for her, and he didn't take too kindly to that. That's when he—"

"The witnesses have testified to the fact that you pushed him in the chest."

"The only witness is Miss Hayes, sir. And she'll tell you that I didn't push him. In fact, he's the one who struck me in the chest trying to get me to brawl."

Sheriff Lockhart breathed heavily through his nose. "There were three other witnesses you failed to mention, young man. I'm sure you accidentally forgot them somehow or other. But two of them were my other sons, and the other was Joe Griffin. So you mean to tell me Mr. Griffin lied?"

"I'm only here to tell you I was attacked, sir."

"I'll tell you what: Rather than play this game, I'm gonna bring you in for some further questioning, alright? Now if ya'll will pardon me, I hate to do this, but the situation requires me to—don't pull your arm away from me, boy!"

"I was attacked, sir."

"We're beyond that now. Now either you can go peaceably, or you can go by force."

"I was attacked!"

"Don't make me yank you out of that chair!"

"I was attacked! Just like you attacked my momma!"

Sheriff Lockhart let go of his wrist. "What in the blazes are you talking about?"

Silas sobbed.

"Speak up, boy!" Sheriff Lockhart hollered. "'Cause now I'm gonna have to commit you to the asylum regardless how this goes! So if you know what's good for you, you best speak up now!"

That was about all Dad could handle. He shut the door. "I reckon it would be a good idea to let the young man talk when he's ready to talk."

Mrs. Sawyer pumped her shotgun. The next thing I knew, the sheriff and his deputy were staring at more than a half dozen barrel ends.

"Now like I said, Sheriff," Dad continued, "the young man will talk when he's ready to talk. And trust me, Deputy Shane's gonna wanna hear what Silas has to say."

Sheriff Lockhart stood there speechless. Deputy Shane held his hands up.

"You'll have nothing to worry about, Deputy," Dad said. "As long as Augie doesn't try pulling off anything fancy. All you need to do is listen, you see—So whenever you're ready, Son."

Silas wiped his eyes and regained his composure. "Like I was trying to say, I was attacked today...just like when my momma was attacked nineteen years ago. Except she wasn't punched in the side of the head like I was. She had her innocence stolen from her. No, not stolen. My momma was robbed. She was robbed when you pulled a gun on her and made her get in that carriage!"

Astonishment stole across the sheriff's face.

"You made her," Silas continued. "You took her captive that night...that night you pawed her and forced her!"

The sheriff cleared his throat.

"I know what you're thinking," Silas said. "I can see it in your face. 'There's no way he could possibly know. There's no way anybody could know about that night. But then how can he be saying all this? How does he know?' Well, it's not just me who knows. It's Miss Slater here who knows as well." Faye emerged from the dining room. "Go ahead, ask her."

Fear and panic gripped the once hardened face of Augustus Lockhart. He wiped his forehead. "This can't be happening," he muttered.

"And if you don't wanna ask Miss Slater," Silas said, "then I'm sure you'll at least wanna hear from Dr. Thompson." The doctor rose from his chair and stood solemnly with his hands folded in front of him. "Dr. Thompson was there the night my poor momma was shot at that nunnery. You wanna know why Dr. Thompson was there?"

Sheriff Lockhart shook his head.

Silas stood up from the chair. "'Cause he saved the baby!"

Sheriff Lockhart stuffed his hands in his pockets and stared down at the floor, shaking his head vigorously now. Beads of sweat formed across his forehead. "So you've come back to this town," he muttered, "to torment me before my time?"

Silas held his gaze. "No, sir."

Sheriff Lockhart finally looked up. "Well, I'm done for...Now if you'll please let me go my way...."

Silas cleared his throat. With tears streaming down his face, he said, "Go."

Sheriff Lockhart turned to Deputy Shane. "I'll be in the car...Sheriff."

The hint did not go unnoticed. Deputy Shane nodded in reply.

Dad opened the door, and Sheriff Lockhart walked out of the house for the last time.

Deputy Shane adjusted his hat. "I'm gonna have to notify the State. As you all know, Augie's been the higher-up around these parts for many years. It's pretty plain what happened; he basically confessed to the entire thing. So I'm gonna go ahead and start on the initial report and get that going. But I'll be in touch with you folks within the next couple days, and we'll see to it—"

Just then, the car started.

Deputy Shane moved over to the window to have a look outside. "We'll see to it that Silas's story gets out...Augie does seem pretty subdued right now. Perhaps, with all you here, I'll be able to talk some sense into him and see if he'll just do the right thing and—hey, where's he going?"

Deputy Shane hustled to the door and ran out of the house.

Sheriff Lockhart had driven away.

We later learned that he veered off onto the lake road and drove all the way down and over the crag, plummeting into the water. When they dredged up the car, they found a revolver in the backseat and a gunshot wound to his head.

Chapter 37

A few days after our famous "get-together," Faye drove Silas and me down to the old convent. The nuns escorted Silas to the spot where his mother had taken her last breath. The spot where he was born. We then proceeded to the churchyard where all gathered around the final resting place. It was identified by a marked grave to the right and a tree to the left, right along the border. Otherwise it was an apparently vacant plot in between.

After Silas's story broke, Mr. Harris of Bryant & Boyd donated a headstone with the name *Clara Moore* on it along with *Matthew 10:28* inscribed underneath. Silas, Faye, Dr. Thompson, and Edna had collaborated on an article that detailed the shameful misconduct of Augustus Lockhart. Sheriff Shane added his own testimony of the exchange he witnessed firsthand. Upon completion, the article was submitted to the *Avondale Times Herald*, put into print, and circulated abroad.

The Ku Klux Klan had already been nationally disgraced a couple years prior due to the despicable deeds of the Grand Dragon. Far from being a defender of morality and a law-abiding citizen, D. C. Stephenson was convicted of the abduction and rape of a young woman who ended up taking her own life. And with all the other horrific accounts of the floggings and the tarring and feathering, people began to see through the pious facade. In the end, most viewed the KKK as nothing more than a mob. Consequently, the overall membership of the organization declined rapidly.

Sad to say, the Klan still thrived in various pockets around the country, including our own part of the state. Thankfully, that all began to change after the release of the front-page story regarding Sheriff Lockhart's "long-kept secret" and "the boy who rose from the dead." Within six months, the bottom fell out of the local chapter. Needless to say, there were no more KKK parades at the county fair.

As you could imagine, it was difficult for Silas after his famous "history lesson." He was still the good-humored man I had known, but there was a distractedness about him over the next few months. I'll never forget the day we were digging post holes together—telling stories, joking around, just having a good time. He plunged his spade into the ground and leaned on it. The smile on his face waned as he stared off into the horizon. He heaved a sigh and said, "My poor momma...Hmm...so hard to believe...." Then he shook his head and went back to work.

Within a week of the bombshell, I was coming out of Cooper's Grocery when I heard someone call my name. I turned around. Jewel was crossing the street from Edward's, waving to me. It was obvious she wanted badly to talk to me; she took no heed of the car driving by and was almost struck. I breathed a sigh of relief and decided to meet her halfway up the sidewalk.

As we drew near to one another, I caught a glimpse of some blotches on her face. To be honest, they were hardly noticeable. It's just that I had never seen any sort of blemish on Jewel's face before. I diverted my eyes and made as if I hadn't noticed.

"Good morning, Jewel."

She looked down at the sidewalk. "Good morning, David."

"Getting a little fresh air?" I hardly knew what to say.

"Yes. I guess you could say that." I wasn't going to bring it up, but she wasted no time. "Pretty horrible about Dominic's dad, huh?"

I nodded. "Sure is."

"And now Dominic's gone, too."

"What do you mean?"

"He skipped town. Left his mother and two brothers to manage by themselves."

I sat down on the bench. "I don't even know what to say, Jewel."

She shrugged her shoulders. "There's nothing to say, really. He already left me anyways. Didn't like my face."

I was taken aback. "I thought he loved the way you looked."

She glanced up at me then quickly back down. "I know you see them. I got these pockmarks a short time ago. He was mad I never got the chickenpox when I was little. Like it was my own fault or something. And here I almost died...."

"But they're not even that noticeable."

"Says you."

That was the first time she had ever spoken those words to me without any feeling. I tried to encourage her. "Well, you'll notice them more because it's your own face, but other people won't pay any attention."

"You really think so?"

"Without a doubt."

After a moment of silence, she asked, "Do you still think I'm pretty?"

I was caught off guard, but I went ahead and told her the truth. "Yes."

She tried to smile but looked away. Her eyes welled up, and she sniffled. "We don't even exist."

I was confused. "You and me?"

"No." She put her hand over her belly. "I just hope it's a boy." I tried my best not to act shocked. I sat up straight and said nothing.

299

"One of me is enough," she explained. "Believe you me, I was just as surprised as you are right now."

"Well, no. It's just that, um...I wasn't expecting to hear that so suddenly, that's all...But best wishes to you. By all means, best wishes."

She wiped her eyes and snickered. "Daddy acts like it's happening tomorrow. In fact, he's here in town picking up a few things for the nursery. He's getting the whole upstairs ready."

I was distracted. "So he knows?"

"Well, of course," Jewel said. "If he's preparing a nursey, that means I broke it to him. If you could've seen the look on his face when I—"

"No, I mean Dominic."

"Oh, Dominic? Of course, he knows. I told him. I might as well have told him the sky was blue, but I told him. There wasn't the least bit of concern on his face. He just said, 'Hmm, I'd better get going now.' And that was that. He never came around anymore and wouldn't even acknowledge me when I bumped into him at Wilson's—and I mean literally bumped into him. He kept right on out the door and wouldn't even look back. As far as Dominic is concerned, we never even happened. Actually, it's worse than that. As far as Dominic is concerned, I'm not even alive."

I rubbed my knees anxiously and looked down.

"So are you still good friends with that girl you were writing?" Jewel asked.

"Oh, you mean Catherine?" I said.

She nodded. "Mae Stone and Mary Brown both told me. Everybody knows."

"Um, yes. We're really good friends."

"Still writing her I assume?"

"Yep. We write each other, um, quite a bit now."

"Like every few weeks or something?"

300

"Um, I guess about every week now. Her and her family are actually coming over to visit in a couple days, so I'm really looking forward to that."

"Oh, I see...You think you two will ever get married?"

"Probably. I mean I couldn't ask for a better friend. And isn't that what you're supposed to be when you're married—best friends?"

"Uh huh."

"So then I imagine so."

"Well, that's good to hear." Another moment of silence and a look around. Then she spoke up: "Well, I guess no one will be seeing me for quite some time...you know, with the baby on the way and all. No one knows yet, except you and the Lockharts, of course. But no one else...so...."

I stood up from the bench and shook her hand. "Well, I wish you the best, Jewel. And if you ever need a friend..." Her eyes lit up for the first time. "...you couldn't find a better friend than Evelyn."

She looked down again. "Thank you, David...And best of wishes to you, too."

She turned around and walked away.

Chapter 38

Despite the rough-and-tumble year of '27, my relationship with Catherine prospered all the same. You can imagine how delighted I was when the Swanson family spent an entire day with us. The best part of it all was that Catherine and I were permitted to sit on the porch alone together. Not that it prevented Carrie from making her rounds to tease her younger sister about being in "the throes of love." Jimmie and Jesse also came by to flash their hunting knives and warn me against laying hands on their sister, half joking and half serious. Not that it mattered to me. I had the support of the most beautiful woman in the world, and I knew that in due time love would be victorious.

I was especially pleased with the way Evelyn treated Catherine. At one point, they were off to themselves, taking their time strolling through the yard together, all smiles and laughter. Evelyn clearly enjoyed Catherine's company, and it made me happy. It was a good time all around. Our families had been friends for years, and there was nothing that could've severed that friendship. We all knew our parents were truly looking forward to the day our families would be related by marriage.

But for now, the spotlight of marriage was on another couple. Stephen and Evelyn were not to be engaged for long. Not only did they loathe the very thought of a lengthy engagement, but Dad wholeheartedly advised against it. "The way you two are ogling each other and cozying up," he said, "you're gonna be tiptoeing off to the struggle buggy in the dead of winter." Hence, October 15 was selected to be the day of the wedding. Evelyn was thrilled with the idea of a fall wedding. "The changing leaves will make the day feel like a colorful dream," she said. Meanwhile, Dad required the two of them not to go anywhere unchaperoned. Stephen was permitted to give Evelyn a single kiss goodbye before departing for the night—with Dad accompanying them to the door.

I doubt Evelyn recalls those months the same way I do. I'll never forget Jack Sharkey's defeat in July. After out-boxing Jack Dempsey for the first six rounds, Sharkey turned his head to the referee to dispute some low blows. Dempsey cashed in on the distraction and knocked Sharkey out. Dad said it was his own fault and that you never leave yourself unprotected, but I was still furious. I ended up losing a half-night's sleep over it.

August begot the kerfuffle about President Coolidge who had handed each of the reporters a piece of paper that simply stated, "I do not choose to run for president in 1928." While frustrating for everybody else, it was hardly as risky as the reenactment of Custer's Last Stand a month earlier when a stampede of horses charged toward the car with him and his wife in it.

We were unaware of it then, but while our family was caught up in the excitement of the wedding, a crowd of eighty thousand admirers gathered to hear Hitler speak on behalf of the Nazi Party. To think that we shared the same globe together!

September was a pleasure though. It began with Babe Ruth hitting his 400th homerun of his career and ended with him hitting his 60th homerun of the season, breaking his own record of 59.

Needless to say, Evelyn had other things on her mind that summer. Though not everything was cheery and chirpy. Beth hadn't responded to a single letter from Evelyn. At first, Evelyn tried to dismiss it. "Beth's busy with her new city life," she said. "I can't blame her. She'll reply when she's got time." On another occasion, Evelyn said, "Beth didn't write me back the last time she was away, yet she still came by to visit." Even so, Evelyn's last letter specifically informed Beth of the exact day and time of the wedding, which was only a month away now. Still, nothing. Evelyn was greatly troubled now.

It so happened Daryl stopped by the workshop one day and told me he wanted to get together. "One last time before moving away," he said. I was flabbergasted. "The plans are finalized. I'm going to live with Beth in New York." He invited me to come over and listen to the boxing rematch between Tunney and Dempsey. "Just like old times," he added. I was still upset over Dempsey's victory over Sharkey a couple months prior and wanted Tunney to put him away, so Daryl didn't have to do much convincing. "It's a deal," I said, shaking his hand.

Thursday evening arrived. I rushed over to Daryl's.

"Good evening, David," Mrs. Mitchell said. "Daryl's in the living room. He's got the radio tuned in already."

"Thank you, Mrs. Mitchell."

She leaned in. "Maybe you can talk some sense into him. Tell him moving to New York isn't such a good idea. His father's not very happy either."

"I think his mind's pretty much made up," I said. "But I'll see what I can do."

She shook her head. "My baby's gone crazy." Then she spoke in her normal tone of voice. "But it's so good to see you, David. You just make yourself at home."

"Sounds wonderful."

I went into the living room.

"Howdy, Mr. Mitchell," I said.

"Howdy, David. Come join us. Daryl's got it all ready."

The pre-fight commentary had already begun.

"The signal sounds excellent," I said, taking my seat.

"Couldn't have a clearer broadcast," Daryl said. "This is gonna be a good one."

"So who do you want to win, Mr. Mitchell?" I said.

"Ah, I gotta go with Tunney," he said, leaning back in his chair. "See if he can hold onto the title. But if Dempsey pulls it off, it wouldn't bother me none. It's hard not to like the guy."

I didn't object out loud, but I certainly thought otherwise.

"I'm rooting for Tunney," Daryl said. "But I know Dempsey wants his revenge for their last fight. The guy's got tremendous power, that's for sure."

"I know I wouldn't wanna be on the other end of it," Mr. Mitchell said.

Before long, the fight officially began.

Mr. Mitchell sat comfortably in his chair, with his hands folded in his lap. Daryl and I, on the other hand, were on the edge of our seats.

Tunney stuck to his usual style of striking from a distance, searching for any holes in Dempsey's guard. It seemed like the fight was to go the distance like the first time they met. I felt confident Tunney was going to win.

Then it happened: Dempsey had Tunney up against the ropes and fired off a series of punches that sent him to the floor.

I sprang to my feet, yelling at the radio. "Good heavens! What just happened? Get up, Tunney! Get up! Get up!" Tunney had never been knocked down before in his entire boxing career.

Despite the referee's directive to move to a neutral corner of the ring, Dempsey was slow to obey, which delayed the count. Even Daryl thought the delay helped Tunney recuperate. I didn't disagree, but it was Dempsey's own fault as far as I was concerned. Besides, I figured Tunney would've gotten up had the count started earlier. Be that as it may, he got back up and survived the round, and that's all that mattered to me.

Tunney seemed to have fully recovered in the eighth round. He returned fire and knocked Dempsey down to the canvas this time. I sprang to my feet again, shouting at the Mitchell radio. Daryl shouted, too. Mr. Mitchell just sat there with a smile on his face.

Dempsey did get back up, but Tunney dominated the final rounds. He ended up winning by unanimous decision, thus retaining the title. I was happy as can be.

And then the reality of the evening began to set in. This was our last time to get together. Daryl was saying goodbye.

We went outside and sat down on the front steps.

"Well, I appreciate you inviting me over," I said.

"Sure. And thanks for coming over," Daryl said. "It was a rare old time."

"Especially with the way it turned out. Ha! It didn't look so good in the seventh, did it?"

Daryl raised his one eyebrow. "That was wild."

We picked up pebbles and threw them at the tree by the road.

"So you and Beth are pretty serious now, huh?" I said.

His expression told me he didn't disagree. "We're good friends."

"I'd say so! You're gonna live with her."

Daryl faintly chuckled. "I guess we're serious."

"She sure liked you all those years. What took you so long?"

"Oh, I don't know. Beth's different now. I like the new Beth."

"She's gotta be happy."

He nodded. "She is."

"Hey, you two might be next."

"Next to what?"

"You know, to get married."

I'll never forget the perplexed look on Daryl's face. "Who said anything about marriage?"

I shrugged. "I just assumed you two were that serious."

"No! I mean, trust me, I like Beth and all—I have to say, she knows how to have a good time—but, ah, there'll be no handcuff."

"Oh." I didn't know what to say.

We continued picking up pebbles, trying to hit the trunk of the tree. I knew time was running out and that I'd better bring up the subject now.

"Hey, Daryl. Could you do me a favor?"

"Sure. What is it?"

"Well, it's not really for me; it's more for Evelyn. Um, Evelyn hasn't heard back from Beth about the wedding. The last they talked, when Beth was home, Beth said she planned on coming back. So she's supposed to be in the wedding...."

"You want me to ask her? I can do that for you."

"That would be great. Evelyn's a little hurt, to be honest. If Beth can't make it, that's fine. Evelyn would understand; you know Evelyn. It's just she's written her several times and hasn't heard anything back...."

"I'll talk to her and ask her. I'll write you as soon as I find out."

"I know Evelyn will appreciate it."

"I understand. No problem at all."

At last, I rose to my feet. "I guess this is it."

Daryl stood up, as well, and shook my hand. "I guess so...Hard to believe...."

"Well, you have a safe trip. I wish you only the best, Daryl."

"Thanks. That means a lot to me."

"I won't forget you. Take care of yourself."

"You, too. I'll be in touch."

I headed to the car. I paused one last time and waved goodbye. Then I got in and drove home.

About a week and a half later, I got a letter in the mail. Daryl had kept his word.

Dear David,

I feel like I've entered another world that is truly impossible to describe. It's hard to imagine this place being here all along with all the hustle and bustle of crowds, the coming and going of cars, the towering structures, all the while we were growing up in little Avondale. Funny how life is!

I'm all settled in now. Beth couldn't be any happier. Her cousin is definitely loaded, and she knows a lot of people! She already has a job lined up for me at S. W. Palmer if I want it. It's really hard work, but we'll see what happens or what opens up from here. I've been told Broadway is one of their biggest customers with all the new construction going on and the constant need to be wired up now.

I did talk with Beth. Unfortunately, she will be unable to attend the wedding, but send Evelyn our love, and good luck to you and all.

Your friend,

Daryl

Chapter 39

"Why? What did I do?" Evelyn said, bursting into tears.

"You didn't do anything, Evelyn," I said. "People are complicated. Life is complicated. Who really knows what's going on? Even if she told you, you know what Dad always says: The issue is rarely the main issue. Only God really knows."

"But she was my best friend, Davey. Why couldn't she at least tell me herself?"

"I don't know. I really don't. I'm sorry, Evelyn."

There was nothing else I could say. I shared the same sentiments, but I didn't want to fan the flames of her anguish. I was really upset with Beth, and I thought it was a cruel thing to do to my sister.

Nevertheless, a blessing came to me unexpectedly. At Evelyn's expense. Not a minute went by and she slapped the letter down upon the table and said, "Fine! Then Catherine's in the wedding!"

"What?"

"If that's the way it's gonna be, then Catherine will take her place."

"But Mattie's still coming. She can be your maid of honor."

"No, Aunt Mary will be the maid of honor."

"So who's gonna escort Catherine down the aisle?"

"You!"

"But you said I was escorting Aunt Mary."

"That was before. I'll pair Andrew with Aunt Mary. Nothing needs to change with Silas and Mattie or Ann and Wayne. They can still be together, but that'll free you up to be with Catherine."

As badly as I felt for Evelyn, I couldn't hold back a smile.

She wiped the tears from her face and eyed me with a smirk. "Ponder that, Davey!" She turned around and left the room.

As if things couldn't get any better for me, the New York Yankees swept the Pittsburgh Pirates to win the World Series. Exactly one week from Evelyn's wedding. "Murderers' Row" included my two favorite batters: Babe Ruth and Lou Gehrig. I'll never forget that week: *The Jazz Singer* had been released a couple days prior to the Yankee's victory. It was the first feature-length movie to have sound, so it was quite the national sensation.

Andrew came home the day before the wedding, at around noon. He hung out at Mr. Bradford's until Dad and I got out of work. As soon as I could, I rushed over to see him. The moment I walked in, he smiled and gave me the biggest hug.

"You look good, David," Andrew said.

"Me?" I said. "Look at *you*!"

"I've put on a few pounds, but I needed them."

"No, you look really good. You seem like you're doing well."

"I am. Mr. Livingston's been good to me. I really owe it to him."

"So the home's working out then."

"It is. Just a great group of guys all around. We've all got our problems, of course, but, ah, just a great group of guys. Boyd's got some of the same problems as me, so we room together and help each other out. The place has electricity, so he sleeps all night with the light on. Helps him with the terrors when he springs out of bed like it just caught fire."

"Man, that's great. I mean, the fact that you've got a good roommate and that it has power and all."

"It is. It really is. Then there's Hardy; he's the prankster. Likes to put soap in Montgomery's shoes. Ha! And Glover's always straightening the shoes and tucking the laces in. Not just his—I mean *all* of ours. You'd think we were in training again. We call him Whizz-Bang Tidy. He's got to put the dishes away, too; can't just leave them out, which is fine with the rest of us if that's what he wants to do. He never stops though. He can't just sit—unless he's playing Chess! Now that's the one time he'd let the house burn to the ground! And he wouldn't budge till someone said *checkmate*. I'm not kidding."

I laughed. It felt good to hear the enjoyment in my brother's voice. His face looked refreshed.

"Oh, and you can't forget Gordon!" Andrew continued. "We call him Jack Johnson 'cause he's got these fists like bear paws and can box like the Galveston Giant. Not the guy you wanna tangle with. We're sitting on the porch and he's gotta name every dang bird he sees or hears even though he's told us a thousand times already. But who's gonna argue with him, right? And then Sanders, well, he's just a great guy all around and funny as can be."

"Sounds like a great group of guys! I'm so happy for you. It's so great to see you, Andrew!"

He smiled. "It's really working out. Mr. Livingston meets with us in the morning and starts the day off with a word of prayer and a verse or two for us to chew on that day. Or we'll read a hymn together—which has kinda inspired me to write my own poetry. I enjoy it like painting now. But anyways, we get together in the evening a couple times a week for chapel. This notebook here, Mr. Livingston encourages us to write our thoughts in it and find some verses to help replace the bad thoughts in our minds. It's been a good practice, so I brought it back with me."

"Well, it's good to have you back home for a few days. Wait till Dad and Evelyn see you!"

"Oh, and speaking of home, I'll tell you what: I wouldn't mind if the Lord used me to open up another home like Mr. Livingston's. That'd be something, wouldn't it?"

I'll never forget those words. My brother had renewed purpose in his life again, and he seemed happy.

Friday night was a delightful time. As soon as Andrew stepped foot in the house, Rouge came scurrying down the stairs and into the room. She romped around his feet, whimpering and wagging her tail, almost knocking over the end table and the lamp. Andrew crouched down and excited her by calling her name and sweet-talking her. She scampered back and forth between the living room and the dining room, running laps and barking excitedly.

Evelyn rushed downstairs and gave Andrew a big hug. Dad stood by, his face beaming with joy. It felt great having the four of us together again.

Andrew proceeded to recount his time at the home while we all grabbed something to eat and to drink. We made our way back into the living room where we spent the remainder of the evening chatting and reminiscing. Evelyn was giddy the whole time and kept saying how she couldn't believe it was her last night having Hayes as her last name. Andrew and I teased her saying it could very well remain her last name, at which point she threatened to punch us.

Rouge was calm now, as contented as can be at Andrew's feet. She would nudge him now and again and entreat him with her adorable expression to be patted on the head or have her belly rubbed.

Ten o' clock arrived. Dad adjourned the family reunion, assuring us that a good night's sleep would be desirable for the special occasion the next day.

I woke up the following morning to a tap on Evelyn's door.

"Good morning, Evelyn," Dad said. "It's your wedding day, honey."

"Good heavens!" she cried. "I'm getting married today!"

"Yes, you are. And just think, in five hours you'll be a Tamas."

"*Thomas*!" Evelyn cried. "Evelyn Thomas sounds best."

"I'm not so sure about that," Dad said, teasingly. "I think Evelyn Hayes sounds best. There's still time to back out, you know."

I jumped out of bed and hollered, "You're still a Hayes!"

Andrew was downstairs, but that didn't stop him from joining in. "I like Istvan and Evelyn. Kinda has a ring to it."

"I certainly think so anyhow," Dad said.

Evelyn opened the door a crack. "It's Stephen and Evelyn, and you guys better knock it off." She shut the door.

"Or what?" Andrew hollered back. "Move out of the house?"

"I've got my ways of getting even," Evelyn said through the walls. "Just ask David."

I stepped into the hallway. "Oh, please."

"Evidently, David knows a little something we don't," Dad said. "Have you experienced the revenge of Evelyn?"

I rolled my eyes. "She's not thinking straight."

Her door flung open. "Need I mention Halloween night a few years ago?"

"Halloween night?" Dad said. "What's this all about?"

I chuckled and headed down the stairs. "Let's just say that Evelyn can be sinister sometimes, that's all."

"Sweet old Evelyn?" Dad cried. "Why, I can't believe such a thing!"

I paused halfway down. "Well, you'd believe it if she had someone frighten you in the dark so badly that you tripped and fell and broke your arm."

"Man alive! Is that how you broke your arm?"

"I don't know. You'll have to ask her."

"Is that how he broke his arm, Evelyn?"

She shut the door. "Maybe."

Dad leaned over the railing. "Do you know anything about this, Andrew?"

"I'm not getting involved with this one," he said, putting his hands up.

"For crying out loud," Dad said. "What else don't I know around here?"

"Don't look at me," Andrew said.

My sister's door flung open again. "David asked for it. He wouldn't stop scaring me. So I had to take matters into my own hands. Right, Davey?"

"And I haven't scared you since, have I?"

"Whew! Smart man," Dad said. "I just hope Istvan knows what he's getting himself into."

"Believe me," Evelyn said, "he knows. He's a very smart man—and his name is Stephen, by the way. Nice try, Dad."

I stood at the bottom of the stairs. "Just so you know, Evelyn, I could get even with you for what you did to me. I could pull the plug on the car."

"You go right ahead, David Millard Hayes! I'll march straight to the church in my wedding dress if I have to. All that matters is that I'm getting married today."

"That's right," Andrew said. "She's gonna be Mrs. Tamas one way or the other—and that's all that matters."

"I heard that, Andy. You're lucky I miss you."

Dad gave her a hug. "Alright, alright, we've teased you enough. We just wanted to make sure you knew what you were gonna be missing from now on."

Evelyn smiled. "And I'm gonna really miss you guys. But at least I'm not moving to Sweden or something."

"That's right," Dad said, offering her his arm. "Now if my beautiful princess of a daughter will allow me...."

314

Dad escorted Evelyn down the stairs. Andrew pulled her chair out and seated her at the table.

My brother and I returned to the kitchen to finish breakfast and brew the coffee. When all was ready, we sat down together and revived the playful spirit of the morning, recalling some of the enduring stories about Evelyn. Like the time when she was three and disobeyed Mom by climbing on top of the dining room table again, insisting it was a boat to keep her safe from all the sea monsters. Or when she threw a snowball at Andrew and caught him right in the face, drawing blood, thanks to the chunk of ice hidden in the snow. Or when she had me stand on a chair to kill a spider, and the chair collapsed, and I ended up on the floor while she laughed at my misfortune.

Time glided by. It always does when you're blessed with good company and enjoying a perfect moment. Before we knew it, it was time to get ready. We got up from the table and parted ways for a short while. Dad, Andrew, and I washed up and changed into our Sunday best, while Evelyn put on her wedding dress and dolled up.

As soon as I finished, I returned downstairs. Andrew stepped out from the kitchen in his suit and tie and met me in the doorway. His hair was combed. His face was clean-shaven. It was an older version of the brother I remembered growing up with. Even Dad remarked about how "fetching" he looked being "spruced up" and "dressed to the teeth."

It was time to head to the church. Evelyn came out in her beautiful white gown, her eyes all aglow. My sister looked divine. She couldn't have been lovelier, and I couldn't have been happier. I helped her downstairs, carrying the portion of the dress that trailed behind so that it wouldn't get tarnished. We proceeded out to the car together.

"Aw!" Dad said, looking up at the sky. "I'm so sorry, honey. I was hoping for sunshine on your special day."

The sky was gray, and it was starting to drizzle.

"That's alright," Evelyn said. "We'll bring our own sunshine!"

Dad smiled and dried his eye.

Andrew opened the car door for Evelyn. She climbed in and got situated, then I handed her the train of her dress. The rest of us took our seats, and Dad started up the car. Then off to the church we went.

We got there early enough, before Stephen showed up. To my surprise, Catherine and her family were already there, waving excitedly as we pulled in. I couldn't keep my eyes off Catherine. She looked breathtaking. Even more beautiful than her bridesmaid dress was her face and charming expression. Her hair was curled, and her eyes sparkled. No doubt, Catherine was my "angel-kitten."

Aunt Mary, Mattie, and Mrs. Richardson immediately conducted Evelyn to one of the Sunday school classrooms where they could touch up her hair and whatnot.

The Tamas family arrived, as well as many of the congregation who came to show their love and support. The Sawyers walked through the door along with Silas who was in his stylish suit and full of smiles. The people were ushered to their seats while Mrs. Hill played the piano.

The prelude opened. The ceremony had officially begun. Andrew offered Aunt Mary his arm, and the two of them walked slowly down the aisle to where Pastor Richardson and Stephen waited at the front. Next were Silas and Mattie. Silas looked like quite the dapper gentleman alongside Mattie. Then Wayne escorted Ann down with her billows of hair let loose, not at all pinned up this time.

Then the moment I'd been waiting for. As nervous as I felt, I had determined not to rush down the aisle and spoil the whole experience. This was history in the making, a preview of what was to come.

I turned to Catherine. We smiled. Then we walked arm in arm, pacing ourselves down the aisle. I cherished the warmth of Catherine's touch and the thrill of closeness we shared because I knew it would be a while before our parents let us get that close again! Then as much as it pained me to do so, I let go of Catherine's arm. We parted ways. She joined the ladies on the left, and I joined the gentlemen on the right.

The wedding march began. The congregation rose to their feet.

Evelyn looked like royalty as Dad escorted her down the aisle. They arrived at the front, whereupon Pastor Richardson asked, "Who gives this bride away?"

"Her aunt and I," Dad said. He lifted the veil and placed a kiss on Evelyn's cheek. Then he presented her to Stephen and took his seat.

Pastor opened with a word of prayer.

Afterward, he reviewed some of the details of Stephen and Evelyn's upbringing, how the two had met, as well as their journey to becoming best friends. A brief exhortation from the Bible followed, reminding us of the sort of relationship built around love and respect.

Rings were exchanged, and the vows were made.

At last, Pastor pronounced them husband and wife. He granted Stephen permission to kiss the bride. Judging by the glow on Stephen's face, he didn't need anyone to twist his arm either. The kiss was wonderfully executed, and Pastor presented the two of them as "Mr. and Mrs. Tamas," which was enough to make Dad, Andrew, and I express our amusement. Evelyn eyed us as she and Stephen proceeded to the back. "It's Thomas!" she said.

We all congregated in the back as well, trading hugs and sharing in some pleasantries. At one point, Jimmy and Jesse approached me to let me know Catherine and I were "about as close as two coats of paint" when we walked down the aisle together. They flashed their hunting knives and asked me if I had anything to say for myself. I said, "Yes. I wished we attended a much larger church." With puzzled looks on their faces, they asked me what for. I replied, "Because I would've had a longer trip down the aisle with your sister."

They were speechless.

Just then, Silas ran up to inform me the bride and groom were "raring to go," and that the car was "all gussied up." Several guys had strung garlands through the windows and attached a sign that read: *Just Married*. They also tied a bunch of loose cans, a couple buckets, "and even Mr. Lee's basin" to the back of the car. Silas said it was enough to guarantee a "good clink and a clank" when the newlyweds drove off down the road.

We conducted the bride and groom to the front entrance. The church doors opened like the curtain of a theater, introducing the next scene as we made our way outside. We were greeted by a view of sunshine breaking through the clouds. The rain had ceased. Some of the clouds rolled back, uncovering pools of bright blue.

Evelyn came up to me, her face beaming with joy. She pointed to the heavens. A little rainbow festooned one of the clouds above. I put my arm around my sister and gave her one last hug before she departed for her honeymoon. We gazed at the beautiful display. Little did we know, as we stood on those church steps together, how much we'd need the promises of God down the road. More changes would come. They always do. In two years, the stock market would crash, and the Great Depression would wreak havoc around the world. But that's "a whole nother story," as Mom would say.

Made in the USA
Middletown, DE
17 June 2021

41812198R00191